CITY OF TIME

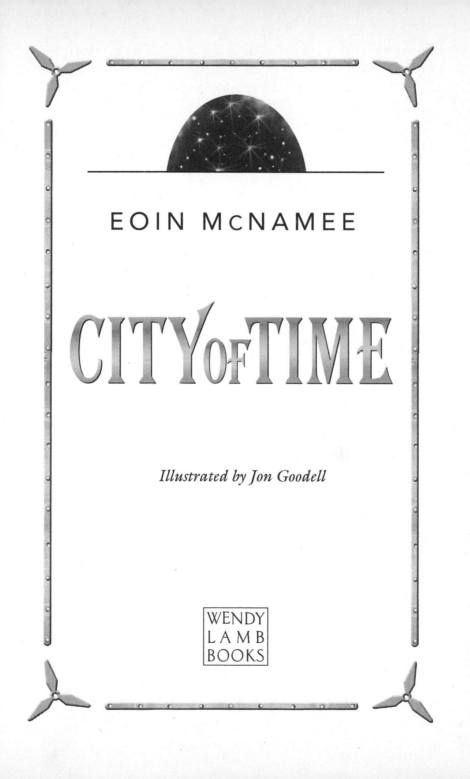

EOIN McNAMEE

CITY OF TIME

Illustrated by Jon Goodell

WENDY
LAMB
BOOKS

Published by Wendy Lamb Books
an imprint of Random House Children's Books
a division of Random House, Inc.
New York

Visit us on the Web! www.randomhouse.com/kids

Educators and librarians, for a variety of teaching tools,
visit us at www.randomhouse.com/teachers

Library of Congress Cataloging-in-Publication Data
McNamee, Eoin.
City of Time / Eoin McNamee ; [interior illustration by Jon Goodell].—1st ed.
p. cm.
Summary: When he receives the cryptic message that "time is running out,"
Owen, known as "The Navigator," summons Cati and Dr. Diamond and together
they journey to the City of Time in order to discover what has gone wrong.
ISBN 978-0-375-83912-2 (hardcover)—ISBN 978-0-375-93912-9 (Gibraltar lib.
bdg.) [1. Time—Fiction. 2. Fantasy.] I. Goodell, Jon, ill. II. Title.
PZ7.M4787933Ci 2008
[Fic]—dc22
2007037131

Book design by Trish Parcell Watts

The text of this book is set in 12-point Galliard.

Printed in the United States of America

10 9 8 7 6 5 4 3 2 1

First Edition

For Arabella, Niamh, Odhrán, and Danny

Owen walked down the riverbank, straddled the log that acted as a bridge over the water, and shinned quickly across. It was a fine sunny day with a brisk cold wind blowing up from the sea. The wind stirred the branches of the trees over his head, where the first colors of autumn were just creeping onto the edges of the leaves.

He stopped at the end of the log as he always did and looked up at the dark bulk of the ruined Workhouse towering above him. It was hard to believe that it had been only a year since he had stumbled across a secret organization called the Resisters who were hidden inside, asleep until the world needed them.

He shivered at the memory of the deadly Harsh, the enemies of mankind and of life itself, who had sought to turn back time, spreading cold and darkness throughout the whole world. They had constructed a device called the Puissance, which was like a huge whirlwind, sucking in time. But the Resisters had emerged and Owen had joined with them to defeat the Harsh, imprisoning the Puissance in the mysterious old chest in his bedroom.

When the battle was over, the Resisters went back to sleep in the chamber known as the Starry, hidden under the Workhouse. They waited there until they were called again. It was his friend Cati's job to watch for danger and to wake them when it came. She was invisible to the ordinary eye, hidden, as she said, in the shadows of time.

"Hello, Watcher!" Owen shouted as he always did, knowing she could see him even though he couldn't see her. He paused and scanned the shadows under the trees, wondering if she was safe and if he would ever see her again. Time, he had learned, was a dangerous place.

He strode briskly along the path toward his Den. Owen had made the Den in a hollow formed by ancient walls and roofed it over with a sheet of perspex he had found. The entrance was cleverly disguised with branches, so it was almost impossible to find unless you knew where it was. He moved quickly. He was late for school, but he had an errand.

He uncovered the entrance and ducked into the Den. Everything was as it had been the evening before. The old sofa, the pile of comics, the battered old kettle and gas stove, the truck mirror on the wall. The only thing that had changed in a year was the empty space on the wall where the Mortmain had hung, the object that he had thought was an old boat propeller, the object that turned out to be the key to defeating the Harsh. It was a magical thing, whose properties he didn't really understand. It resembled a battered piece of brass a little larger than a man's hand, with three leaves coming out from the center. When activated, it transformed into an object of wonderful intricacy and power. The Mortmain was now in his bedroom as well, acting as a lock to keep the Puissance in the chest.

Owen looked at himself in the mirror. His face had filled out and the thin, worried boy of last year had gone. His brown eyes were still wary, but that wasn't surprising, given the danger he'd gone through.

Quickly he opened the small box he had left on the old wooden table. He reached into his pocket and took out what looked like a jagged stone, one that glowed bright blue. It was the piece of magno that Cati had left as a keepsake, the stone filled with a power that the Resisters harnessed like electricity. He had taken it home with him the evening before, but he wasn't comfortable leaving it in his bedroom. It belonged in the Den, close to the Workhouse. He shut the magno in the box, took a last glance round, then left.

Once outside, he climbed up the side of the bridge onto the road. His mother had forgotten to give him lunch again, so he ran toward Mary White's shop. He had to stoop down to get into the tiny dark shop with the whitewashed front. As always, Mary was standing in the gloom behind the counter wearing an apron and pinafore, her hair in a bun.

"Have you been down at the Workhouse recently?" Mary asked. Owen remembered that the Resisters had spoken of her and seemed to have a great deal of respect for her. How much did she know about them and their battles with the Harsh?

"Be careful down there," she said. "Be very careful." For a moment the shop seemed to grow even darker and Mary's face looked stern and ancient. Then she smiled and things went back to normal.

Owen bought a roll and some ham. He put the money on the counter and Mary looked at his hands, which were unusually long and slender for a boy. *Just like his father's,* Mary thought. *Hands that were made for something special.*

Things had been easier at school since Owen had fought alongside the Resisters. No one knew about his adventures with the Resisters, or that if they hadn't defeated the Harsh, everyone would have vanished from the face of the earth, but he had grown up a lot during that time and his classmates sensed it. He was still a loner, but he was respected. It also had something to do with the fact that his mother was not as depressed and forgetful as she had been, so no longer sent him out in clothes he had outgrown or cut his hair with the kitchen scissors. Now he had the quiet air of a boy who could solve problems, and the younger children in particular often came to him for help.

At lunch he sat in the shelter outside. He had forgotten to buy a drink, so when Freya Revell sat down beside him and offered him a sip of her smoothie, he gratefully accepted.

"Look at the moon," she said. "It's so clear today."

"So it is," Owen said.

"You can see the man in the moon," she said.

Owen looked up and saw she was right. Then he turned back to Freya and felt his blood run cold. Instead of Freya's pleasant features, he saw the face of an old woman, more than old, ancient beyond counting. He felt himself recoil.

"What is it?" she said. "Is there something wrong?"

Owen rubbed his eyes. When he opened them again, Freya's face was back to normal. "I just . . . I just felt a bit dizzy," he said, knowing that didn't sound very convincing. "I have to go now."

He backed away, feeling Freya's eyes following him, her expression puzzled and a little hurt. He looked up again and for a moment the man in the moon did not seem like the kindly face from the nursery rhyme, but instead looked hard and cold.

After school, Owen walked slowly home, trying to

rid himself of the image of Freya's face, how it had changed. Was there something wrong with him, or had it been a kind of waking dream?

No. It had happened, and there was no one he could tell.

If only Cati were here.

When he got back home, his mother was in the kitchen. She looked careworn, but she smiled to herself from time to time as though she remembered something funny. It was an improvement on the way she had been, he thought. She had put out tea for him. Well, he thought, she had tried. There was a rubbery fried egg, which looked as if his fork would bounce off it, a bowl of porridge that had set like cement, and tea that came out as hot water because she had forgotten the tea bag.

Owen didn't mind, though. After his father was lost when his car crashed into the sea, his mother had sunk into a terrible depression, barely recognizing even Owen. But when he had broken the hold that the Harsh had on time, his mother had recovered a little, although Owen didn't understand how. She was vague and sometimes hardly seemed to be there, but she was happier.

He put the egg between two slices of toast and gulped it down, then grabbed his schoolbag from the corner, kissed his mother gently on the cheek, and went upstairs.

Owen spread his homework out on the bed, but he

couldn't concentrate. When it got dark he climbed up onto the chest underneath his window and stared out at black trees whipped by the wind. Then he got down and examined the chest, as he did almost every night. It was a plain black chest with brass corners and what looked like an ordinary brass lock and yet he dared not open it. The terrifying whirlwind that had turned time backward and threatened to destroy the world was trapped in it. The tarnished brass lock, the Mortmain, could look dull and uninteresting, as it did now, but Owen knew it was ornate and complicated. *Not made just to be a lock on a chest,* he thought. *No matter how important the chest is.*

He pulled off his trainers and lay on the bed. He shut his eyes, but Freya's old-woman face was the first image that came into his head. Then he saw the moon, with Freya's wizened face on it. He drifted into a troubled sleep in which images of the chest and the Mortmain flowed and merged into each other.

Owen wasn't the only one thinking about the chest. At the far side of the garden there was an ash tree, and in its branches a heavy figure was perched holding a brass telescope in one hand. The man had a broad red face, large sideburns, and a sly look. His name was Johnston and he was a sworn enemy of the Resisters. He was a scrap dealer, but the previous year he had stood shoulder to shoulder with the Harsh, the cold enemy who had tried to crush Owen and his friends.

He peered through the telescope into Owen's room. Reflected in the dressing-table mirror he could see the chest and the dull gleam of the Mortmain. It had taken Johnston all year to work out that the chest contained the Puissance. The Harsh were eager to get it back. He lowered the telescope. This time Owen would not stand in his way.

Cati also lay awake. For a long year she had been the Watcher. There was always a Watcher—one member of the Resisters who stayed awake while the others slept.

She lived in the Workhouse on the river below Owen's house, taking food from the cavernous storerooms and cooking it in the vast empty kitchens. Every day she walked the crumbling battlements of the Workhouse, the Resister headquarters, which just looked like an old ruin to human eyes. She could see traffic moving up and down the road, but the drivers could not see her. She wondered what they would think if they knew that there was an army sleeping in the old building.

Watching other people going up and down the road was lonely enough, but worst of all was seeing Owen going to and from school or walking to his Den, his brown hair blowing in the wind from the harbor. She loved it when he waved and said hello even though he couldn't see her. She longed to call to him and walk along the river, to laugh and talk the way they had before.

Cati sighed. Her father had been the Watcher before her, but he hadn't said much about what it was like to be awake when everyone else slept. He had never mentioned the loneliness. He'd merely told her that it was a bit like being a night watchman. She sat up in bed. She knew that she wouldn't sleep that night, so, pulling on her clothes and boots, she made her way toward the stone staircase that led to the top of the Workhouse. *If I'm the Watcher,* she thought, *then I might as well go and watch.*

It was a crisp clear night, with a full moon that seemed to fill the sky over the harbor. Cati shivered and pulled her collar tight around her neck. She listened to the gentle murmur of the river far below. Then she heard the sound of wings. A vast skein of wild geese were flying low and hard toward the harbor. They were flying in a V formation from north to south and Cati could hear them honking. She watched them cross the face of the moon until they were framed in its circle. *They are free and I am not,* she thought sadly.

Then she froze to the spot. A second before, there had been birds on the wing. Now they turned to skeletons, the flesh and feathers gone! For a moment they

10

hung in the sky, a great silent flock of the dead, their bone wings fixed in flight, their beaks agape but noiseless. Then they turned to dust, which fell earthward in a great plume until it was swallowed by the darkness below.

Cati felt as if her heart had stopped. For a long moment she stood staring at the moon, wondering if she had hallucinated the whole thing. But the geese had been real; nothing could have been more real than their wild honking high in the sky. She forced herself to think. No weapon could have reduced the geese to dust. No storm or wind or lightning strike. Only one thing could have happened. Somehow, time had changed them and they had aged many years in a single second.

Her job was to watch for a threat to the fabric of time and to wake the other Resisters if they were needed to defend. Was this one of those times? Her heart told her that it was. She turned and plunged down the stairs.

In two minutes she stood at the doors that led to the Starry, the great chamber where the Resisters slept. As she fumbled at the lock, doubt began to creep into her mind. What if she was wrong? She thought about Samual, one of the Resister leaders. The warrior was a brave fighter, but his tongue was acid and he had not approved of Cati's friendship with Owen. She could almost hear his sarcastic words. *Geese turning to dust? You woke us because you had a silly dream?*

But it wasn't a dream, she said to herself. *It wasn't.*

11

Cati turned the slender key in the lock and the stone doors opened.

Before her in semidarkness were hundreds of wooden beds, and in each bed lay a Resister. What light there was came from the ceiling, which was domed and covered with tiny lights like a night sky. The air was warm and still and she could hear gentle breathing sweep the room like a great sigh. She looked at the sleeping faces, recognizing every one—young and old, friend and opponent.

She checked on the Starry once every three or four days. It was part of her job, although no one had ever told her so. Her visits were brief: a glance to make sure all was well and no more. To see so many familiar faces only made her loneliness worse.

She had seen her father wake the Sleepers before. He had simply touched each person's forehead and after a moment the Resister would wake, looking around, a little bewildered until they realized where they were. Whom would she wake first to tell about the geese? *Contessa,* she thought. Contessa, who ran the great kitchens in the Workhouse, who was gentle and wise, a mother to them all. She would know what to do.

Cati walked between the rows until she found her. Contessa was tall, elegantly dressed in a wool gown. Her hands were folded on her breast and even in sleep there was a calm authority to her face. Hesitantly, Cati reached out and touched her forehead. She stood for a moment, feeling the warm skin, waiting for her eyes to open.

Without warning, Contessa started to writhe, her back arching, pain written on her gentle face. "No," she moaned, "stop . . ."

Cati jerked her hand back. Contessa's body fell to the bed and she was asleep again, breathing heavily, beads of perspiration on her forehead.

Something was wrong. Cati placed her hand on another Resister's head, a dark-haired young man. He twisted and moaned as if her touch burned him. She snatched her hand away. What was wrong? She should be able to wake them.

Even as she stood there, bewildered and alarmed, Cati could feel sleep start to steal over her, as it did if you remained too long in the Starry. But this sleep felt different. It seemed . . . *stale*.

She turned swiftly and walked toward the door. As Watcher, she knew it was not the time to fall asleep. She closed the door behind her and locked it, then ran outside, welcoming the cool night air on her face. Outside it seemed as bright as day. The moon over the Workhouse roof shone with a light that was almost dazzling.

Cati sat down on a rock. Something was terribly wrong. There was only one option. She knew that her father had sometimes called upon special people in the ordinary world. She thought that the shopkeeper, Mary White, was one of them.

Owen was another. His father had known the Resisters and Owen had joined them to defeat the Harsh. Owen was called the Navigator, for reasons she didn't quite understand, and it was a title that the other Resisters seemed to respect; even, in some cases, to fear.

She would never try to contact him under normal circumstances. But these were not normal circumstances. She jumped up and began to run.

Owen didn't know what woke him. A gust of wind, he thought, or a dog barking? As his eyes got used to the dark he lifted his head from the pillow. Everything in his room was the same as before. His guitar propped against the wall, the model plane hanging from the ceiling, the old chest under the window. Outside the wind stirred the trees. *That was it*, he thought, *the wind*.

He allowed his head to fall back onto the pillow. It was cold and he gathered the blankets around him. He was about to close his eyes when he noticed something odd. He sat up. The air in the middle of the room looked strange. It was shimmering slightly. He rubbed his eyes, but when he looked again, there was still something different. The room looked distorted, as if he was looking through old glass. He felt the hairs on the back of his neck rise as he sensed a presence in the room, and his heart started to beat faster.

Then he thought he heard a sound, a voice. There *was* somebody else in the room.

Without knowing how, he was out of bed now. The shimmering air was between him and the door. He started to edge around it. He heard the sound again, like a voice, but far, far away, as if in a cave or down a well. The words were mournful and distorted. He tried to squeeze between the wall and the shimmer, but it moved toward him.

He stepped back, stumbling over his trainers, and instinctively put out an arm to save himself. The arm touched the moving air and to his amazement it felt warm and solid, like a living thing.

He jerked his arm away and backed toward the bed. Something was resolving itself in the middle of the room. Suddenly there was a large flicker and he realized that it *was* a person, someone he recognized. He saw a clever girl's face with dark curly hair, then a body wearing a faded uniform with epaulettes on the shoulders. His heart leapt.

"Cati!" he gasped. He could see her lips moving but could not understand the words, which still sounded distant. He grabbed her arm. Immediately he could hear her voice. It had been a year since she had disappeared back into the mists of time, but if he thought that she was going to exchange memories with him like two old comrades, he was sadly mistaken.

"Hold on to me, you idiot," she hissed. "It's the only way I can stay stable in your time." Owen grasped her with both hands. The flickering stopped and at last she was standing in his room, flesh and blood. Her expression was serious, but as always, there was a mocking look in her strange green eyes.

"Cati," he said again. "I missed—"

"Never mind that," she said. "There isn't time. I need you to come down to the Workhouse and meet me."

"What's happening? Is it the Harsh?"

"Come to the Workhouse and I'll explain. It's easier to stay stable there." As she spoke, Cati began to flicker again. One moment Owen had hold of solid flesh, the next there was nothing. But just before she faded completely, he saw a cheeky, lopsided grin on her face and thought he heard the words "Missed you too . . ."

Hastily, Owen yanked on jeans, a sweatshirt, and a jacket and fumbled for his trainers. Then he opened the door into the hallway. It was flooded with moonlight. From the room at the end he heard his mother's soft breathing. As quietly as possible, he crept along the landing and down the stairs.

Outside it was chilly and he was glad he'd grabbed his jacket. Everything was quiet and still and he could hear the sound his trainers made on the grass. He ran lightly across the two fields that separated his house from the river and from the dark shadow of the Workhouse. Its crumbling brickwork and dark empty windows were forbidding enough to send a shiver down his spine. He remembered being inside and seeing cold ghostly shapes moving through the field as the Harsh attacked. He remembered Johnston's men attacking the Workhouse defenses.

When he reached the riverbank he leapt lightly onto the fallen tree. He ran across and jumped down on the other side. It was darker here and hard to see where he was going. He should have brought a torch.

"Cati?" he called out, his voice sounding a bit weak and scared in the darkness. He cleared his throat and tried again. "Cati?" In the darkness something rustled. He ran to the Workhouse door.

"Cati," he hissed, "is that you?" There was a scrabbling sound from inside, like stones and rubble falling. In the darkness he could see the staircase, almost blocked with rocks. Then a small figure dashed around the bend in the stairs, carrying a strangely shaped magno gun in one hand.

She slid to the ground in front of Owen. "I nearly shot your silly head off," she said, starting to brush dust off her trousers.

"I wouldn't have put my head up if I'd known you were armed," he said. "What's going on anyway?"

"I don't know," she said, looking troubled. "If only the Sub-Commandant was here . . ."

But Owen knew that the Sub-Commandant, Cati's father, would never be there again. In the final battle with the Harsh, he had been sucked into the time vortex they called the Puissance and been lost, leaving Cati to inherit his role as Watcher.

Cati turned her face aside and passed her sleeve over her eyes. "You miss him too?" she said, her voice almost pleading.

Owen nodded. The small, stern man had believed in Owen when everyone else seemed against him.

"Anyway," Cati said with an effort, "let's get inside somewhere where we can talk."

"What about the Den?"

"All right," she said. "I should be stable there. Let's go."

They walked along the riverbank, then dived through the bushes into the Den. Inside Owen took the piece of magno from its box and placed it on the table. The blue light illuminated the room.

Cati threw herself wearily down on the old sofa. Owen went to the little box where he kept food and took out tea bags and a packet of biscuits. He had added a camping stove to the Den and Cati watched with interest as he lit it. Owen made the tea and waited until she had drunk half of it before he spoke.

"So what is it, Cati?" he said. "Why did you come looking for me?"

She rubbed a hand wearily over her face and he saw

the dark shadows under her eyes. "I didn't know what else to do," she said slowly. Then she told him about the flight of geese she had seen and how they had turned into skeletons and then into dust.

"That's like what happened to me!" Owen said. "A girl in school. Freya Revell. I was talking to her and for a moment she turned really old. I mean, her face looked ancient."

"So I didn't dream it!" Cati exclaimed. "It must have happened!"

"I think so," Owen said. "It sounds as if it's something to do with time going weird. You should wake the others. . . ."

Cati shook her head. "I tried, but I can't. There's something wrong."

His heart went out to his tired-looking friend. "Maybe I can . . . ," he began. Cati looked up at him hopefully. He knew that he possessed a strange power to awake those who were in the long sleep, although he didn't understand it.

Cati nodded. "That is why I called you. I don't know if it's wrong or not. There may be consequences. But when I couldn't wake them I didn't know what else to do."

"You did the right thing," Owen said, hoping it was true.

"Do you think you can wake them?" Cati asked eagerly.

"I can try," Owen said, frowning. He had awakened

people before, but it had felt like an accident. He didn't know if he could wake the whole Starry.

"Come on, then," Cati said, jumping to her feet, her tiredness forgotten.

Owen barely had time to put the cup back on the table before she had hauled him through the gap in the bushes and out onto the path. Within minutes they were standing before a wall of rock. Cati put her hands against it and the outline of a massive door appeared, delicately carved with small, ancient-looking figures and decorations. Cati produced a tiny key and inserted it into an almost invisible lock. Silently the massive door swung open.

Owen stared at the sleeping people. Part of him thought of the Resisters as a dream, but now that he saw them, memories came flooding back.

"Come on," Cati said. "We'll try to wake Dr. Diamond."

Owen nodded approvingly. If anyone would know what to do, it would be the scientist and philosopher. They slipped between the rows of sleeping people and he recognized many of them. Here and there, one of the simple beds was empty. Defending time was a dangerous business.

Finally they came to Dr. Diamond's bed. The scientist's chest rose and fell gently as he slept, and there was an expression on his face somewhere between a smile and a frown, as though he was on the verge of solving a particularly tricky problem that had cropped up in a dream. The pockets of his faded blue overalls bulged with mysterious objects.

"Will you try?" Cati whispered. Owen nodded.

He gently placed his hand on the man's forehead. There was a faint tingling in his fingers, but nothing more. He straightened up. A simple touch had worked before, even when he didn't know he had the power. He tried again, with the same result.

"Call him," Cati said. "Call out his name in your mind."

Owen bent forward again. This time he put both hands on the man's forehead and closed his eyes.

"Dr. Diamond," he whispered, then formed the words in his mind. *Dr. Diamond, Dr. Diamond.* Suddenly he felt as if he was sinking in a deep well, going down into the darkness.

"Dr. Diamond," he whispered again. Something was wrong. He felt staleness in the atmosphere, and in the spaces his mind reached out to. He found himself gasping, as if all the air had been sucked out of the Starry. He tried to detach his mind. Then, in the distance, he felt another presence. A warm presence, calling his name, groping its way toward him in the darkness.

Owen had the feeling that another mind gripped his like two strong hands and propelled him upward, out of the darkness and into the light.

"Owen! Owen!" It was Cati's voice. Owen came to and found himself on the floor of the Starry. He sat up and shook his head, groggy. Cati's face swam into focus. She looked both anxious and relieved.

"What happened?" he asked. "I was calling Dr. Diamond. . . ."

"And I heard you," a voice said.

Owen looked up. Dr. Diamond was sitting on the edge of his bed, looking down at him. There was a half smile on his face.

"Then that was you . . . ?" Owen said.

"Who came and joined my mind to yours? Yes, indeed. I don't think either of us could have awoken on our own."

"We'd better get out of here," Cati said, her eyes heavy, "before the Starry sends us all to sleep."

"Yes," agreed the doctor, stretching. "It gets very musty in here after a year or so."

More than musty this time, Owen thought. He watched Dr. Diamond looking carefully around the Starry, as though there was something wrong that he couldn't quite put his finger on. He was definitely worried.

Ten minutes later they were sitting on the sofa in the Den with Dr. Diamond examining the camping stove. "Ingenious," he said. "Now, Cati, tell me everything that has happened in the past year."

Cati went quiet. How could she explain how it had felt, autumn stretching into winter? Standing under the trees as they changed, then lying awake at night listening to the wind howling through the Workhouse battlements. How could she tell him about the time it had snowed, and how in the stillness she could hear the voices of children playing? How there was no one to talk to when she was worried or scared?

"Nothing much happened," she said finally. "It was just . . . a little bit lonely sometimes." Owen reached out and touched her hand.

They both know what loneliness is, Dr. Diamond thought. *That is why their friendship will endure.*

"And what happened then?" he said eventually, his eyes shrewd and penetrating. "What happened that you reached out of the shadows to contact Owen? Is time under threat?"

"I was watching on the battlements," Cati said. "There was a flight of geese that turned to skeletons and then to dust." She looked defiantly at Dr. Diamond as though he might disbelieve her.

"I saw something the same," Owen said. He told Dr. Diamond about the girl in school who had changed in front of his eyes.

"I tried to wake the Resisters, but when I touched them it was as if my fingers were hurting them," Cati continued. "I didn't know what to do, so I called Owen."

Dr. Diamond looked grave. "You did the right thing," he said. "Something or someone is interfering with time. That is why you saw what you did, and why the Sleepers could not be woken."

The scientist looked at Owen and Cati over the top

24

of his glasses. "I don't know what is happening yet, but I do know one thing, my two young friends. There is a mystery here. And where there is mystery there is an adventure. Now, where is my pencil?"

"I think it's behind your ear," Cati said, exchanging a smile with Owen. Dr. Diamond produced a notebook from his overalls, licked the tip of the pencil, then started to write at lightning speed. This action had a strangely soothing effect and Owen and Cati both felt their eyelids grow heavy. Within minutes they had both fallen asleep, as Dr. Diamond had intended they should.

The doctor got up, lifted their feet onto the sofa, and covered them with sleeping bags. Then he sat down with his notebook again.

"Night good," he said, speaking backward, as he tended to do when distracted. He bent his head and began to write.

4

Dr. Diamond woke Owen at six o'clock. There was no sign of Cati.

"Cati has gone to check on the world. Her 'morning round,' she calls it," Dr. Diamond said. "You had better get home before your mother misses you."

"But—" Owen began.

"It's better if you carry on as normal. Go home, then to school, and come back here this evening before dark. We have much to plan." Owen jumped up. At least he would see his friends again that evening.

He ducked out of the Den into the chill morning air and ran along the riverbank. As he crossed the river on the old tree trunk he heard someone calling. Cati was standing on top of the ruins of the Workhouse. He waved at her and she waved back, then disappeared from view.

After school, he came straight back to the Workhouse without returning home first. Approaching the gaunt ruin, he found it hard to believe the building had ever come alive when time was threatened, and that it had teemed with people. If you looked closely, you could see the outline of the defenses along the river and some of the scars left by exploding ice lances during the battle with Johnston and the Harsh. But otherwise the building was sunk into decay and dereliction.

The wind funneling down the river valley toward Owen was cold, but it was the kind of cold he didn't mind, where you pulled your scarf around your neck and looked forward to sitting at a warm fire. Not the terrible cold that the Harsh had used as a weapon, the chill that froze your heart as well as your limbs.

He couldn't see any sign of Cati or Dr. Diamond, so he followed the riverbank to the Den. He pulled aside the bushes at the entrance and paused. There was something strange in the air, something different. Not danger, definitely not danger. He moved cautiously forward.

The first thing he saw was Cati, fast asleep on the battered sofa. As he went over to wake her, he spotted something lying on the table. At first he thought it was a cornflower. The Resisters used them as tokens of remembrance and Cati had left one in exactly the same place for him when she had faded back into the shadows of time. But then he realized that it was in fact a cornflower brooch, very old and beautifully made from silver and enamel. He turned it over in his hand.

"Where did you get that?"

Owen turned. Cati was sitting bolt upright, her eyes unnaturally bright. "It was on the table," he said.

"Give it to me!" She sprang up and snatched it from his hand.

"Take it easy," Owen said. She was staring down at the brooch and Owen saw tears in her eyes. "I'm sorry," he said. "I just saw it lying there. I didn't mean any harm. Where did it come from, anyway?"

She didn't answer. Her hands were trembling.

"Cati?" he said softly.

"I don't know how it got on the table," she said, her voice shaking, "but I know where it comes from."

"Where?"

"My father," she said. "He was here, Owen! It belonged to my mother. He carried it on a chain around his neck."

Owen looked at her. His heart was beating so loudly that he thought she could hear it. He had seen what had happened to her father, the Sub-Commandant, how he'd been sucked into the Puissance, the maelstrom that had been draining time from the world. He could never have survived.

"He wasn't killed," Cati said, as though reading his thoughts. "Just lost in time."

28

"Forever," Owen said. "Remember what he said. He was saying goodbye to you forever, Cati. You know that."

"Stop it!" Cati cried. "He left the brooch! He's not gone. You don't know what it's like."

"I do," Owen said quietly. "I do know, Cati."

"I . . . I'm sorry," Cati said.

"Don't be," Owen said. "I'm glad he's out there somewhere. But we have to think what this means, Cati. Your father wouldn't have done this for no reason."

"It wasn't for no reason," Cati said. "It was for me."

"Yes, Cati. But . . . you know what type of man he was."

"Kind and loving and—"

"Yes, but he knew his duty too. There has to be a message here somewhere, Cati. About time. Can I see it?"

Cati handed over the brooch. "Ouch!"

"What is it?"

"The pin stuck into me. It's all bent."

They examined the brooch. The pin at the back was badly bent, turned almost at right angles to where it should have been. "I wonder how that happened," Cati said, sucking at her sore finger.

"I wonder," Owen said. "Hang on a second. . . ."

The late afternoon light coming through the perspex roof of the Den made dust motes dance above the table. But it was the surface of the table that had caught Owen's eye, the fresh scratches in the battered wooden top.

"That's why the pin is bent!" Cati said. "It must have been used to scratch a message."

They bent over the table together. The scratches were definitely words gouged into the surface. They were hard to read; the wood was splintered and the letters uneven and clumsy.

go to the city of time
not enough time   *a tempod*

"Do you know what it means?" Owen asked.

"No." Cati frowned. "I've never heard of a city of time. And what does he mean by 'not enough time'? Not enough time for what? And what is a tempod?"

"I don't know," Owen said, "but he went to a lot of trouble to get the message to us, so it must be important." He looked at Cati. She was tracing the letters with her finger, a dreamy smile on her face.

They found Dr. Diamond in his laboratory, the Skyward. The Skyward was a glass building fixed to the top of a metal column called the Nab. When the Workhouse was fully awake, the Nab opened out like an old-fashioned telescope, becoming a slender column that stood high above the building like a metal lighthouse, the Skyward on top. But now the Nab was folded away deep under the ground.

Owen had followed Cati through one of the hidden openings to the interior of the Workhouse. This one

looked like a badger sett. It opened out into a damp earthen corridor that led steeply downward and they stumbled over rocks and tree roots on the way. Small pieces of magno set into the wall cast a dim light, but it wasn't bright enough to see properly.

Finally Owen saw the outlines of the Nab, the brass body going downward into a dark aperture in the ground. Above it were the glass walls of the Skyward, lit from within.

They had to climb a rickety wooden ladder to get to the door. When the Nab stood high above the Workhouse the top revolved, so you had to wait for the inner and outer doors to line up, but now the doors were already open. Cati and Owen stepped inside.

The interior of the Skyward was familiar and com-forting. Much of Dr. Diamond's equipment was made from objects he had found and recycled. There was the old fridge that produced temperatures so low that it took things weeks to defrost. There was the old airplane seat. Next, the vacuum cleaner with mysterious pipes flowing into it. A submarine periscope hung from the ceiling that you could use to see backward or forward in time. There were odors of strange chemicals and varnish and hot solder, and a delicious smell of baking. Dr. Diamond was an excellent cook and Owen knew there must be a cake in the little oven.

The middle of the room was taken up by a big clock with five faces. Dr. Diamond was standing in front of it with a notebook, frowning. Owen remembered that the clocks all moved at different speeds. Now, though, three of the clocks weren't moving at all. Of the two remaining clock faces, one was moving slowly and steadily, while the hands of the other one were spinning round at immense speed.

Dr. Diamond scribbled furiously in the notebook, then sucked the end of his pencil.

"Dr. Diamond!" Cati burst out. "We got a message from the Sub-Commandant!"

The scientist wheeled around to look at them. Owen was uncomfortably aware of how penetrating the gaze from those kindly blue eyes could be. "That is impossible—"

"It's not impossible!" Cati exclaimed. "It happened!"

"If you will let me finish," Dr. Diamond said patiently. "It *is* impossible, but there are other impossible things happening. Look at the clocks."

Owen studied them. He always felt a little stupid in the Skyward. Dr. Diamond had said that there were at least five different kinds of time and that was why there were five clocks, but Owen didn't really understand it.

"The clocks are slowing down," Dr. Diamond said, "and that should be impossible. And now a message from my old friend the Sub-Commandant. What does he say, Cati?"

Cati told the doctor how they had found the message scratched on the table, and showed him the cornflower brooch.

"Yes, of course," Dr. Diamond said softly. "Your mother used to wear it. She looked very beautiful."

"Did she?" Cati said.

"Yes." Diamond ruffled Cati's hair fondly.

Owen had never thought about Cati having a mother before. He wondered where she was and what had happened to her. But now was not the time to ask. He told Dr. Diamond what had been scratched in the table.

"City of Time?" Diamond said sharply. "Are you sure it said City of Time? Those words exactly?"

"Yes," Owen said.

Dr. Diamond got up and began to pace. "City of Time and not enough time," he repeated to himself. "Obviously, he didn't have the strength to spell out exactly what he meant. It is a long while since I heard the City mentioned. And I wonder why we need a tempod? Wait here. . . ."

With bewildering speed, he disappeared through the door at the back of the Skyward that led into his private quarters.

"What do we do now?" Owen said, staring after him.

"Don't know," Cati said. "It feels late. Are you going home?"

"No." He knew his mother would be asleep, unaware that he was out.

Cati sniffed the air. "You know what?"

"What?"

"You think Dr. Diamond would mind if we checked the cake?"

34

"Just in case it burns?"

"Just in case it burns."

Across the fields someone else had noticed it was getting late. Mary White's little thatched shop was just down the road from Owen's house. Mary was a good friend and neighbor to Owen and his mother. Often when Owen did not have enough money for groceries, Mary had given him food, saying he could pay later. She was much older than anyone suspected, and much wiser, and could see things that others couldn't.

She had stood behind the counter of her shop all day, and now she locked the door and turned out the lights and went into the parlor behind the counter. It had been a long day and she moved slowly, but she knew there was something that must be done. Something that could not wait.

There was a grandfather clock in the corner of the parlor. She went over to it and opened the glass door below the clock face. A brass pendulum hung there, apparently unmoving. But if you looked deep into the case you could see that it *was* in fact swinging, making a tiny motion, almost a tremble. Not quite still, but almost.

All year Mary had watched the pendulum get slower and slower. She stood there for a long time looking at it. Looking *beyond* it, for if you gazed closely you could see that there was no back to the case; instead there was a velvet blackness studded with pinpricks of light. It was like looking into deep space, the blackness going on

35

forever and ever, as though the grandfather clock contained all of eternity.

Mary closed the glass door gently and locked it, removing the long thin key. She went to the mirror on the wall beside the door and twisted a length of her gray hair around her fingers, using the key to fix it in position. It looked like an ornate hairpin, perfectly hidden.

She bolted the back door, took her coat from the peg, and went out through the shop at the front. As she reached down and opened the shop door she looked through the glass panel. She stopped and the hand that held the door key trembled. She quickly relocked the door. It was dark outside but she recognized the truck that was parked on the other side of the road. The battered and filthy scrap truck that went up and down the road every day. The truck driven by Johnston, the Resisters' mortal enemy.

Mary slipped back behind the counter and into the parlor, where she sat down heavily on the sofa. She had no idea that things were so bad. Never before would Johnston have had the nerve to post a guard on her front door. Without thinking, she put her hand to the little key that she had concealed in her hair. There was something she had to do, something she had promised herself she would do a long time ago. She hoped it wasn't too late.

D r. Diamond came back into the room as Owen and Cati were helping themselves to cake. "Not enough time," he muttered to himself. "What did he mean? Is it too late? Is that why the Resisters won't wake?"

"What is a tempod?" Cati asked, thinking about the final odd word of her father's message.

"A tempod is a strange thing, not much understood," Dr. Diamond said. "It looks like a hollow rock, by all accounts, but it is capable of storing a large quantity of time."

"Speaking of time, what time is it?" Owen asked.

"That is an interesting question," Dr. Diamond said, turning to look at him.

"No," Owen groaned, "I meant is it morning or the middle of the night? I can't tell down here."

"Oh," Dr. Diamond said. "About eleven o'clock p.m., I think." An idea struck him and he strode to his blackboard. He swiftly wrote out a long sum with lots of fractions, looked at it, then seized the duster and wiped it out.

"No good." He sat down, glum. "I can't figure out why he left that message in particular. 'Not enough time.' What does it mean?"

"What about . . . ," Owen said slowly, almost afraid to be laughed at. "What if he just meant that there wasn't enough time?"

"Precisely!" the doctor cried. "But not enough for what?"

"No," Owen said, sure now that Dr. Diamond would laugh out loud. "What if it meant that there *really* wasn't enough? I mean, not enough to go around. Say the world or universe, or whatever, is filled with time, but that it has run short or something, so that there just isn't enough of it. . . ." He ground lamely to a halt. Dr. Diamond was staring at him. "It's just a theory," Owen said. "Probably pretty stupid."

"A theory?" Dr. Diamond said, finding his voice. "You've hit the nail on the head, Owen! That was *exactly* what the message meant. It makes sense now. That is why the clocks are all slowing down. That was why your friend's face changed in the playground, although fortunately the change wasn't permanent. That was why the geese turned to dust. There isn't enough *time*. And that's why he told us about the City."

38

"What *is* this City of Time?" Cati asked.

"It is called Hadima in the old books," Dr. Diamond said. "Years ago there was a lot of coming and going between the Workhouse and Hadima. There used to be an entrance. . . ."

Cati noticed a strange expression on Dr. Diamond's face. His eyes fell on Owen and stayed there, as if lost in a dream.

"The City of Time, Dr. Diamond," Owen reminded him gently.

"Oh yes. Well, to cut it short, it is a trading city, you might say; a city with its roots stretching back in the past and far into the future."

"What does it trade?"

"Time," Dr. Diamond said. "It trades time itself."

"That's why my father is telling us to go there," Cati said excitedly. "To get some time. There isn't enough, so we have to get some."

"Is that right, Dr. Diamond?" Owen asked. Time, after all, wasn't something you went out to a shop and bought.

"Yes," Dr. Diamond said slowly, "I think Cati may be right."

"So, that's easy then," Owen said. "Cati's dad is telling us to go to Hadima and get a tempod containing time, and . . . and . . ."

"And release the time here." Cati completed his sentence.

"But you cannot," Dr. Diamond said.

"Why?" Owen demanded.

"The entrance is sealed. The Resisters sat in Convoke—you remember the Convoke, Owen? Where we all gather together and decide things? And at this Convoke a long time ago, we decided that the entrance should be sealed and should stay sealed."

"But why?" Cati asked.

"We were afraid that the Harsh might use it to travel from the City to here. There were rumors. . . ."

"But the Harsh got here anyway!" Owen said. "When they attacked last year!"

"I know, Owen," the doctor said, looking troubled, "but there was another reason. Your father was traveling between here and Hadima. The Convoke thought that he was bringing trouble with him. That he was meddling in things he did not understand."

"But now . . . now we need it," Cati said. "We need to get to Hadima!"

"I'm sorry," Dr. Diamond said, "but I cannot repeal the decision of the Convoke."

They heard a faint rumble beneath their feet. The Skyward swayed gently for a moment and then was still.

"What was that?" Cati jumped up.

Dr. Diamond stood and walked over to an instrument in the corner that had started to spout out rolls of paper. He examined it. "Earth tremor," he said. "Two point three on the Richter scale. Caused by the moon, I would say."

Cati and Owen looked at each other. Cati opened

her mouth to speak, but before she could Dr. Diamond said sternly, "The decision of the Convoke is final. The entrance to Hadima has been sealed with the sign of the fleur-de-lis and will not be reopened!"

Next morning they ate breakfast at Dr. Diamond's workbench. The scientist fried bacon and sausages, and they had them with fried potato cakes and crusty bread, all washed down with mugs of tea.

"Now," said the doctor when they had finished, "we need a plan. But first, what about your mother, Owen? Will she not wonder where you are?"

"She'll think I've gone to school already. She doesn't really notice much."

"Don't be too hard on her," Dr. Diamond said. "We never really know what is going on in someone's head."

"What shall we do first?" asked Cati.

"I think we need to wake some of the others," the doctor said. "Do you think you can try, Owen? I know it's dangerous, but we need more help. How about Rutgar and Pieta? They both have strong minds and should be able to reach out to you as you wake them."

Rutgar was the head of the Workhouse guard, solid and dependable. Pieta was the subtle and dangerous warrior who had followed Owen to the north when he had been taken by Johnston's henchmen. Owen still remembered the magno whip she had wielded with deadly force.

Owen took a deep breath. He remembered what had happened when he had woken Dr. Diamond, and he wasn't eager to experience it again. But then he found himself saying, "Yes, of course I will."

"Start with Rutgar," Dr. Diamond said.

"Maybe I should wake Wesley," Owen said. "The Raggies are younger. They might be easier to wake."

Cati's heart lifted at the thought of seeing Wesley and the Raggies again. The Raggies were Resisters too, but slept in their own Starry in warehouses near the harbor. They were children who had been abandoned in time by a ship's captain who had been paid to look after them. The older children, like Wesley, took care of the younger ones. They dressed in rags and never wore shoes, but they were proud and resourceful, and were experts on anything to do with the sea.

Dr. Diamond frowned. "That is the problem," he said. "They are young. Rutgar is an experienced fighter."

"It has to be Wesley," Owen said stubbornly, "or I won't do it."

Cati looked at him. It wasn't like Owen to behave so childishly.

"All right," Dr. Diamond said quietly. "If you fear to risk waking Rutgar, then Wesley it is."

There was another rumble beneath their feet and the Starry swayed again. The doctor leapt up and examined the machine in the corner. "Two point four on the

Richter scale!" he exclaimed. "We must hurry! Go and wake Wesley if you can. I must think."

"We need a magno gun," Owen said.

"Then take one," Dr. Diamond said, "but hurry!"

Fifteen minutes later, Cati and Owen found themselves walking down along the river, Owen carrying a magno gun under his arm. He glanced at the tiny glowing blue chip that was fixed in the middle of the gun and wondered for the hundredth time how the Resisters had harnessed the power of magnetism, using it the way ordinary people used electricity.

It had rained during the night and the river was in full spate, tumbling over the rocks. The leaves of the overhanging trees had turned red and brown and had started to fall, so the path was covered in them.

"Why do you want to wake Wesley so badly?" Cati asked.

"I don't," Owen said. "I just wanted to get down here."

"I don't understand. And you never asked for a gun before. What are you up to?" Cati asked suspiciously.

"I think Dr. Diamond gave it away."

"Gave what away?"

"The location of the entrance to Hadima."

"But he didn't say anything. And it doesn't matter because the entrance is sealed."

"Maybe I can unseal it," Owen said, patting the barrel of the magno gun.

"You can't do that . . . it's dangerous."

"It wasn't dangerous for my father."

"But the Convoke! The Resisters will turn against you if—"

"There won't *be* any Resisters if we don't do something," Owen said angrily. "And your own father sent us the message to go there. So are you with me or against me?"

Cati took a deep breath. "I'm with you," she said at last. "So how did Dr. Diamond give it away?"

"He said it was sealed with the sign of the fleur-de-lis."

"So?"

"Look!" Owen said, pointing to the gable of a building that backed onto the river. On the wall there was a blue neon sign. "Look at it," he said. "The shape is a fleur-de-lis!"

Cati looked. The sign did indeed seem to be a fleur-de-lis if she closed her eyes and squinted. "Come on, Owen," she said. "That's just a bit of old advertising. For a shop or something."

"There is no shop around here. Nothing else either," Owen said quietly. "Look more closely."

"I can't see anything."

"Concentrate."

Cati stared until her eyes hurt, but still could see nothing besides the glowing neon tubes of an advertising sign. Then suddenly she saw it. "The sign is made from magno," she breathed.

"Yes," Owen said, "and look at the wall. The stonework is newer than the rest. It has to be the entrance to Hadima."

"What are you going to do?"

"I'm going to try to blast it open."

Cati gulped. "Are you sure that's a good idea?"

"No," Owen said cheerfully, "I'm not sure at all. Take cover!"

Cati had barely time to dive behind a rock as Owen raised the gun and fired. A glass bulb filled with magno shot from the end of the gun and arced toward the wall just below the sign, where it burst with a crash and a gout of blue flame. Cati peeped out. The wall was blackened but otherwise there seemed to be little damage. Owen pulled another glass bulb from his belt.

"How many of those do you have?" Cati asked.

"Three more." He fired again. This time the mortar binding the wall cracked a little. He fired the third projectile and the cracks deepened.

"One left," he said. Now he moved much closer before firing. He recoiled from the heat of the blue flame that flicked back and almost enveloped him. As it died down, he ran forward. The wall was severely cracked and stones had fallen out in places, but there was no sign of it having been breached.

Owen sighed with disappointment. "We'll never get through it. Even with a hundred shots."

He turned away, and as he did so there was a low rumble and the ground below his feet moved.

"Earthquake!" Cati shouted.

Before Owen had a chance to move, the whole world shook. He grabbed at the wall, then looked up in horror. Great pieces of masonry were falling all around him. He tried to move, but the ground was shaking too violently. Another earth tremor, much stronger this time. In the nearby town he could hear the sound of car alarms going off. He glanced up again. The whole wall was about to fall on him!

He felt a strange sensation around his feet. The path he stood on was covered with water up to knee height. Water was pouring up the river, topped with dirty yellow foam. A geography lesson about underwater earthquakes causing tsunamis came into his head.

"Owen!" Cati shouted above the roar of the water. Then a wall of water hit him. In seconds he was tumbling, being driven upstream, bouncing along the riverbed. Once again he heard Cati call his name and thought he felt her hand grip his, but he could not hold on. Her fingertips glanced against his and then she was gone. With one great shuddering breath he filled his lungs and the water claimed him.

He couldn't say how long he was underwater. His lungs burned and his body ached from being hit by stones and boulders. He knew that he could no longer hold his breath, that he had to exhale. He felt consciousness starting to slip away, and as it did so a distant memory formed in his mind. How as a baby he had been with his father when their car crashed into the harbor. How his father had rescued him. He could almost feel two strong hands closing around his waist. . . .

Then he felt the terrifying wave that had carried him upriver start to ebb, receding with startling speed. A great eddy bore him to the surface. He opened his eyes and realized that he was being carried along, high above the riverbed where they had walked moments before, being swept now toward the sea. With a bone-shuddering impact, the water threw him against the stone sides of the river, pushing him higher and higher. Weakly he reached out, seeking any purchase. Just as his strength was fading, he found something to grip. Scrambling with both hands, he tried to lift himself to safety.

Not until a fresh wave of water caught him did he manage to get his hands and then his elbows onto the edge of what was the opening to a tunnel. He drew a gasping breath and then another. But even so he might have fallen back had not a great surge lifted him and propelled him into the tunnel itself. The water followed him in and rose to the level of his neck. He forced himself farther into the tunnel on his hands and knees, scrambling upward, until finally he was beyond the water's reach.

Panting, Owen heaved himself upright and lay back against the wall. There was a faint light coming from up

47

ahead and he could see that the tunnel was big enough to stand in. He got to his feet, his clothes soaking. The water surged toward him again, so he turned and ran as fast as he could in the opposite direction.

The tunnel walls were slimy and the stones underfoot were slippery, but there was enough light and the going got easier as the tunnel widened. He could feel fresh air on his face. The tunnel suddenly curved to the left and opened out. Owen stepped out of the tunnel, feeling the autumn sunshine on his face.

He looked around and saw he was in a small court-yard. It was enclosed by shops and outbuildings, but it was obvious that no one had been there for many years. Doors sagged off their hinges and the windows were opaque with dust and cobwebs. Several old cars lay abandoned in the center of the courtyard, cars that were perhaps thirty or forty years old. Beside them was an old truck with canvas sides. Both of its doors were open, as though it had been abandoned in a hurry. There was a stillness to the place. Owen had the feeling that no one had disturbed the silence there for many years.

He walked cautiously around the courtyard. There was a shop selling old-fashioned mountaineering gear, the ropes now moldy and useless. Another sold camping gear, a rotted tent erected in the window. Next door the shop advertised auto spares, puncture repair kits, and things that you might need while traveling. A small shop whose front had collapsed had carried tinned food. Hundreds of tins had spilled out over the courtyard.

This was a place where people stocked up for a long journey, Owen realized. And he had a good idea where that journey might lead.

The final shop seemed older than the others. The big window was completely obscured with dirt. Owen wiped it with his sleeve to peer inside and revealed a large gold *G* printed on the glass. He wiped again, revealing other letters. They looked familiar.

He held his breath as he wiped the rest of the glass, revealing a name: *J. M. Gobillard et Fils.* The same name that was on the mysterious chest in his bedroom!

Owen stepped back to get a better look at the shop. There didn't appear to be any door and when he looked through the glass he saw only darkness. Then he realized there were wooden doors beside it, double doors large enough for a car to get through.

He hesitated before taking hold of the big rusted bolt that held the doors closed. It screeched loudly as he forced it open, and he glanced nervously around the courtyard, feeling an air of disapproval in a place that had lain undisturbed for so long.

With one final effort the bolt slid back. Owen swung the doors open and found himself looking into an opening. The ground was battered and rutted, the walls scarred and scraped. Graffiti in strange languages covered the notched plasterwork of the walls, and huge broken lamps hung from the ceiling.

A battered wooden sign pointed into the tunnel. Owen traced the letters with his finger. HADIMA.

There was no mistaking that it was the entrance to a road, one that led down into the darkness. As he stood at the gateway, a cold, vigorous wind blew from the depths, carrying with it the smell of mountains and of snow.

Owen ran back down the tunnel. There was no sign of the flood that had swept him to it, except for damp rubbish and debris. The end opened onto the river five meters above the water. Nor was there any sign of the masonry that had hidden it, or of the fleur-de-lis.

Then he caught sight of Cati. She was sitting on the riverbank, half hidden by a tree. She got to her feet and called his name, then sat down again, looking hopeless.

"Cati!" he yelled. She leapt to her feet, looking frantically up and down the river. "Cati! Up here."

She looked up. Relief spread across her face. He swung off the lip of the tunnel and dropped onto a pile of fresh seaweed on the ground below. Cati was on her feet now, and he knew what was coming. For several moments he stood with his head meekly bowed as she told him off.

Then he interrupted. "I found it!"

"Found what?"

"The entrance! The way to Hadima."

"What? You're joking! Where?"

"Up there, in that drain," he said. "The earthquake brought the wall down and the water swept me there." Quickly he told her what he had found. Cati looked up. The entrance was barely visible. You had the impression of a shadow on the wall, nothing more.

"We have to tell Dr. Diamond," Cati said.

"Yes," Owen said firmly. "But first we need to make sure that the Raggies are all right." Squelching in wet clothes and shoes, Owen told Cati about the hidden courtyard on their way to the harbor. They could hear the sirens of fire brigades and ambulances in the town, but the river curved away and the sound soon faded. As they walked, Owen noticed that sometimes Cati shimmered and almost dissolved from sight.

"Are you invisible to other people at the moment?" he asked.

"I don't think so." Cati looked worried. "Whatever is happening to time has made me visible to everyone."

Owen wanted to ask more but Cati hurried on. They could see a group of what appeared to be derelict warehouses up ahead. But these warehouses were home to the Raggies.

"Hurry up," Cati said.

They ducked under the fence that separated the warehouses from the rest of the harbor area.

"They are sleeping in the far building," Cati said. "I checked on them the other day."

Owen followed Cati to the farthest warehouse. The buildings were more run-down than he remembered. Last time he'd seen them, they'd been full of children's voices and running feet. At the back of the warehouse a small stone staircase led to a basement.

The door was small and made of wood studded with nails. Cati took a key from around her neck—the same key that opened the Starry in the Workhouse. She opened the door and pushed Owen inside, closing it quickly behind them.

Owen found himself in a smaller version of the Resisters' Starry. The ceiling glittered with what seemed like stars on a dark blue background. Small beds stood throughout the room and on each bed a child slept. Owen recognized Uel and Mervin, the brothers who had reluctantly fought for the Raggies when they had sailed forth with Cati and Dr. Diamond. He saw Silkie, the brave, resourceful oldest girl, her features more delicate than he remembered. At the top of the room his friend Wesley slept soundly, a frown on his face.

"Something's wrong," Cati said. "Can you smell it?"

Owen sniffed the air. There *was* something odd, more noticeable than at the Workhouse Starry. There at least the air smelled dry and clean—like sleep, if sleep had a smell. Here there was an odor of decay, sweetish and sickly. Some of the children were breathing rapidly. Others had cold sweat on their brow. Then, in the darkness, someone moaned, the frightened sound of a child having a nightmare.

"This isn't good," Cati whispered. "The air is stale."

"It's not the air," Owen said. "I think time itself is stale. Stale and old . . . I have to wake Wesley!"

He stumbled through the rows. He found Wesley at last. Wesley looked even thinner and more undernourished in sleep. But Owen knew the great strength Wesley's thin frame concealed. He put his hands on his friend's forehead, and closed his eyes. Wesley seemed very far away, at the bottom of a deep well where nightmarish things lurked. Owen could feel the darkness entering his own mind, smothering his thoughts, dragging him down and down, until panic overwhelmed him. He struggled to get back to the surface but couldn't. The darkness would take him and hold him there forever.

And then he sensed Wesley's presence reaching out to him. With a final terrible wrench, Owen turned away from the dark and forced his mind to wakefulness, Wesley with him. He staggered back and fell against Silkie's bed, his hands brushing her face and bright hair.

Owen straightened up, as weary as he had ever been. As he looked down on his friend, Wesley's blue eyes opened. In one single movement, he threw himself on Owen, his arms flailing.

"You won't take us!" Wesley shouted. "You won't!"

"Wesley!" Cati shouted. He stopped and looked

around, bewildered. He rubbed a hand slowly over his thin face, then reached out and touched one of the children beside him.

"What's happening, Cati?" he said. "What's happening to us Raggies?"

Owen looked out over the harbor. Cati had persuaded Wesley to leave the other children in the Starry and go up into the warehouse above. The warehouse was chilly and unwelcoming, bearing no resemblance to the warm and friendly place that Owen knew. Cati got Wesley to light a driftwood fire in the grate to dry their clothes, which were still wet from the flood. As he worked, Cati told him everything they knew, about the message from the Sub-Commandant and the City of Time, and the flood that had swept Owen up the river.

"First thing I seen when I woke up," Wesley said. "The moon's not in the right place. Something is bad wrong. The Raggies ain't doing too good."

"It's because they're afloat in time, I think," Owen said. "They're like fish in a tank. It's as if the water is running out and the little bit that is left is getting stale and dirty."

Normally Wesley was tough and resourceful, but now he looked lost.

"Don't worry," Cati said, taking him by the arm. "We'll sort it out." Owen wished that he felt as confident.

Wesley disappeared outside. Owen stood in front of

the fire, watching the steam coming off his still-damp trousers. When Wesley came back he brought several fresh fish, cleaned and ready to cook. He put them on a stick and started to grill them over the fire. As the smell filled the room, Owen realized he was starving.

Cati had brought some bread in a leather bag that had somehow remained almost dry. They ate the fish and bread with their fingers, in silence. Owen couldn't remember eating anything more delicious.

When they had finished every scrap, Wesley stood up and stretched. His ribs showed through his ragged clothes and worry made his face look even more gaunt than usual.

"We should get back to the Workhouse," Cati said. But Wesley had gone to the window and was staring out to sea. "What is it?"

"Look!" he said. In the distance a group of seals was racing across the ocean surface. "Killer whales chasing them," Wesley said. "Which is odd. Too far north for a whale this time of year."

Owen joined them at the window. He could see the whale fins cutting the water behind the seals, who raced frantically toward a shoal of rocks. Just when he thought they had made it, a killer whale burst from the water beneath the seals. It seized one in its jaws and rose high in the air, the seal writhing frantically.

"The poor seal," Cati breathed.

"It's the way of the sea," Wesley said.

The whale rose several meters from the water and

turned as if to crash down nose first. But as they watched it they found they were watching not a live whale but the enormous skeleton of a whale, hanging for a moment in midair, the seal still held in the jaws of bone. Then, with a strange, muted splash, the bones plunged to the ocean and were gone.

Wesley stared at Owen and Cati, grim-faced. "We're in big trouble, ain't we?"

Mary White knew that it had to be now. She had gone out to her garden that morning. Usually it was her favorite place at this time of year, full of ripe fruit and autumn reds and browns. But now all was gray and withered. Normally she kept the radio on for company, and this morning she caught snatches of it coming through the window. They were talking about unexplained crop failures, deaths of livestock.

It is happening quickly, she thought. Her contribution would be small and would cost her dear, but she had to move now.

She checked the front of the shop. Johnston's truck was no longer there. He probably had plenty of spies around during the day to let him know if she ventured out, but she didn't care if they saw her. All she had to do was get to Owen's house. It didn't matter what happened on the way back. She put on her coat and grabbed a walking stick from the stand in the hall. Then she took a deep breath and stepped out into the road.

It was quiet. The road was never busy. Mary put her

hand up to her hair, to make sure the ornate hairpin was still there, and started to walk. She could feel her heart beating in her chest. The world seemed more alive than she had ever known it, and more under threat. *You just do your part,* she said to herself, *and let others worry about the rest of it.*

It was only a few minutes to Owen's house, but it seemed to take forever. And the garden gate squealed so loudly. *Fit to wake the dead,* Mary thought, then shuddered at the idea. She followed the overgrown garden path around the corner of the house and slipped in through the kitchen door. She heard a gentle humming sound from the living room and followed it.

Owen's mother was standing at the table arranging a vase of flowers. The room was untidy and dusty. There were dirty dishes on the floor and one of the curtains hung limply from a broken rail. But Owen's mother did not seem to notice. In contrast, the flower display was beautiful and delicate.

"Hello, Martha," Mary said gently.

Owen's mother turned round, smiling when she saw the old woman. "Mary, it's good to see you!" she said. "Come into the kitchen. I'll make you some tea." She looked worried then. "I'm not sure if there is any tea. But anyway. You look great."

"So do you," Mary said, though Martha looked pale and in need of makeup and a hairbrush. When Owen called at the shop, Mary always asked after his mother and his silence told her that things were not well. As she watched, Martha moved her hands in front of her face distractedly, almost as if invisible cobwebs were hanging in her face and tickling her.

"Come over here and sit down," Mary said, taking Martha by the hand. She led her to the sofa, where she had to clear old magazines and clothes from the cushions first. "Tell me, what do you remember?"

Owen's mother's eyes met hers. "Remember?" she asked. "What do you mean? I . . . What do I . . . ? I was married once. Mary, do you remember him? We got married in . . . Where did we get married?"

Mary sighed. There was a lot to do. Martha's mind had been frozen all the way through. But she had to be brought back and it would take all the strength Mary possessed, that and more perhaps. With a surprisingly strong grip, she took hold of both of Martha's hands and started to talk.

After a few minutes Martha began to shake her head, trying to break the old woman's grip, but it was no good. Tears streamed down her face and then she began to wail.

Owen, Wesley, and Cati moved upriver swiftly and silently. They didn't see any more signs of what was happening to time. They didn't need to. Owen thought that the sight of the skeletal whale would stay with him forever.

When they reached the Skyward they found Dr. Diamond surrounded by dusty volumes piled high on the floor. The walls were covered in maps. Some of the books were ancient, with strange astronomical symbols. Others looked more modern, with titles such as *Strata in Time: A Mapmaker's Approach* and *Time Trails of the Late Period*. One book was a thumbed paperback; the cover showed a wintry city scene and the title was *Hadima: A Street Guide Including Restaurant Supplement*.

Owen was bursting to tell Dr. Diamond what he had found, but had to wait as the man shook Wesley's hand gravely. Wesley told him about the sleeping children and the decay that surrounded them.

Dr. Diamond nodded. "Something similar is happening in our own Starry. We have to move quickly. I've been checking the books. They all point toward the same thing. The flow of time into this world is slowly but surely drying up—"

"Owen found the entrance to the City of Time," Cati interrupted.

"Did he now," Dr. Diamond said, wheeling around sharply.

Quickly Owen told him about the earthquake and the water that had swept him into the storm drain, and what he had found beyond it.

"So the tremor unsealed the entrance?" Dr. Diamond asked, his shrewd eyes flickering from one to the other.

Owen looked the doctor in the eye. "No," he said. "I guessed where it was and fired at it with the magno gun, which weakened the wall."

"You heard what I said about not reopening it?" Dr. Diamond said. Cati had never seen him like this. His eyes bored into Owen.

"I heard," Owen said quietly.

"It was forbidden," Dr. Diamond said. He turned to Cati. "Your father would never have permitted this!"

Owen could see tears spring to her eyes. "I didn't ask

for permission," he said angrily. "It was nothing to do with her! Besides, her father sent the message."

Dr. Diamond glowered at him. "You will have to answer for this to the Convoke."

"There won't be any bleedin' Convoke if we don't do something!" Wesley broke in. "What's done is done. Let's get on with it!"

"Owen, your father was impulsive too," Dr. Diamond said, almost to himself, the fire fading from his eyes, "and we do not know if he did good or evil. Very well. The tunnel is open. We will go to Hadima and find a tempod and perhaps set the world to rights. For now."

Owen looked away, unable to meet Dr. Diamond's eyes.

"What about the Sleepers?" Wesley said.

"We can do nothing for them until we fix time. You will have to watch the Workhouse, Wesley."

"On my own?"

"Owen will have to wake Pieta," the doctor decided.

Owen got wearily to his feet. Since he had roused Wesley in the Warehouse he'd felt tired, almost as if a little of the darkness he'd penetrated to reach Wesley had seeped into his mind. And he knew that Pieta would be harder to wake. Would her mind help him or fight him?

"Let's go," he said. "I can try to wake one more at least."

"Go with him, Wesley," Dr. Diamond said. "Cati can help me get ready here."

"Get ready?" Cati said.

"Yes," Dr. Diamond said. "Can you not feel it? Time is exhausted here. If we are going to the City, we must go soon."

After Owen and Wesley left, Dr. Diamond started to pick out maps and books from the pile on the floor and pack them into a leather attaché case with his initials on it.

"Now, to be practical, Cati," he said. "Both ovens are full of fresh bread and cakes we can use for the journey. I want you to pack them into this!" With a triumphant flourish, the doctor produced an ancient rucksack. The canvas was faded and the whole thing smelled of mothballs, but it was enormous.

Resisting the temptation to hold her nose, Cati took it from him and started taking loaves from the oven, putting them on a rack to cool. Out of the corner of her eye she could see the scientist packing all sorts of strange instruments and devices. She had known Dr. Diamond all her life, but there were times, like now, when his blue eyes hid more than they revealed.

A few miles away, Mary White was almost at the end of her strength, but she had called Owen's mother back and healed her. Martha was sleeping now. Mary unfastened the pin from her hair. Her gray hair cascaded down and in the dimness of the room she saw her reflection in a mirror and recognized the shadow of the long-haired, wild young girl that she had been long

63

ago. Despite her weariness she smiled to herself, then bent and fastened the pin in Martha's hair. She could do no more.

Outside, Mary went slowly down the path. It was dusk now and the white shapes of moths flickered in the hedges. She stopped at a field gate and looked down toward the river. A pale mist was covering the fields and when she looked up she saw a full moon low in the sky. She frowned. The full moon was not due for another three weeks.

Slowly and painfully she walked on. Turning the last corner, she saw the shop in front of her. She moved forward, and as she did so Johnston stepped out of the shadows, teeth bared in a wolfish grin.

"Where are you going, Mary White?"

"I am going home, Mr. Johnston," she said, her own voice sounding faint and far away.

"Do you like the moon, Mary?" Johnston said, his grin widening.

Mary shook her head. She was tired and confused and could no longer see clearly. Johnston watched as Mary pitched forward onto the roadway. Her hands reached out for a moment as if to fend something off, and then she was still.

At the Workhouse, Dr. Diamond looked worried. He had a model of the solar system that moved in sequence. Powered by magno, there were no strings to keep the planets in the air. Cati and Dr. Diamond both heard the clattering noise from it. When they looked at the model, they could see that the motion of the planets was distorted, with the moon in particular swinging in a wild orbit that loomed nearer to the earth.

"What is it?" Cati asked.

"Time and the fabric of space are intimately connected," Dr. Diamond said. "When one is out of shape, the other is also affected. Quickly now, get three sleeping bags from the back room and pack them. What is keeping Owen and Wesley?"

The two boys were at the river. Wesley stood looking across the fields while Owen ducked his head into the cold stream. He felt as if he could lie down and sleep. Waking Pieta had been even harder than he had thought. Wesley had unlocked the concealed stone door of the Starry for him and they had gone in. The Resisters sleeping there did not seem as disturbed as the Raggie children, but Owen could now sense an unease in the air, a feeling that things weren't quite right.

They found Pieta slightly apart from the others, sleeping with her two children on either side of her. Her face was stern and beautiful. When Owen bent over to wake her, her mind fought with his and mocked him by slipping off into deeper and darker spaces. Where the others had sought help, Pieta's sleeping mind twisted away. Only when he was at the absolute limit of his strength did she come toward him.

When her eyes snapped open, he fell back exhausted.

A sardonic smile creased her face and she swung her legs off the bed in an easy catlike motion, looking first for her weapon of choice—the magno whip she wielded with such fearsome power.

"Must be some fighting to be done, if you're waking me first," she said.

"Reckon so," Wesley said.

"What about the others?" Pieta said, looking at her children.

"I can't," Owen said. "I don't have enough strength."

Pieta looked at him long and hard, then reached out and took his chin in her hand. "Make sure you come back later and wake them then, young Owen. Do you hear me?"

He nodded dumbly. Pieta bent swiftly and kissed each of her children on the forehead, then turned and strode out of the Starry without looking back.

Wesley helped Owen to his feet. "A thank-you would have been nice," Owen said, rubbing his back where he had fallen.

"Not our Pieta's style," Wesley said, looking after her admiringly. "But she's a good one in a fight."

Leaning on Wesley's shoulder, Owen made his way to the door again. He was glad to leave the stale atmosphere in the Starry and felt nothing but relief when Wesley turned the key in the door. Then he felt guilty when he thought of his friends still sleeping in there—

Rutgar and Contessa, even the subtle and dangerous Samual.

After Owen had ducked his head in the stream, the two boys ran back to the Workhouse. Owen worked hard to keep up with Wesley, who ran lightly in his bare feet, oblivious to the stones and branches that littered the path. They had just reached the Workhouse when what looked like a long coil of blue flame licked the ground in front of Wesley's bare toes. Wesley stopped dead and looked up.

Pieta returned her whip to her belt and dropped to the ground from the branch she had been sitting on.

"You want to watch out with that whip," Wesley said. "I need them toes."

"I need to know what's going on," Pieta said, "so get talking, fish boy."

"There's not enough time," Owen said.

"What?" Pieta's eyes narrowed.

"There isn't enough time left to keep our world going," Wesley said. "So Dr. Diamond says, anyway."

Pieta moved her head from side to side, sensing the air. "Time doesn't feel right," she said.

"Stale. Is that what you feel?" Owen said.

"Yes," she said. "Stale and old and still. This is not something I can fight with my whip, boys. This is beyond Pieta."

Owen and Wesley looked at each other. She sounded worried, even afraid.

· · ·

Moonlight streamed in through the windows and woke Owen's mother where she lay on the sofa. She snapped awake, instinctively listening for signs of danger. All she could hear was the drip of a tap somewhere and, outside, the rustle of some little night creature in the bushes.

She shot bolt upright. It was wrong that there should be no noise in the house. Where was Owen? Where was Mary? All of a sudden memory came flooding back. Memory that had been locked away for years, sharp and painful. What had happened? How long had she wandered round in a fog?

Martha recalled the years she had spent in this tiny house with Owen, barely able to function, all that she had been locked away in her mind. She remembered everything now. The trip to the City. The Workhouse. Owen's father. Grief stabbed her. He was gone. His car had driven into the harbor when Owen was a baby. She bowed her head and felt the tears spring to her eyes.

But beneath it all there was a resolve that had not diminished with the years. Martha straightened again and stood up. She had to find Owen. She moved to the bottom of the stairs and listened, then mounted the stairs, instinct telling her not to switch on the light.

His room was empty. She had expected it to be. Her eyes swept over it. The old model plane hanging from the ceiling. Owen's guitar. Then she saw the trunk under the window and knew it at once. Swiftly she knelt in front of it. It was Gobillard's trunk, and in place of a lock, the Mortmain. She placed her hands on the trunk. She knew that catastrophe had been removed from the world and been sealed in the trunk. But by whose hand?

Surely, she thought, *not Owen's? He's only a boy. But where is he?*

She sat on the bed and tried to think. Her son was out there in the world on his own. She had neglected him for too long. Lifting his pillow, she held it to her face so that she could smell him. She put her arms around it and held it, as if the pillow was Owen.

Mary, she thought. It had been Mary who awakened her. Perhaps she knew something?

Martha went quickly down the stairs and out the front door. She had never seen the moon so bright. She could see the road clearly. Trees and bushes cast strange shadows across it. She walked fast, all of her senses alert to danger. This state reminded her of the way she had once been, when every waking hour had seemed full of peril. Every few meters she stopped and listened, but she was alone.

Then she rounded the bend before Mary's shop. She thought the shape on the ground was a shadow, until she realized it was a body. She ran forward. It was Mary.

Martha put her hand on Mary's face. It was very cold and at first she thought it was the chill of the grave. But as she bent to put her ear to Mary's chest, the old woman moaned and her eyes opened. Martha looked into them. Mary was trying to communicate, but she didn't have the power to speak. With a strength that belied her slender frame, Martha stooped and lifted the old woman.

In Mary's cottage, Martha lit a fire and placed Mary on a chair near it. She heated some soup and held the cup to the older woman's mouth. "It'll warm you up."

"No, what chills me will never be warm again," Mary said faintly. "Johnston used the Harsh cold against me."

Martha shivered. The name of the great enemy and their world stirred a cold memory.

"But the Harsh are not the immediate danger this time. . . ."

Mary's breath rasped and Martha could see the great effort she was making to speak. Mary took Martha's hand. "Time . . . is in danger. I'm sorry, Martha, I couldn't wake you until now. . . ."

"Why not?" Martha asked. There were tears in her eyes. "And where is Owen?" But Mary's eyes had closed again and she did not reply.

Martha sat with the old woman. And as she watched, her memory became more complete. She remembered things that made her smile. Owen as a baby looking up at her and laughing for the first time. She remembered things that caused her pain, that made tears of regret and longing spring to her eyes. And she remembered some things that were so hurtful she almost wished that Mary had not wakened her.

The hours passed, but Mary did not speak again.

When Martha touched her skin it was colder than it seemed possible for skin to be. But still the old woman's breath came.

Martha stood up. She had to stay with Mary, who was the only person who could tell her where Owen was. She stretched and ran her hands through her hair.

"Ouch!" she exclaimed. She had pricked her finger.

Carefully Martha reached up and removed the long, thin key that Mary had hidden in her hair. She turned it over in her hand, frowning. The key also stirred a memory, something she couldn't quite grasp.

When the boys returned to the Skyward, Dr. Diamond barely greeted Pieta. He had dragged a large blackboard into the middle of the room and was working frantically on it. Owen could see equations interspersed with arcs of what looked like planets.

Cati watched Dr. Diamond. "What's going on?" she whispered to Wesley.

Suddenly Dr. Diamond threw down his chalk and strode toward the door. "Follow me!"

Puzzled, they did so, even Pieta. Outside it was almost as bright as day, the moon huge in the sky. They followed the doctor to the roof of the Workhouse, where he stood with his hands on the crumbling parapet, looking up into the sky.

"She's too close," Wesley said quietly. "Ain't that right?"

"Yes, Wesley," the scientist said. "The shortage of time means many things, all of them serious, but this is the most immediate problem."

"What is?" Cati asked.

"The fabric of space and time is loosening," Dr. Diamond said, "and as it does so, gravity is distorting. In this case, getting stronger. The earth is starting to pull the moon closer."

"Gravity keeps the moon in orbit around the earth," Owen said.

"That's right," Dr. Diamond said, "and compared to other planets, the moon is very close to us. At the moment too close. You can see how large it is."

"What do you mean by too close?" Pieta said.

"Soon gravity will bring the moon to within a few hundred miles of the earth, and then—"

"It'll hit us?" Cati said, staring at the moon as if she'd never seen it before.

"It won't need to," Dr. Diamond said somberly. "When the moon is so close it will cause havoc— massive tides, tsunamis . . . The earthquakes have started already. But yes, Cati, eventually it will strike the earth."

"When, Doctor?" Owen said. "How long have we got?"

"I don't know exactly," Dr. Diamond said, "but I think it is only a matter of days."

Dr. Diamond equipped Owen and Cati with magno torches, almost like lanterns with handles. He fetched warm leather flying jackets for both of them and flying hats with flaps that went down over their ears. Cati already wore a pair of leather boots and the doctor sent her to get a pair for Owen.

When Owen was dressed he looked up and saw Cati and Wesley grinning at him. "I feel ridiculous!"

"You look . . . wonderful," Cati said, choking back a giggle.

"Put your own hat on," Dr. Diamond said. "From what little I've learned about where we're going, we'll need warm clothing." He was wearing the biggest flying jacket that Owen had ever seen, and his flying hat had goggles attached. "Pieta . . ."

"I was wondering when you'd get around to me," the tall woman said.

"I want you and Wesley—"

"To guard the Starry and the Raggies, and to poke the moon away with sticks if it gets too close."

"If you can, yes. And watch out for Johnston."

"Wait," Pieta said. She took the doctor aside, her face serious. "This is too sudden. Do you know where you are going and what you are going into? The old stories describe Hadima as a dangerous place."

"It's not like you to be cautious, Pieta."

"There is a difference between taking a risk and being foolhardy. You have told me nothing of what you intend."

"I'm sorry, Pieta. Things have happened so fast." And he told her about the Sub-Commandant's message.

"I see," she said, frowning. "You have to find this tempod and release the time from it. But even if you find it, how will you know what to do?"

"We'll cross that bridge when we come to it," the doctor said.

"I shouldn't be going. I am the Watcher," Cati suddenly burst out. "I should stay and watch."

"Your watch here is over for now, Cati," Dr. Diamond said gently, "and you cannot defend the Sleepers as Pieta can. We need you with us. And Owen—"

"Is the Navigator," Pieta finished his sentence. "But you don't have anyone who can defend you."

74

"I don't think our task will be resolved by fighting," said the doctor softly. "There is no choice. Guard this place for us, Pieta, so that we have somewhere to come back to. I am sure Johnston is up to some mischief."

Pieta looked at him long and hard. "I don't know if you're right, but I don't know that you're wrong either. If there was more time . . ."

"If there was . . ." Dr. Diamond nodded and let the sentence hang in the air.

Pieta sighed and nodded too. She stepped back and put her strong arm around Wesley's thin shoulders. He looked surprised at the gesture. "Well, fish boy, looks like you and me holding the fort."

"I wish I knew what they mean when they call me the Navigator like that," Owen whispered to Cati.

"Why don't you ask?" she whispered back.

But Owen stayed silent. The title had some connection with his father and he was never sure whether this was a good or bad thing.

"We must go," Dr. Diamond called softly. "Look!" At first Owen couldn't see what he was pointing at. Then he saw the way the river seemed to be flowing the wrong way in the moonlight.

"It's the tide!" Wesley exclaimed. "The moon made it do another surge."

They stared in silence at the gushing threads of water that shone silvery in the moonlight, spilling into the hoofprints where cattle drank at the river.

"The surge is dying," Wesley said. "You'd best be off before it comes up again."

They set off in single file walking downriver, away from the Workhouse and Owen's house, Dr. Diamond burdened under his huge rucksack and attaché case, Owen and Cati carrying the magno torches, although they didn't need them yet.

Owen turned back and saw Pieta and Wesley silhouetted in the moonlight. Wesley raised a hand in the air, but Pieta stood without moving as if she had been carved there. Then the friends turned a bend in the river and they were gone.

"The Resisters are in good hands," Dr. Diamond said. "Now, Owen, tell me more about this place you found."

Owen drew level and started to describe the tunnel opening, the courtyard, and Gobillard's shop. The doctor questioned him closely about the truck that was sitting in the courtyard. Were its tires punctured? Did it look as if it had been used recently? Were there fresh tire tracks?

Before long they reached the place where the river started to flow through the town. The high walls on either side cut out the light from the moon, but Dr. Diamond wouldn't let them use the magno torches yet.

"There are too many people about," Dr. Diamond said. "Look."

A couple leaned over the bridge, looking down at the water. The man said something and the woman laughed softly. Owen found himself thinking of a photograph of his parents when they were younger.

Dr. Diamond made them wait until the couple had gone, then they moved forward again. The going was slow and treacherous now. There were pools caused by the tide where there had been none before, and channels gouged in the path by the rising water. Owen heard a splash and Cati muttering a curse as she slipped into the water. The river even smelled different, of seaweed and tidal pools.

"We need some light," Owen said. "It's hard to see."

Dr. Diamond looked cautiously around, then let Owen light his magno torch by sliding open a small window in the side. A beam of intense blue light shone out.

Owen scanned the wall above his head until he saw the tunnel a little downriver. It looked dark and gloomy. They moved downstream until they were directly under the opening.

"How do we get up there?" Cati asked.

The doctor didn't answer but took his rucksack off and fished around in it, coming out with a line with a hook on the end and a little motor. Swinging the hook around his head expertly, he threw it upward until it caught on the edge of the opening. He attached the motor to the line and turned it on. Humming quietly, the motor shot to the top of the line and stopped. Then he looped the rope quickly round Owen's waist and gave the line two sharp tugs. Owen felt himself hoisted quickly upward by the little motor.

At the top, Owen unfastened himself and threw down the line. While he was waiting for Dr. Diamond and Cati to ascend, he stared apprehensively into the tunnel. He caught a hint of the smell again, of snow and cold mountain air.

Soon his companions were up there too, and Dr. Diamond packed the hook, line, and motor back into the rucksack. "Useful little thing." He smiled. "Come on."

He took the magno torch from Owen and plunged into the darkness. Cati followed him with a shrug. Owen found himself standing on his own, watching the blue light of the torches recede into the dark. Owen started to follow them, then realized he had left without even saying goodbye to his mother!

Suddenly he felt the ground beneath his feet begin to shake again, and looked up. A crack was forming in the ceiling of the tunnel. Half running, half crawling, Owen forced himself to go up the tunnel.

Dr. Diamond grabbed his hand and urged him on. Behind them there was a great crash, and they were flung to the ground. The quake grew momentarily more violent before it went away. The three companions looked behind them. Through the dust they could see that the roof of the tunnel had collapsed.

"There is no way back," Cati murmured.

"Not this way, anyway," the doctor said.

Cati picked her way up the tunnel behind him. Owen shut his eyes and saw his mother's face. Then he opened his eyes again, turned heavily, and followed the others.

In the warm darkness of the warehouse Starry, the Raggie girl Silkie awoke. Her head was pounding and she felt breathless and hot. Around her the other children were tossing in their sleep, some muttering. She remembered . . . what? Someone had touched her head. There had been a long and difficult wakening while the strange, black, clinging sleep had kept her under its surface. But someone had called her without meaning to, and she had been able to wake only because of that touch. A touch from someone she had watched shyly from the first time he had arrived in the warehouse.

Silkie sat up. At once she sensed the odd, sickly atmosphere in the Starry. She looked over toward Wesley, as she always looked to him for guidance, but his bed was empty. Quickly she got up and went over to feel the blanket. Cold. He'd been gone for a while. She looked around, her mind in turmoil. Something was badly wrong.

She went to the window, where she could see the harbor. The moon blazed unnaturally bright, illuminating the high tide spilling over the dock wall. Then her eyes were drawn to a burly figure striding along the dock, carrying a torch in one hand and a container in the other. Johnston.

As Silkie watched he approached the warehouse

door, looked around furtively, then placed the torch and container on the ground and took a crowbar from inside his coat. He forced open the old door, the wood giving way with a loud, protesting sound. Quickly Johnston slipped inside.

Silkie ran to the hatch that gave access to the rest of the building, trying to stem the panic rising inside her. The Starry could wait; Johnston was a more urgent threat.

She ran into the main part of the warehouse. It was pitch-dark, but she knew her way around without lights. Although it was cold outside, the warehouse was warm, with a sweet musty smell that reminded her of the barefoot children who lived and played here when they were awake. She moved swiftly to the door where Johnston had entered and darted up the staircase opposite.

Silkie was at the first floor now, moving quietly on the dusty floorboards. As she neared the front of the building she stopped and listened. She could hear a voice. Whatever Johnston was up to, he was *singing* to himself as he did it, his voice a deep rumble rising from below. She could see light from his torch shining through the chinks between the floorboards and hear footsteps as he moved about the room.

She was in the room where they cured and stored fish. The room Johnston was in was where the Raggies dried their damp clothes after a fishing expedition. Both rooms smelled of fish, but there was another, stronger smell now. Silkie remembered smelling it on the river once, spilled from a passing boat. Petrol, Wesley had said it was, flicking a match into it so the surface of the water flared up and burned with a blue flame.

There was a trapdoor in the floor and Silkie eased it open. Below she could see Johnston in one corner. He was pouring liquid onto the floor from the container until it was empty, still humming loudly. When he straightened, the smell of petrol was overwhelming.

He walked across the room. As he passed the window the moonlight caught his face, his red complexion appearing pale and ghastly under his thatch of wiry black hair. At the doorway he turned and started searching his pockets.

Matches, Silkie thought. *He's looking for matches. He's going to set fire to the place.* Frantically she wondered what to do. Then her eye fell on the fish pot—a cast-iron pan that they used to wash the catch. She was always telling the younger ones off for not emptying it, but now she was praying that it was full. Quietly she scampered over to the pot and slid the lid off. It was half full of oily water, and she recoiled from the stench of year-old fish.

"Where are those damn matches?" she heard Johnston growl from below. Silkie put her arms around the pot and heaved it off the ground. Stinking water slopped over her arms and chest and she gasped, her knees buckling under the weight as she heaved it to the trapdoor.

She looked down. Johnston had found the matchbox. He struck a match and as it flared, he held it up to his face, gazing almost lovingly into the flame.

With all her strength, Silkie upended the pot. Johnston looked up just as the torrent of rancid liquid reached him, sweeping the match from his hand, plastering his hair to his head and drenching his clothes in vile, fishy water. Silkie stared down at what she had done. Johnston looked almost comical, his mouth agape, his small eyes blinking out from a thicket of wet hair and slime. She lost her grip on the pot and the heavy iron vessel slipped from her hand. It bounced off the edge of the hatch with a clang, then plummeted down, striking the side of Johnston's head with a sickening thud.

Johnston swayed. An ugly white-lipped gash appeared on his temple and blood started to ooze from it. His head turned very slowly until he was looking directly into Silkie's eyes. He didn't say a word, but he held her gaze. She wanted to look away but couldn't. It made her feel like crying.

Johnston smiled a grim little smile to himself, then turned and left, moving more quietly than Silkie would have believed possible for such a big man. He left behind only a pool of water on the floor and the stench of old fish and petrol.

Johnston might not have spoken, but his eyes had

given Silkie a clear message: that he knew her now and he would not forgive her, and that he would return. She slumped back against the hatch cover. The moonlight cast her shadow against the wall and it loomed over her, as if to remind her how alone she was.

Dr. Diamond stood in the little courtyard, a delighted expression on his face. He paced about, examining the moldering shop fronts, the deep ruts in the ground. Even the very dust seemed to fascinate him.

"It's a bit *musty,* isn't it?" Cati asked.

"Kind of," Owen said.

"I mean, what is this place, anyway?" Cati said.

"It's a . . . it's a frontier, a border," Dr. Diamond said. "Or it was at one time."

"Like going from one country to another?" Owen asked.

"Exactly. That's a very intelligent observation, Owen."

"Really?" Owen said, feeling more confused than intelligent.

"This proves that there were comings and goings between this place and the City of Time in years gone by. That there were trade, traffic, commerce. It seems that the traffic came to a halt for some reason, and the Resisters forgot about it. It was what your father maintained, Owen. He said that there could be commerce again. I . . . we . . . were worried about it . . . he was inclined to exaggerate sometimes."

"At least he was right about something," Owen murmured sourly.

"And then there is this . . . this . . . absolute marvel!" Dr. Diamond's outflung arm indicated the old truck in the middle of the yard. Cati and Owen exchanged glances. Whatever the truck was, the word *marvel* didn't quite seem to apply.

"Now show me the passage you found," Dr. Diamond said. Owen led him to the gates beside the Gobillard et Fils shop. The doctor helped him to swing them fully open. They creaked and protested and flakes of rust fell off into Owen's hair, but in the end the three friends were looking down the passage, the ground underfoot rutted by countless wheels, the walls battered and scarred. And there was that smell again, of mountains and snow. They stood in silence.

"The way to Hadima," Dr. Diamond said, putting a protective arm around Cati's shoulders. "To the City of Time."

"Do we walk or what?" Owen asked.

"No, I wouldn't think so. Let's take a closer look at that marvelous truck."

The doctor led them over to the vehicle. He opened the hood latches and peered inside. Owen looked over his shoulder. The engine was a tangle of oily pipes and half-exposed wires, some with insulating tape wrapped around them. Deep in the heart of the engine he could see a faint glow of blue, indicating the presence of magno.

"A Prentiss twin-cam eight-stroke," Dr. Diamond said, patting the fender. "An absolute beauty. Needs a bit of work, though."

Owen felt Cati shiver as she stood beside him. He saw that her face was gray with tiredness. For the first time since they'd been reunited he remembered how the Harsh had blasted her with eternal cold. It was said then that she would never fully recover from it.

"Dr. Diamond," he said.

The scientist looked around, concern filling his eyes when he saw Cati. "It's late and you need to rest," he said. "Come on." He led them to the rear of the truck, pulled aside the canvas flaps, and unfolded a small metal ladder. Full of misgiving, Owen followed him up. His idea of rest wasn't the back of a smelly old truck. He slipped in under the canvas and stood in the dark while Dr. Diamond fumbled with a switch.

Owen blinked when the lights came on. It wasn't like the interior of any truck he'd seen. One wall was covered with racks for carrying freight, but the rest of it was kitted out like a comfortable if slightly eccentric room. The walls were covered with red velvet, which gave it an Eastern feel. There were four bunk beds against the other wall, with deep sides so you didn't roll out. There were worn but beautiful rugs on the floor. Against the bulkhead between the cargo area and the driver's cab, there was an ornate iron stove with wood piled beside it. A bent chimney led up into the ceiling. There was an opening into the cab with sliding wooden doors, and beside that, a row of bookshelves full of battered paperbacks.

"Very cozy," Dr. Diamond said approvingly. "Everything on gimbals as well, to absorb motion."

He knelt to examine the stove and moments later had it lit. There were warm-looking red blankets and sheets on the perfectly made bunks. Owen knelt to examine them, expecting them to be musty, but they smelled only of dried lavender. Cati blinked sleepily and went over to the stove to warm her hands.

"First time I ever saw a truck with a stove in it," Owen said.

"This vehicle has a lot of surprises," Dr. Diamond said. "The two of you get comfortable and get an hour's sleep if you can. I need to do some work on the engine." With a wave of his hand he slipped out of the back.

Cati yawned noisily. "Don't go to sleep yet," Owen said. He had opened a little cupboard beside the stove and found it full of cooking implements, as well as a teapot that reminded him of something. He fished in his pockets and brought out a handful of tea bags. Dr. Diamond's rucksack was propped against the tailgate and from there he took out a flask of water, butter, and some scones.

It wasn't long before the kettle was whistling merrily on top of the stove while the scones warmed in the oven. Dr. Diamond must have heard it, for he came in, his face and hands covered in oil.

"Wonderful engineering!" He beamed.

They sat in silence in front of the stove, eating the scones as butter ran down their fingers, drinking tea from tin cups. When they were finished Cati could barely keep her eyes open, and Owen wasn't far behind.

"Get some sleep," Dr. Diamond said. "We must start out before dawn. And we have no idea how far we have to go." He took a pouch of tools from the rucksack, dimmed the lights, and went out to his engine.

Yawning, Cati pulled off her boots and lay down fully clothed on the nearest bunk. Owen didn't remember getting into bed and pulling the bedclothes up around his neck. But just before he went to sleep he heard Cati's voice.

"This is a bit of an adventure, isn't it?"

"It is," he said.

"Long as we don't get killed," she murmured. "Night, Owen."

But Owen didn't reply. There was something about

this journey, a hope that had flickered to life and had been fanned by one thing in the truck: that teapot. Did he recognize it? *Don't be silly,* he told himself. Experience had taught him that most hopes turned out to be false. On the other hand . . .

"Cati?"

"Mmm?"

"Do you think my dad ever drove this truck? Dr. Diamond said that he had been to Hadima."

There was a long silence. Owen could almost feel her frowning in the dark. Then, "I don't know. He might have."

She doesn't really think so, Owen thought. *But that teapot has the same pattern as the tea set in the kitchen cupboard at home. The tea set with the missing teapot.* And the idea that his father might have been in this very place comforted him as he drifted off to sleep.

Although she was exhausted, Martha did not sleep. Mary's breathing had become more irregular. Martha watched the woman and brushed the hair back from her face, wondering at how young Mary had seemed to grow in the last few hours. The wrinkles had faded from her brow and there was a flush in her cheeks.

Martha shook her head. How stupid could she be? She'd lived in a fog for so long that she'd forgotten that the world existed. A doctor! That was what Mary needed, not somebody moping over her. She jumped to her feet, looking for a phone. She found an old-fashioned black one on a low table by the fire. She lifted the receiver, but as she did a voice stopped her.

"Martha?" Mary's voice was strong and Martha turned to her. Mary's face was youthful now, and there was a sparkle. Martha went over to her and took her hand.

"It is a key," Mary said.

"What?"

"It is a key." Martha looked at the hairpin she still held in her hand. "Take it over to the clock and open it."

Martha did as she was told. The clock case opened easily. Martha gazed at the clock face and it was a moment before she thought to look down. Her eyes widened. The infinity within drew her, the blue-black depth without end in which tiny lights glinted.

"Is this it?" she said, hardly comprehending the words coming out of her mouth.

"Close the case and lock it," Mary said. Martha did so. "It is what you think, an entrance into time itself. An ingress, it is called. I have guarded it."

"But why didn't you tell—"

"Whom would I have told, Martha? And what good would it have done, except to betray its location to Johnston, perhaps? But my time is very short now and I can't explain everything. The Navigator must go to the City of Time."

"The Navigator . . ." Realization dawned on Martha's face. "No! Not Owen. He is too young."

"Young, perhaps, but also brave. There are things

you do not understand. Your mind was put to sleep because it was frozen and wounded. You were not properly awakened until tonight. I am sorry that it took so long."

"Owen isn't ready!"

"He has already fought and beaten the Harsh once while you slept. He is ready. And in your heart you know that the Navigator is the only person who can heal this world. He must go to the City of Time. It is the only place he can find what he needs. He may already have gone," Mary said. "Diamond. Dr. Diamond will realize that there is no other way."

"No!"

The light was fading from Mary's eyes and her voice was weakening. "Listen to me," she said urgently. "Keep the key safe. It will be needed. The Workhouse will need you. It is badly manned."

"But Owen . . . ," Martha said, and there was anguish in her voice.

"Is the Navigator," Mary said. Then her breathing changed.

"Mary?" Martha bent over her, but the old woman's eyes had closed and she did not answer.

Martha ran to the phone and this time nothing stopped her from making the call. She sat down to wait for the ambulance, her mind in turmoil. Owen was the Navigator? His father's quest to be the Navigator had done terrible damage to all their lives. What would happen to his son?

A curious groaning noise awoke Owen. It sounded like an old sheep. He heard it again. He swung his legs out of the bunk and slipped on his boots. Outside it was still dark. He went around to the cab, where Dr. Diamond was sitting at the wheel. As Owen reached him he heard the noise again, but this time there was a spluttering sound, then with a gout of smoke from under the hood the engine burst into wheezy, clattery life.

Dr. Diamond beamed down at Owen. "Breakfast!" he shouted over the noise of the engine. "Quickly. Then we go."

Owen wakened Cati and they made hot chocolate on the stove and had bread and honey.

"I still don't really understand where we're going," Cati said.

"I'll tell you what I know on the way." The doctor's voice was light but Owen could sense worry underneath it. He realized that the scientist had not slept.

They clambered through the hatch and into the cab, which was roomy with one long bench seat. "Here goes." Dr. Diamond started the engine and put the truck into gear. It lurched toward the open gates beside Gobillard's shop.

The truck cleared the gate, the tunnel walls throwing the engine clatter back at them, and they plunged downward. Dr. Diamond turned on the headlights.

After a while the tunnel leveled out but continued to curve to the left, so they couldn't see far ahead. As the tunnel widened, the truck's headlights cast eerie shadows. Peering through the gloom, Owen could see abandoned vehicles at the sides of the tunnel. Trucks like the one they were driving, what looked like motorcycle sidecars, and odd, old-fashioned-looking cars.

After five more minutes the tunnel began to climb. Owen saw the remains of old signs hanging from the ceiling, but they were too dirty and tangled to read.

"Looks like we're coming out," said the doctor. As he spoke the tunnel straightened and the truck clattered into the open. Dr. Diamond slowed to a halt.

They had come out at what looked like a border crossing. Five or six lanes of traffic led into a line of glass kiosks. There were crash barriers and overhead gantries with arrows to direct traffic. But it was deserted. The kiosk windows were dirty and cracked. The lanes were empty and the traffic signs swayed and clanked in the breeze. The roof of the tunnel disappeared into darkness above their heads. Owen opened the door and got out, followed by Cati and Dr. Diamond.

"This is spooky," Cati said. Owen rubbed his hand across the top of one of the traffic barriers. It came away coated in dust and grime. They looked around.

"There's no one here," Dr. Diamond said.

"I wouldn't be too sure about that," Cati said as a movement caught her eye. A small dark shape was darting swiftly behind one of the barriers. Cati dropped to a crouch, scanning the surroundings, a Watcher on the alert.

"Two more," she said as shapes flitted behind the glass kiosks.

"Get back to the truck!" yelled Dr. Diamond. Before he could move, a jagged rock hurtled out of the darkness and struck him on the temple. He crumpled and fell. Now more shapes were moving from behind the barriers. Another rock flew past Owen's head and hit the truck with a clang.

"Quick!" Cati shouted. "Grab his feet." Owen ducked another rock and took Dr. Diamond's legs while Cati lifted his head. A tall figure stepped out from behind one of the kiosks. The man was dressed in black, but his hair was white. With one easy movement he inserted a rock into the slingshot he held and swung it round his head. The rock hurtled straight for Owen's face. Owen spun away from it, but the rock caught him full in the back. The leather jacket absorbed some of the impact but the pain was excruciating. He stumbled and almost fell.

"Come on," Cati yelled. Half shielded by the open door, they swung the unconscious Dr. Diamond into the cab. Cati climbed in and caught Owen's hand as another rock ricocheted off the door frame. Owen pulled the door shut behind him and slammed down the lock with his elbow. Cati shot through the opening into the back and he heard a rattling noise from the interior.

Owen turned to check Dr. Diamond. He was bleeding from the head wound.

Cati slid back in. "I've secured the back doors. Who or what was that?"

A pale face appeared at the windscreen, staring in at them, while long white hands felt at the glass. Owen recoiled from the windscreen as he stared at the expressionless face. The eyes were a curious violet color. The man started hitting the window with a jagged rock. Other hands pulled at the door handle beside him.

"What are they?" Cati shuddered.

"Never mind that, the windscreen's going to break," Owen said, his voice rising with panic.

"That glass seems pretty tough to me," she said. "Look, the stone isn't even chipping it. Let's have a look at the doctor."

Cati felt Dr. Diamond's pulse and lifted one of his

eyelids. "Out cold," she said. "I hope he's not con-
cussed."

Other hands were now hammering at the windscreen, not damaging the glass, but making so much
noise that Owen couldn't hear himself think. There
were scratching noises from the top of the cab as well.
Another face appeared at the windscreen—a girl with
long white hair. The thick, dark mascara around her
violet eyes made her appear sad and beautiful in a
cold way.

"Look at her hands, lover boy," Cati said dryly. The
girl's nails were covered with sharp chrome talons, long
and curved and deadly, and as Owen stared they shot
toward his face, rebounding off the glass with a vicious
clatter. The violet eyes looked disappointed.

Violet eyes, Owen thought. *I wonder . . .* Frantically,
his hands searched the dashboard. The symbols on the
switches were strange to him.

"What are you looking for?" Cati said. "The windscreen wipers won't get rid of them."

There were three switches together with a round
symbol on them. Owen flicked them all, one after another. There was a shriek from outside. The creatures
shrank away, covering their eyes, turning their backs to
the truck's suddenly blazing headlights and spotlights.

"They're albinos," Owen said. "They can't bear the
bright light!"

"I think you're right!" Cati said as they watched the
creatures scuttle back behind the kiosks and barriers.

"That got rid of them," Owen said, but he spoke too soon. A stone flew out from behind the kiosks, then another and another, until a hail of slingshot rocks was raining down on the cab.

"Any more bright ideas?" Cati shouted above the din.

"Well, you didn't—" Owen began crossly, but broke off as the whole area began to light up, starting from the tunnel entrance behind and spreading toward the kiosks, massive lights coming on overhead. They were hanging from the same gantries as the signs. Many were broken and useless, but the ones that did work were immensely powerful. There was another shriek from the albinos, and then they were gone.

"Now, that's what I call light," Cati said with a glint of amusement in her eye. "Look."

There was a low wooden structure to the side that they hadn't noticed before. A sign over the door said CUSTOMS and underneath that OFFICE. A man had emerged, wearing a black uniform with soiled braid on the cuffs and a grubby peaked cap pushed back on his head. In no particular hurry he walked over to the truck. His eyes were red-rimmed and his plump face needed a shave. He stood by the cab, looking off into the distance in a bored way.

Owen lowered the window a fraction. "Hello?"

The man held out a hand. "Papers," he said, shifting his weight from one foot to the other.

The friends looked at each other. "Sorry?" said Owen.

"Papers," the man repeated. "Import cert, export docket, duty-paid duplicate, end-user cert, or other documents pertaining to and contiguous with the shipment of goods, temporal instruments, and carriage thereof."

"I don't think we have any of those," Cati said. "Who were those people?"

"Albions," the man said.

"I told you," Owen said, "albinos."

"Albions," the man said. "Also I require sight of personal documents, passports, national identity cards, laissez-passer, and other documentation to wit and likewise."

"Our friend is hurt," Cati said.

The man sighed and peered through the window at Dr. Diamond. "There's not much point in putting up signs if people don't read them," the man said, pointing to an almost illegible sign reading DISMOUNTING IN THE RED ZONE IS STRICTLY FORBIDDEN.

"He needs help."

"Nothing I can do. Show me your papers and get on your way. You're blocking the intersection."

"The traffic is piling up behind us. I can see that," Owen said sarcastically.

"Listen, we don't have any papers," Cati said.

"Then you can't come through."

"We're not going back," Owen said.

"Certainly not." The man nodded. "That is not permitted without a quarantine certificate."

"We'll just have to stay here, then," Owen said, exasperated.

"Stay here? On public property? In the middle of the red zone? I think not," the man snorted.

"Well, if we can't go on and can't go back and can't stay here, what can we do?" Owen said.

The man said nothing. He just stood there with his hand out.

"Wait!" Realization began to dawn on Cati and she fished around in Dr. Diamond's jacket pockets. Triumphantly she pulled out an overstuffed wallet and flicked it open. It was full of a bewildering array of currencies. Dollars, dinars, rubles, bahts . . . Cati rifled through them, selected twenty Australian dollars, and placed them in the man's outstretched hand.

The man didn't move. He cleared his throat suggestively. Cati peeled off another twenty dollars and placed the bill on top of the first one. The man's fist closed and the notes disappeared into the pocket of his greasy trousers. "On your way now," he said gruffly.

"Hold on a second," Owen said. "What about those albinos?"

"*Albions*," the man said. "Keep moving and they won't bother you. Bandits is all they are."

"What were they after?" Cati asked.

"Magno," the man said. "Go mad for the stuff, so

100

they do. They can't be bothered to go into the mountains and dig it up like everybody else. Magno's in pretty short supply these days."

Owen thought that the man didn't look as if he spent much time digging in the mountains, or anywhere else, for that matter.

"Must be very quiet around here," Cati said. "I mean, how many people come through here these days?"

"Haven't seen nobody for near four years, and not many before that. Last crew I saw were in a tearing hurry and all. Barely time for the, eh, formalities," he said, with a meaningful look at the wallet still in Cati's hand. Then he took in the truck as if for the first time. "This wagon looks familiar. Could've been the one they were driving . . ." And he looked at Owen as though reminded of something.

Just then Dr. Diamond moaned and stirred and tried to sit up.

"I think . . . I think I'm all right," the doctor said. "Just a bit dizzy." He peered through the window. "Who are you?"

"Customs inspector," the man said. "Import cert, export documents—"

"It's all taken care of," Cati interrupted.

"And it's time you stopped blocking up the red zone," the inspector said.

"We're not moving until our friend is better," Cati said.

The man stepped back from the cab and reached under his jacket. He pulled out a large and very rusty revolver. "I'm authorized to use deadly force to ensure the free flow of traffic in the red zone."

"It's all right," Dr. Diamond said hastily. "I can drive." He eased himself into the driver's seat. "How far to Hadima?"

"Two days," the inspector said. "Last I heard."

"You don't know?" Owen said.

"As far as I can tell," Dr. Diamond said, "time and distance won't mean quite the same here."

"I see," Owen said, not really seeing at all. The inspector cleared his throat in a menacing way.

"OK, OK, we're going," Cati said.

Wincing, Dr. Diamond eased the truck into gear and the truck rolled forward past the kiosks toward a tunnel. The inspector watched them pass without expression. When Owen looked in the mirror he was already halfway back to his office.

As he turned his glance to the dark road ahead, he caught the smell of cold mountain air.

Wesley was restless. To give him something to do, Pieta had sent him out to patrol the river. She didn't think he would find anything there, but he was getting under her feet. When the full Workhouse was up and running there were hundreds of people about and the place buzzed with energy. But now it was quiet and shadowy.

He walked down the river toward the bridge. The ash and alder trees formed an arch over the path, and brown leaves falling from the branches swirled about his feet. On a fresh autumn day like this it was hard to believe there was anything wrong with time.

As Wesley got closer he noticed a woman standing on the bridge. She was frowning. She walked over to the parapet and stared at the Workhouse. Then her gaze moved downward and Wesley realized she was looking straight at him. And it was perfectly clear that she could see him!

He was about to dart away when she called out softly, "Don't run. I'm Martha, Owen's mother. You must be one of the Raggies."

Wesley was suspicious.

"Look at me," said Martha. Wesley saw the family resemblance and knew she must be telling the truth.

"But Owen said . . . I mean . . ."

"He said that I was lost and didn't know what was going on around me?" Wesley nodded. "I was, but not any longer. What is your name?"

"Wesley. But Owen's not here. He's gone to the City of Time."

"I know," sighed Martha. "When did he leave?"

"This morning. There's not enough time in the world, which means the moon is going to crash into the earth, and Owen and Dr. Diamond and Cati have gone to try to stop it," Wesley said in a rush.

Martha stared at him.

"I don't right understand it myself," Wesley said.

"Dr. Diamond is with Owen. That is good. And the girl?"

"Cati. Her dad was the Sub-Commandant. The Watcher. She's it now. The Watcher, I mean."

"Even better. But Hadima can be a dangerous city. There are many dark places."

"Have you been there?" Wesley asked.

"Been there?" Martha laughed. "I was born there."

"Wesley!" The voice was like a gunshot. Wesley spun round to see Pieta standing there, the magno whip swinging dangerously in her hand.

"It's all right, Pieta," Wesley said. "This is Owen's mum!"

Pieta slowly lowered the whip. She walked up to Martha and looked into her face. Martha thought it was like being looked at by some graceful and dangerous animal—a cheetah or a puma, perhaps. "Hello, Pieta," she said.

"Martha," Pieta said simply.

"We find ourselves in danger again," Martha said. "The town is in chaos because the earthquakes have caused fires. Reports say there could be a tsunami at any moment and people are moving to higher ground."

"Then you had better come to the Workhouse," Pieta said.

"We won't be safe even there," Martha said.

"I know," Pieta said, "but we can defend the Sleepers for as long as possible. Come!"

Silkie hadn't got any sleep that night. She had waited in a high window, watching in case Johnston came back. But by dawn she had dozed off and midmorning awoke stiff and hungry.

She fetched a fishing line, then went out the back of

the warehouse, where she couldn't be seen from the harbor. She went down to the water's edge, noticing with puzzlement that the tide line was much higher than she had ever seen it before.

She caught a fish within minutes and was glad to return to the shelter of the warehouse. Soon she was frying a large fish fillet she'd dipped in flour. She found a few wizened potatoes and made rough chips in another pan. Then she sat in front of a driftwood fire and a warm glow spread through her as she wolfed it down. She sat staring into the fire, wondering why she was still the only Raggie awake, until a noise outside caught her attention.

Coming down the quay toward the warehouses was a large blue bulldozer with Johnston at the controls, the wind whipping his hair out behind him. His face was fixed with a grim determination.

Silkie could see the big waves that had started to roll over the surface of the dock. Not that the bulldozer would be swept away by a few waves.

She ran outside and was drenched straightaway. The salt spray made her gasp and foam from the waves rolled around her ankles. She had no idea what she was going to do. The bulldozer was halfway along the quay now, and she could see that Johnston was grinning, showing those big tombstone teeth. She ran toward the bulldozer.

Johnston stopped several meters away. "Get out of the way, little girl," he boomed over the noise of the wind and the waves, "or I'll run right over you and push you into the sea along with all your skinny little pals."

Silkie stopped dead with her arms outstretched. Johnston laughed, then bent down and fiddled with something under the seat. Loud music suddenly blared from a speaker on the front of the bulldozer.

"That's Wagner," Johnston said. "You like Wagner? No? Ah well. Children are philistines." He revved the engine, laughing loudly. "Let's clear some vermin!"

The machine lurched forward. Silkie shut her eyes. As she did so the whole dock swayed and she fell to her knees. There was a rumble, then a crash, then the screech of bulldozer tracks on concrete. Silkie opened her eyes. The big waves, the earth tremor, and the weight of the bulldozer had combined to undermine the dock in front of her. A massive section had simply collapsed into the sea, so several meters now separated her from Johnston's bulldozer, perched precariously on the very edge.

The warehouses were now on a proper island. Johnston's eyes bulged with surprise as he looked at the chasm that had opened in front of him. He moved in his seat and the bulldozer swayed alarmingly.

His expression was so funny that Silkie choked back a giggle. But then his eyes met hers. "Just you wait," he growled. "Just you wait."

The square of light in front of the truck became bigger and bigger. Owen could see that the tunnel they were in was opening into fresh air. As they reached it Dr. Diamond slowed the truck and they coasted out of the tunnel into daylight, daylight so bright after the murky customs post that they had to shade their eyes against the dazzle of cold winter sun reflected from snow. They had emerged onto a snow-covered mountain landscape, into a pass running between two vast craggy mountains rearing on either side. The snow lay thick and deep on the mountains, on the pine trees on the slopes, and on the road, barely visible in front of them. A gust of wind stirred the surface of the snow and carried a miniature snowstorm toward them, then subsided.

"Look at the snow!" Cati breathed. She went to open the door but Owen stopped her.

"The Albions," he warned.

"Don't be silly," she said. "They couldn't take the light." Cati climbed out of the truck and took a handkerchief from her pocket. She made a snowball, wrapped it in the cloth, and climbed back up to give it to Dr. Diamond. "Hold it against your head. It'll help bring down the swelling."

Dr. Diamond took it gratefully, while Cati told him about the Albions.

Owen meanwhile examined the terrain in front of them. He could make out the road under the blanket of snow. There were even signposts. He got out and knocked the snow off one to reveal a rusty enamel plate reading HADIMA. But the road sloped steeply downhill and Owen wasn't sure the truck would manage the descent in the deep snow.

While they were stopped, Cati warmed up the rest of the hot chocolate. She and Dr. Diamond sat on a nearby rock to drink it while Owen climbed into the empty cab and scanned the switches underneath the steering wheel. Spotting one bearing a faded emblem that looked like a skier in a downhill pose, he flicked it upward. There was a groaning noise; then the truck lurched from one side to the other. Alarming clattering noises came from underneath, and a cloud of old rust flakes flew out, staining the snow dark orange. With much grinding and squeaking of metal against metal, two long skis unfolded from under the truck, replacing the rear wheels.

Cati and Dr. Diamond looked on openmouthed and Owen grinned. "Anyone for skiing?"

Even with the skis, the going was now very slow. Dr. Diamond was groggy from the blow on the head and he found the road hard to follow. "I lost my contact lenses when I was hit on the head. I should have brought a spare set."

"Resisters have contact lenses?" Owen was openmouthed.

"Yes, I hate to lose them. They take weeks to make."

"It's starting to snow again," Cati said. Great fat flakes were falling, getting thicker by the minute. Soon Dr. Diamond couldn't see the road at all.

"I know where it is," Owen said. "I'll tell you where to go." He moved in beside the scientist and calmly directed their progress. Cati looked at Owen. How could he tell where the road was when they could barely see beyond the end of the hood? If Dr. Diamond thought it was odd, he didn't say so.

It was a long day. Cati climbed through to the back and started to look through the paperbacks. There were titles such as *Cuisine of the Three Mountains,* featuring strange recipes for things like roast argosy. There were boring-looking books called *Time: Past or Present?* and *Increase Your Temporal Taste Buds.* Then she took down a volume written in a strange, jagged script, which contained drawings of ornate buildings, a towering palace, and a vast hall with a domed ceiling. She couldn't understand the words but felt sure that these buildings were in the City of Time.

Dr. Diamond called back, "As long as you're in there, why don't you whip us up something to eat?"

They sat in the warm cab eating bread and cheese. The doctor continued driving, and Owen's voice calling out the directions had a hypnotic quality. Soon Cati was asleep.

When she awoke the snow had stopped. They were driving through a dense patch of tall pine trees, each branch laden with snow. The headlights were on, casting their yellow beams on the snowy road.

"What time is it?" she asked.

"Almost night," Dr. Diamond said. Cati looked up apprehensively at the trees that pressed in around the truck.

"Look!" Owen said. Someone was standing at the edge of the road, a small dark person just under the trees up ahead.

"It can't be anything good," Cati said, shivering.

As they drew closer, they saw it was someone bundled up in a black fur coat. They couldn't see a face. But the black-gloved thumb at the end of an outstretched arm was unmistakable.

"A hitchhiker!" Owen said.

"Don't stop!" Cati said as the doctor eased on the brakes.

"It would be wrong to leave anyone out here at this time of the evening," Dr. Diamond said. He slowed to a halt and opened the window. "Can I offer you a lift?"

"Too right you can," a girl's voice piped up from under the hood of her coat. "Thought you wasn't going to stop for a mo'." Without hesitation the girl walked around and clambered in through the passenger door, elbowing Cati aside with a "Move over, can't you?" Cati moved, trying to put some distance between herself and the stranger.

"Nice and cozy in here," the girl said.

"Where are you going?" Dr. Diamond asked.

"Hadima, bless you," the girl said. "Nothing much else around here unless you want to cuddle up with the Albions."

"They're not very cuddly," Owen said, warming to the girl, although he hadn't even seen her face yet.

"Phew," the girl said. "Mind if I take my coat off?" She disrobed, a process that involved half standing up in the seat and poking her elbow into Cati's eye. "Sorry about that, pet."

Cati stiffened. She didn't like being referred to as *pet*, particularly by some urchin they'd picked up by the side of the road. She stole a look at her. The girl had jet-black hair and her eyes seemed to be the same color, set above an upturned nose and a cupid's-bow mouth. She was dressed more for a party than for the mountains, wearing a black silk jacket with a gold clasp, and a straight skirt over stockings. Her shoes were patent leather with a high heel. Her gloved hands were covered with rings, Cati noticed as the girl took a makeup mirror and lipstick out of her pocket.

"Got to apply the old war paint," she said. "The name's Rosie, by the way."

"Pleased to meet you, Rosie," Dr. Diamond said, putting the truck into gear.

"Who's the funny-looking geezer with the bump on his head?" Rosie whispered loudly.

"Dr. Diamond," Cati said. "I'm Cati, and this is Owen."

"If you don't mind me asking," Dr. Diamond said, "what are you doing out here on your own?"

"Magno hunt," Rosie said. "What else? Walked a bit far yesterday, though."

"Yesterday?" Cati said, but thought, *In those shoes?*

"Yeah, took a lift with a trader. He never seen me holding on the back."

"Did you find any magno?" Owen asked.

Rosie eyed him suspiciously. "Why? Who's asking?"

"I just—"

"You just nothing," Rosie said. With her back to the door, she slipped one hand under her jacket and brought out a long slender knife.

"No one wants your magno, Rosie," Dr. Diamond said softly. "We have our own. It's not what we're here for."

Rosie glared at them, the long needle-like knife glittering in her hand.

"I was only trying to be polite," Owen said.

"Put the knife away, Rosie. Please," Dr. Diamond said.

"All right, all right. I suppose if you wanted to rob me, you would just have run me over back there and took what you wanted," Rosie said. The knife disappeared again. "But you can't be too careful. The place is full of bandits."

"Please!" Cati said. "Do we look like bandits?"

"*You* do," Rosie said.

Cati folded her arms firmly and stared ahead out the window.

Dr. Diamond suppressed a grin. "There's some chocolate in the back," he said. "Why don't you get it, Owen?"

Owen found the massive bar and broke it into four. Rosie sniffed her piece cautiously, then bit into it and devoured it with an expression of ecstasy.

"Enjoy that, did you?" Cati said.

"Ain't had any for years. Not since rationing."

"There's rationing in the City?" Dr. Diamond asked.

"Not for ordinary food, but for anything posh, like chocolate. I reckon it all goes to the Terminus."

"What is the Terminus?"

114

"Where the ones are as is in charge."

It was now completely dark outside and Owen found himself yawning. Up ahead Dr. Diamond spied a rotting wooden noticeboard that showed a picnic table under trees. He turned there and they saw a tumbledown building that might at some point have been a toilet. Of picnic tables there was no sign.

"Time to stop for the night," Dr. Diamond said. "I'm not sure how safe it is to travel in the dark."

"Are there Albions around here?" Owen peered into the dark.

"You get them in the mountains," Rosie said, "and there's a different gang near the city. Should be safe enough here, though."

Dr. Diamond killed the engine and they climbed through the hatch into the back of the truck. Rosie looked around her with approval. "Not bad," she said, nodding.

"You mentioned rationing in the City," Dr. Diamond said. "Are things bad there?"

"They're not good," Rosie said, "and that's a fact. Everything's low. Magno stocks are drying up. There's only the likes of me goes up to the old mines and finds a little bit. Then there's the time famine."

"What's that?" Dr. Diamond asked.

"Ain't no time coming in. They got nothing to trade in the Bourse. Reckon it's all bought up or stole."

"The Bourse?"

"You know. Where they buy and sell time."

"How can you buy and sell time?" Owen said.

"That's the problem," Rosie said. "If there ain't any, you can't. The City isn't happy. There was riots last year. Now the Specials is on the street all of the time. Looking for your papers and that sort of malarkey.".

Owen took a large hunk of cheese from Dr. Diamond's rucksack. "I'll make cheese on toast for supper," he said. "Here. Cut this up with that knife of yours."

He threw the hard lump to Rosie. She caught it, then flinched and gasped with pain, which she tried to disguise as a cough.

"What's wrong?" Cati said.

"Nothing," Rosie said.

But Dr. Diamond could see the tears in her eyes. He moved to her side. "Let me see your hands." The scientist seemed to tower over Rosie and his voice was full of authority. Rosie looked as if she was about to resist, then she met his stern gaze and slowly stretched out her hands.

With great gentleness Dr. Diamond removed her rings, then slid off the black gloves. Owen gasped. The girl's fingers were twisted and distorted, and ugly sores and cankers covered every inch.

Cati's look softened when she saw the terrible injuries. "What happened?"

"The magno, I'd guess," Dr. Diamond said. Rosie nodded dumbly. "In its raw state, magno is a dangerous thing. And volatile. It emits a force that penetrates flesh and bone. I presume you're picking it from slag heaps at those mines?" Rosie nodded. "I've heard of this. Burns, distorted bones, eventually . . ."

"Your hands have to be took off else they fall off," Rosie said, her voice almost defiant.

"Yes," Dr. Diamond said with a pitying look.

"Why do you do it, then?" Cati burst out.

"No choice." Rosie shrugged. "My brother got took hostage in the Terminus. They left me free to raise the ransom. That's what they do."

"That's terrible," Cati said.

"Works two ways," Dr. Diamond said. "They raise money on the ransom, and it keeps the population quiet."

Rosie put her head down so they couldn't see her eyes, but Owen caught the glint of tears. She started to pull the gloves back on.

"How much do you need?" Cati said.

"A lot more than I have," Rosie said, her voice muffled. Cati felt her heart melt. What pain she must be enduring to try to free her brother.

"I have some ointment that might help," Dr. Diamond said.

But Rosie would have none of it. She pulled on her black gloves and, with her hands safely hidden, seemed to recover some of her old spark. "So, you lot never been to the City before?" she said.

"A few days ago I didn't even know it existed," Owen said.

"It's a tough old place for them that doesn't know their way about."

"We could probably use a guide, yes," Dr. Diamond said.

"I could guide for you," Rosie offered.

"We don't know anything about her!" Cati said, her pity reverting to suspicion.

"I don't know nothing about you neither," Rosie said. "I mean, where d'you come from? And what's your business in the City? Tell me that. I don't wanna put myself in the employ of rebels or traitors."

The friends looked at each other but didn't say anything. Rosie was amused. "Y'see? My reckoning is you want to get into the City dead quiet and go about your business, whatever that is, without nobody nosing around."

"We'll decide in the morning," Dr. Diamond said. "Now we should get some sleep. And we'll need to set watches. We don't know what might be lurking around out here. I'll take the first one."

Owen took a walk outside before settling down. It was a clear night and he could see great spiraling galaxies in the sky, and once a shooting star that burned across the sky from north to west. The forest stretched off to the left, dark and still.

When Owen climbed back inside the truck, the girls were in their bunks and had turned down the light. He could see Dr. Diamond's head through the hatch; the scientist was sitting in the driver's seat. The doctor had taken out some of the books Cati had been looking at earlier and was reading by the light that he wore on a strap around his head.

Owen climbed into his bunk. "Night, Cati. Night, Rosie," he said.

"Night," Cati replied, but there was no answer from Rosie.

Soon Cati could tell from Owen's even breathing that he was asleep as well. But Cati lay awake, thinking about Rosie's hands, how terrible they looked and how painful they must be.

13

Owen wakened to the smell of frying bacon. Dr. Diamond was busy with the pan over a roaring stove. Owen realized that he must have kept watch all night, without waking them.

"Wake up, lazybones," Rosie said.

Owen blinked out through the hatch at the windscreen. It was completely white. "It's snowing again."

"Going like the clappers for an hour," Rosie said. "Too heavy to drive through."

"We could be stuck here for days," groaned Owen, his heart sinking. He wasn't sure if the rest of them felt the same urgency he did. He'd been dreaming about that huge moon crashing into the earth.

"Weeks," Cati said.

"We could find out," Rosie said.

"Yes, let's go and buy a newspaper," Cati said sarcastically.

"Better than that." Rosie wriggled forward into the cab and began fiddling with buttons and dials on the dashboard. Suddenly there was a burst of music.

"A radio station?" Owen said.

"Course," Rosie said. "What, do you think we're backward round here or something?" She twirled the dial until they heard a man's voice.

"We'll be going to Metro news next," he said, *"but first the weather for the Tri-land area. The City and boroughs remaining cold with scattered snow showers. Temperatures remaining low in the Sound also, with pack ice reported off the south shore. Heavy snow this morning in the north county"*—"That's us," Rosie whispered—*"which will give way to clear skies within the next hour."*

"We're about five miles north of the Speedway," Rosie said.

"What's that?" Owen asked.

"You'll see." Rosie grinned. "Now, that was useful of me, wasn't it? So have you made up your minds about me being a guide?"

"Come here," Dr. Diamond said. His shrewd eyes met Rosie's. She held his gaze steadily, until the doctor reached out his right hand. "You're hired."

Rosie spat in her palm and, despite the fact that it must have caused her great pain, she shook the doctor's hand vigorously. "We'll discuss terms later," she said, and then she was suddenly all business. "We need to get going as soon as the snow stops. We don't want to get caught outside the City gates after dark. Once we're in there we'll play it by ear. You haven't got any papers, I suppose? Ah well, Mrs. Newell will know what to do with you."

Before Owen could ask who Mrs. Newell was, Dr. Diamond had held up his hand for quiet. They listened as the radio presenter spoke.

"Mr. Magnier, chairman and Chief Seller of the Bourse, said that the supply situation was critical. Raids were carried out in inner-city districts overnight by Terminus Special Police in operations aimed at detecting those hoarding heirlooms."

"The Specials," Rosie hissed disdainfully.

"Who are they?" Cati asked, feeling a bit like the country cousin in front of the big-city girl.

"The police," Rosie said. "Everybody hates them."

"Terminus spokesman Mr. Headley earlier today said that the hostage issue would have to be revisited. In a prepared statement he said that executions were being considered."

Owen looked at Rosie, whose face had gone very pale, but she turned away before anyone else could notice. The news ended with a traffic report that mentioned several multiple-vehicle pileups on the Speedway.

Owen and Cati exchanged nervous glances. Then the radio started playing opera, which made Owen feel queasy because it reminded him of Johnston.

But the forecast was accurate. Within an hour the

snow had stopped. Dr. Diamond stood outside shading his eyes and looking into the forest.

"Are you ready to go?" Owen asked.

"I am," the doctor said, "but there is one problem."

"What's that?"

"I still can't see properly, Owen. I can drive slowly with you guiding me, but that won't work in City traffic."

"What are we going to do?" Owen said. "I can't drive. Neither can Cati."

"But I can," came a voice from above. Rosie was looking down at them from the tailgate, a broad grin on her face. Cati was standing behind her, looking dubious.

"All right, Rosie," Dr. Diamond decided. "You drive the next few miles and see how you get on." Then, catching Cati's expression, he added, "Right now we have no other choice."

Cati and Owen watched nervously as Rosie climbed in on the passenger side. She adjusted the pedals. Then she put a cushion on the driver's seat so that she could see over the top of the steering wheel. But she turned the key and put the engine into gear expertly. They moved off with a jolt that rattled Owen's teeth, but at least they were under way.

After a few miles it became clear that Rosie knew what she was doing. "Where'd you learn to drive?" Owen asked.

"Me and my brother, Les, used to drive the slop truck," Rosie explained proudly.

"What's the slop truck?" Cati said.

"Well, it's not the best job in the world." Rosie

grinned. "People bring their slops to it. Any kind of old rubbish—veg and meat and sour milk and stale beer."

"Kind of like recycling?" Owen asked.

"Kind of," Rosie said cheerfully, "but there's other stuff too. We picked up at the hospital, and from the Terminus. You wouldn't believe some of the things that people—"

"What's that noise?" Dr. Diamond interrupted. Despite his limited vision, he didn't seem to be downhearted, although Owen was worried about him.

"What noise?" Cati said, then she heard it too—a noise that was somewhere between a hive of huge bees and buzz saws, with loud clangs and screeching noises thrown in.

The road had narrowed and angled downward. Then another road came into view, one that could not have been more different from the calm, snow-covered stretch on which they were traveling. Owen couldn't make out how many lanes of traffic there were, but it didn't matter anyway because nobody was using them.

There were all sorts of vehicles: battered trucks, motorcycles with sidecars, tractors with tall swaying funnels, motorized tricycles, cars stripped down to just a chassis and an engine, rust-streaked amphibious vehicles covered in barnacles, army personnel carriers with tracks and machine gun ports. What they all had in common was that they were packed side by side and bumper to bumper, traveling at a breakneck pace on a road pitted with potholes and littered with cast-off machine parts. The sides of the road were piled high with the mangled debris of a thousand car wrecks.

The din was indescribable. The roar of engines and blaring of horns mingled with the screech of brakes and grinding of metal as each vehicle jockeyed for position. Over the whole road hung a mist of polluted air and dust and half-frozen particles of ice.

"You're not taking us into that," Cati yelped. But Rosie just accelerated with such force that they were thrown back against their seats. Owen dived forward and hit the ski button and the truck slewed sideways as the skis retracted.

"Watch out!" Rosie shouted, grinning from ear to ear.

With a roar the truck shot from the end of the side road into the traffic. At once they were surrounded by swerving cars and trucks and cursing drivers. Owen had never heard such bad language, even from Rutgar's troops at the Workhouse, and certainly not in such a variety of languages and accents. A truck beside them swerved violently, dumping half its load of tomatoes into the road, to be hit by the next tanker so hard that a red spray of crushed tomato enveloped that lane. Rosie laughed and gunned the engine, and the front bumper struck the sidecar of the motorcycle in front of them. The motorcycle veered sideways and almost overturned before the rider got it under control.

Rosie stuck her head out of the window. "Speed up or shift over," she bellowed. "Rosie's coming through."

The occupant of the sidecar, a small man wearing a large leather jacket, turned and gave Rosie an evil grin. He opened the jacket to show an array of throwing knives fixed to the lining.

"What's happening?" Dr. Diamond asked.

"You don't want to know," Owen groaned. Cati's knuckles were white where she held on.

The truck lurched as it struck an immense pothole. Rosie wrenched the wheel sideways to stop what looked like a small snowmobile from cutting in front of them. "Now we're on our way," she shouted cheerfully. "You have to throw your weight around a bit when you join the Speedway or you don't get nowhere."

It was true. The vehicles around them now seemed to be giving them some space, even if that space could only be measured in inches. Every few moments the truck's wheels crashed into a great rut in the road, and it swayed from side to side and groaned.

"Traffic's moving well," Rosie said. "Shouldn't take too long to get to the City."

"Either that or get killed," Cati said.

"That could happen too," Rosie admitted as she eased the truck in front of an eighteen-wheeler.

Owen could hear an enraged bellowing. The trailer was full of bulls, tossing their horns and stamping their feet. He looked across the line of traffic, blinked, and looked again. He saw what looked like a small wolf leaping from vehicle to vehicle—a wolf that appeared to be moving on two legs. "What's that?" he said, and pointed.

Rosie glanced out of the side window. "Trouble," she said shortly. "Dogs."

She began to accelerate through the traffic, barging through tiny gaps. There were more Dogs now, moving across the speeding lanes of traffic, jumping onto hoods, balancing on bumpers. They seemed to be children, but they were wearing dog's-head masks. They carried large bags slung over one shoulder and, as they leapt nimbly from one speeding vehicle to another, were stealing anything they could.

Owen saw one reach inside an open car window and pull out a purse. A passenger of the car pointed a gun through the window at the Dog. Without faltering, the Dog snatched it and dropped it into the bag too. They stole hood ornaments, boxes of produce, and tinned goods. They snatched hats off drivers' heads and wing mirrors off doors, and whipped sandwiches out of drivers' hands. They moved with incredible speed and daring.

One Dog descended on an open engine and emerged with a handful of wires. Another seemed to be siphoning olive oil from a tanker into a flask. Owen watched with horror as one climbed onto the tow hitch of a huge truck. The Dog tugged the pin connecting the trailer to the truck until it came loose. He held it up to the light in triumph, then dropped it into the bag and skipped onto the hood of the car alongside. Owen watched as the trailer slowly veered away from the truck. With an earsplitting crash it struck another truck and flipped over. Other vehicles swerved to avoid it and crashed into each other. The last sight Owen had as they sped on was debris, car wheels, and pieces of bodywork flying high into the air.

"Better check the back is closed up," Rosie said.

Cati climbed through the hatch. It was dark and it took her eyes a moment to adjust. She had just decided that everything was fine when she saw a hand with long, clawlike fingers coming through a gap in the canvas flap. It worked rapidly at the ties and the flap fell open. Before Cati had a chance to move, a Dog's head came through the flap. Cati knew it must be a mask, yet the way the head cocked to one side and the eyes gleamed was eerily real in the gloom.

The Dog spotted Dr. Diamond's rucksack and Cati could have sworn that its ears pricked up. Another hand came through the canvas, followed by a wiry body dressed in rags. The Dog began to creep across the floor toward the rucksack. Cati knew she should do something, but she felt paralyzed.

"Everything all right back there, Cati?" Owen shouted through the hatch. The Dog started, and for the first time looked in her direction. Just as a real dog would, its lips curled back from its teeth and it gave a low, threatening growl. It began to creep toward her.

Cati looked around frantically. A saucepan was sitting on top of the stove. She grabbed it and swore as it burned her fingers, then flung it toward the Dog. Hot liquid splashed the dog's fur before the pot hit it firmly on the nose. The Dog yowled and ran toward the exit. Just as it reached the canvas, the truck lurched over a pothole. The tailgate caught the Dog in the back of the knees. It tottered, then with a whimper fell backward out of the truck.

Feeling sick, Cati rushed to the tailgate and looked out. Behind the truck thundered a line of grim vehicles, barely inches apart. The scarred tarmac raced past between the wheels of the truck. There was nowhere for the Dog to go except under the rushing wheels. Cati sat down on the tailgate, shocked. *It didn't deserve to die,* she thought.

She thought how thin its limbs had been, and how it had whimpered pathetically as it fell. She felt responsible for its death. As she lifted her eyes from the road, she looked through the windscreen of the tractor following behind. It was being driven by a muscular woman with a thatch of flattened blond hair and prominent teeth.

She couldn't work out what the woman was staring at, and looked up to follow the gaze. Her stomach lurched as the Dog swung down from the roof of the truck, where it had been hiding. One long-nailed hand caught in her hair and began to haul her upward and outward. For one sickening moment Cati slipped out of the back of the truck, dangling precariously by her hair over the Speedway. Frantically she grabbed at the canvas and swung herself back inside.

The Dog hauled on her hair and she gasped in pain but managed to keep her grip. The other clawlike hand caught her shoulder painfully. Then the Dog reached for the hand that gripped the canvas, striking so hard that it tore the material. Her hair felt as if it would come out by the roots. She couldn't hold on much longer.

"Cati!" She heard Owen's voice.

"He's on the roof!" she gasped. "Hit him with something!" The claw found her shoulder again.

Owen appeared beside her. He had the rope and hook that Dr. Diamond had used to get into the tunnel from the river. He threw the hook out of the back of the truck. It landed right on the roof of the tractor coming behind and caught among the lights there. The blond woman shook her fist, but there was nothing she could do. As fast as he could, Owen knotted the other end of the rope around the Dog's wrist where it held Cati's hair.

He turned back into the body of the truck. "Rosie!" he shouted. "Put your foot down!"

With a roar the truck leapt forward. The rope tightened around the Dog's wrist and an almost comical look of alarm grew in its small black eyes. The rope snapped tight and the Dog was yanked from the roof, releasing Cati's hair. It plummeted toward the ground headfirst. This time, Cati thought, it would surely be run over, but just before it struck it twisted in the air and bounced off the ground, spiraling up to land on the roof of the tractor. It crouched there barking furiously.

Owen examined Cati's face and shoulder. Her face looked bad, but the scratches weren't deep. Owen washed her wounds out, then, following Dr. Diamond's instructions, found his medicine box in the rucksack and shook penicillin powder into the cuts.

When Cati clambered shakily back into the cab, Rosie looked concerned. "Dirty old things, those Dogs," she said.

The landscape by the side of the road had changed from snowy trees to small settlements. There were poor-looking neighborhoods with houses that were barely more than shacks, but sometimes Owen caught a glimpse of older streets, with shops and restaurants, and people bundled up against the cold eating hot food. Once he saw a skating rink with children on it.

"It's getting dark." Dr. Diamond frowned. "Or is it my eyes?"

"No," Rosie said, "it gets dark good and early around here in winter." She was quiet for a minute before she lifted a gloved hand and pointed. "Look," she said softly. "Hadima!"

Ahead of them, through flurries of snow and the golden light of the setting sun, rose a conical mountain covered in stone buildings. The winter light flashed off wet slate roofs, marking the lines of streets climbing toward the peak. But although the light was still good and there was no fog, Owen couldn't make out the very top of the City. Every time he tried it slipped out of focus.

Rosie glanced at him with a wry smile on her face. "They're pretty tricky folk on the top of that hill," she said. "Hard to pin them down."

Despite this, there was a beauty to the city on the hill. The houses clung tightly to the slopes, with smoke coming from chimneys. It had an air of mystery, its tightly packed streets disappearing into little squares surrounded by bare trees.

"Looks better from here," Rosie said. "Can get a bit smelly close up."

Owen looked at Cati and found her asleep against his shoulder. The scratches on her face were red and angry. He touched her forehead. It was feverish.

The drivers speeded up on seeing the City. Even Rosie had to keep her eyes on the road, constantly alert to another truck or a tricycle trying to barge its way through. "Getting dark, getting dark," she muttered to herself, "and these folks got no papers. It'll have to be the underground."

"What's the underground?" Owen asked, but Rosie didn't answer. The Speedway veered to the left and swept around the City. There was a massive concrete wall to one side and a dead drop to the other. But there were gaps in the wall and Rosie seemed to be counting them off.

Suddenly she wrenched the wheel to the right. The truck went careening across all the lanes of traffic.

Brakes shrieked. A tricycle clipped the bumper and almost toppled. A speeding dragster had to deploy its parachute to avoid crashing into the side of them. Drivers roared and shook their fists and at least one tried to train a gun on the truck. Owen shut his eyes.

"Why am I glad I can't see properly?" Dr. Diamond said mildly.

Fighting the wheel, Rosie plunged toward the gap in the wall. Owen opened his eyes to see wooden roadwork barriers blocking the way. "Look out!" he shouted, but Rosie didn't stop. Splintered timber flew high into the air as she gunned the truck into the darkness. It careered down a nearly vertical slope, then, with a sickening bang from the suspension, leveled out.

Rosie braked hard. Owen saw a wall coming toward him. The tires shrieked and the wall loomed up until, with inches to spare, the truck came to rest and Rosie turned the engine off.

Owen looked around. The truck was standing on some iron rails next to a platform covered with rubbish and building debris. "Where are we?" he said shakily.

"Abandoned underground station," Rosie said. "Welcome to the City."

Martha had walked through the town earlier that day. People stood in huddles outside shops, talking in hushed voices and looking up at the moon, which was clearly visible in the daytime sky. There were two or three earth tremors each day now and some buildings had collapsed. The television showed fires raging unchecked in other cities. Some claimed that the earth was being punished for man's wickedness and that it was time to repent. A group of people had set up a camp on the cliffs overlooking the harbor and were holding round-the-clock prayer services. *They should be praying for Owen and Cati and Dr. Diamond,* she thought, her mind returning to Owen, as it did day and night. The City was dangerous and he was so young. Her heart ached for him.

Enough, she said firmly to herself. There was nothing she could do to help him. Her job was to help look after the Workhouse and the sleeping Resisters until he got back.

Martha had begun to piece together her lost past, although it seemed so strange that she wondered if she had dreamed it, and there was no one to ask if it was otherwise. She remembered Owen, of course, and realized how much he had looked after her in recent years, and how much he had taken on his young shoulders. She remembered being young and meeting a handsome young man. They had got married quickly, but so much after that was still a blur.

She remembered finding out that there was more to him than she'd first known. She'd thought he was involved in a revolution or an underground movement or something. There were secret meetings at night, strange visitors, things he could not tell her about. Then one night he'd sat down with her at the kitchen table and told her a story about the Workhouse, and Resisters, and how time itself had to be constantly defended.

And now everything was a jumble. There had been a journey. Then there had been pain and the sleep from which she had only just awoken.

The chest. That was it! It was something to do with the chest in Owen's room. She reached for understanding, but it slipped away into the void. And in her heart she knew what the void was: that her husband was gone. His car had driven into the harbor. The baby, Owen, had been rescued, but her husband was gone.

Silkie went to the window. During the night the tide had carried more of the dock away. *Safer that way,* she thought.

There were other new things as well. The moon stood high in the sky, as bright as the sun. And there was a large white tent on the cliff overlooking the harbor, with people coming and going.

Where's Wesley? she wondered. Wesley would have an explanation for all of this. She splashed water on her face, then went to the Starry to check on the sleeping children. They still slept, in the same fretful atmosphere she had felt before. She felt helpless, looking down at the troubled, sleeping faces.

I have to guard them, she thought. *About all I can do, so I better do it well.*

She went into the big room downstairs where the children used to gather. There was a box in the corner that only Wesley was allowed near. But Wesley wasn't there. The box was locked, but she got an old piece of metal and used it to force the lock. She reached in, took out a magno gun, and loaded it. Then she went to the highest window of the warehouse and stood there, a lone sentinel on guard over an island of sleeping children.

After the turmoil of the Speedway, the old underground station was quiet and peaceful. Owen got down
from the cab. The platform walls displayed posters for
cough medicines and holidays, but they were so tattered
and faded that he couldn't make out any details.

"What happened here?"

"Magno got too dear to run it," Rosie said, shrug-
ging. "Besides, there's only poor people down this end
of town. The Terminus don't really care about us.
Rather keep us down here and poor than have us running about uptown, getting in their way."

"What do we do now?"

"I have one contact that might be promising," Dr.
Diamond said. "I got it from one of the guides. The
owner's name is familiar."

"Where is it?" Rosie asked.

"The Museum of Time. Do you know it, Rosie?"

"I think so," she said, frowning. "Down near the end of Desole Row. But first things first. We need to get out of this tunnel. Wouldn't want Dogs to come across us down here. Nor the Specials, for that matter. I don't like them, and they don't like Rosie, no sir."

"Well, then, let's get going," Dr. Diamond said.

"I'll take you as far as Cyanite Place, where I live. It's safer than most areas and you can get anything there, as long as you pay for it."

"Is there a doctor?" Dr. Diamond said. "I'm worried about Cati."

Owen looked at his friend guiltily. He had almost forgotten about her encounter with the Dog. She was sleeping peacefully, but every so often her limbs twitched and she whimpered. Owen knelt beside her.

"Don't wake her," Dr. Diamond warned. "Sleep is probably the best thing for her."

They got back into the truck and Rosie drove slowly through the abandoned tunnel. Now that they were in the City, Owen started to think about the task ahead and felt a wave of depression wash over him. How were they to find out where all the time had gone? And if they did, how would they put it back? And would that prevent the moon from colliding with the earth? It seemed as impossible as reaching out with a hand and pushing the moon away.

He wondered if the Harsh were behind it. Was this

yet another attempt to plunge his world into darkness and emptiness?

Beside him, Dr. Diamond hummed tunelessly. If he was worried by the scale of the task in front of them, he wasn't showing it. The tunnel opened out and they came to another deserted, vandalized station.

Rosie stopped the truck. "Come on," she said, and Owen followed her out of the cab. Beyond a wooden barrier lay a darkened street. "No patrols about," Rosie said nervously. "Good. Help me with this."

Together they lifted the barrier out of the way and went back to the truck. Rosie turned the lights off. "There's not supposed to be traffic in this zone," she said. "If the Specials see us, they'll take us for smugglers."

Keeping the revs low, Rosie eased the truck out into the street. Owen peered around, trying to see what the City looked like. There were ornate wrought-iron streetlights, but the glass had long since been smashed and the cabling wrenched out. The buildings had beautiful carvings, but the windows were broken and doors sagged on their hinges. Once they saw a blue light in the distance and Rosie killed the engine. They waited for ten nervous minutes before creeping forward again.

After half an hour Rosie pointed to a red circle painted on a gable wall ahead of them, beyond which were lights. She accelerated toward it.

"That's my district. No curfew there."

As soon as they passed the red circle, people appeared

142

on the streets: men in fur hats, women with long coats and tall hats. Everything was patched and darned, Owen noticed, but they wore the clothes proudly. The houses and shop fronts were old and in need of repair, but lights shone from windows and children were playing on front steps. Everywhere there was somebody selling something—old clothes, battered toys, secondhand furniture.

People stood around glowing braziers, warming their hands and chatting. There was food too—chickens being turned on a spit, potatoes roasting in the ashes, bowls of hot soup, roasted meats and fish on long skewers. The tempting smells were almost overpowering.

Rosie was grinning broadly. She opened the window and leaned her elbow on it like a truck driver. People waved and shouted to her as they passed. "Like the truck, Rosie!" "Where'd you steal that?"

They passed down several busy streets, then turned into a quieter area. She swung the truck under an arch and they emerged into a courtyard.

"Welcome to Cyanite Place."

Cyanite Place was a square of tall, crooked buildings with odd bent chimney stacks. The center was dominated by an ancient elm tree surrounded by stone seats. In the corner was a small pub, the Whin Bush Inn. As Rosie turned off the engine, a woman came to the door of the inn, drying her hands on a towel. She was small and broad and wore a blue crocheted shawl, and her jet-black hair was piled on top of her head in the tallest bun Owen had ever seen.

"I'm back, Mrs. Newell," Rosie said, "and I've brought some guests."

"Paying guests, I hope," the woman said in a deep voice.

"I have a fund of notes in many denominations and currencies to put at your disposal, madam," Dr. Diamond said. "I am Dr. Diamond and I am pleased to make your acquaintance."

"Got manners anyhow," Mrs. Newell said. "How d'you do, and who else have you got with you?"

Rosie introduced Owen and Cati. Mrs. Newell gave Owen a curious look but said nothing. Then she came over to the truck and looked in at the sleeping Cati. "What's wrong with her?"

Rosie told her what had happened and a black look came over Mrs. Newell's face. "Why didn't you tell me that first!" she cried, swiping at Rosie with the towel.

Mrs. Newell wrenched the cab door open. "Don't just sit there," she said, poking Dr. Diamond. "Carry the poor child inside."

With Owen guiding him, the doctor lifted Cati and carried her across the courtyard to the inn. They ducked under the doorway and entered a long, low-ceilinged room. A fire burned in the grate and its flickering light reflected from polished brasses and china.

There were several dark wooden tables and chintz sofas, and battered but comfortable leather armchairs. There was a small counter at the end of the room, and beside it was a large black stove on which pots bubbled softly.

Mrs. Newell led the way through a door beside the counter. They followed her up a narrow, twisting staircase with uneven steps and into an even lower-ceilinged bedroom. Under the window was a bed with feather pillows and a bright red quilt.

"I'll put her to bed," Mrs. Newell said. "Take this lot down and give them some stew, Rosie. That lad looks half starved."

While Mrs. Newell fussed over Cati, Rosie led them downstairs. She ladled stew into deep plates and put them on the table. Then she found hunks of fresh white bread. There was silence for five minutes while they tucked into the delicious hot food, using the bread to mop up the last drops of gravy.

A radio was playing behind the counter. The volume was low and Owen hadn't really been aware of it, but Rosie sprang to her feet and turned it up. Voices crackled out.

". . . *subversives.*" Owen heard a harsh male voice.

"*Where'd they come from?*" said another.

"*Down the Speedway. A boy, two girls, and a weird-looking man. Reckon the Albions had a go at them on the way.*"

"That's us!" Owen said.

"They in the City?" the first voice went on.

"Hard to tell. Might've gone down one of the old underground tunnels."

"Told you we should've blown those places up."

"That's the Terminus' call."

"Too cheap to pay for the explosives."

"Could use a few of them hostages—they could do with a little bit of exercise," the second voice said with a harsh laugh.

"Over and out."

Rosie turned down the radio again. "Mrs. Newell keeps an eye on the Specials' radio. She likes to know what's going on."

"We were noticed," Dr. Diamond said.

"That we were. We'll have to be careful."

"We need to find a tempod quickly," Dr. Diamond said.

"The traders used to bring them down the river," Rosie said. "To sell them in the Bourse."

"The Bourse?"

"The exchange. For buying and selling stuff."

"Of course. You said. Where is it?"

"Uptown. I can show you, for a price. Speaking of which, I ain't got paid at all yet."

Dr. Diamond produced his wallet. He opened a side pocket and shook out some silver coins. "Is that enough?"

"I don't want no foreign currency," Rosie said. "No

146

good around here." Then she picked up one of the coins and stared at it. There was the faintest of blue glows from it, as though magno had been used in its making. Quickly the coins disappeared into a pocket of her dress. "That'll have to do," she said, although Owen had the impression that she had been very well paid indeed.

Just then Mrs. Newell came down the stairs.

"How is Cati?" Owen asked anxiously.

"I don't know," Mrs. Newell said, frowning. "There's no infection as such, but wounds from a Dog bite or scratch can have very strange effects."

"What sort of effects?" Owen demanded, but Mrs. Newell merely shook her head.

"I gave her a drink and her temperature is down. More than likely she'll be right as rain in the morning."

"I think we should—" Owen began, but Rosie cut in with a warning look.

"Mrs. Newell knows what she's doing."

The woman's arms were folded and her lips pursed. "That's not all," she said. "That child has felt the breath of the Harsh in the past. There is a cold in her bones."

"She has. I was with her when it happened," Owen said.

"And who are you, young man?" Mrs. Newell said. "Why would the Harsh take such an interest in you and your friend?"

"We just . . . we just got in their way, I think," Owen stammered. He wasn't sure if the fact that he was called the Navigator would mean anything to Mrs. Newell, but he felt reluctant to let her know about it.

"Specials were on the scanner," Rosie told her. "They know we got in."

"Specials aren't that interested in the likes of you," Mrs. Newell said. "It's about time some business got done here. Including which, that stew needs paying for."

Dr. Diamond produced his wallet. He took Mrs. Newell over to the counter and they talked in low voices. When he came back he had arranged for them to stay.

Mrs. Newell left the room and returned with a wooden box. She put it down on the table and opened it. It was full of eyeglasses, many of them with bent frames on cracked or missing lenses. "The late Mr. Newell kept a market stall," she said. "He used to sell glasses, among other things."

Owen tried to keep a straight face as Dr. Diamond tried on different kinds of glasses, including pince-nez and monocles. Eventually he settled on a pair with big black frames and the thickest glass that Owen had ever seen. Even Mrs. Newell looked startled when he turned to look at her with his eyes magnified to three times their normal size.

"That's better," he said. "Now, Rosie, can you take us to the museum?"

"You'd better walk," Mrs. Newell said. "That truck sticks out like a sore thumb."

"It's late. The museum might be closed," Owen said, sipping at the piping hot tea that Mrs. Newell had placed in front of him.

"We have to try," Dr. Diamond said.

"This'll be more money," Rosie said with satisfaction.

"What about Cati?" Owen asked.

"Best let her sleep," Mrs. Newell said. "Don't worry, I'll keep an eye on her."

"Go up and see her," Dr. Diamond said to Owen, hearing the worry in his voice.

He climbed the narrow stairs once more and went into the little bedroom. Cati was sleeping peacefully. He sat on the bed beside her for a few moments, then got up to go.

As he did so her eyes opened. "Navigator," she said, and her voice was strong.

"Cati! You're awake!"

Her eyes were clear. "I'll be all right," she said. "I'm just a little sore. But I'm much better. You need to find the whatsit, the tempod."

"I'm worried about you."

"I am the Watcher," she said, her voice stern. "And my father before me."

"Yes, ma'am," he said with a grin, and saluted. She lifted a pillow from the bed and threw it at him weakly.

"I'll report in later," he said, the relief clear on his face.

"Go on," she said, smiling.

After he left Cati lay thinking for a few moments before her eyes closed and she drifted off to sleep. When Mrs. Newell looked in an hour later, Cati was still asleep, but frowning and making small troubled noises.

Outside a biting wind was blowing through the archway. Owen got hats and scarves from the truck, and they set out. There were fewer people on the street, but still Rosie exchanged greetings with shopkeepers and stallholders. If they were curious as to who her friends were, they didn't ask. They passed houses where the faint strains of music could be heard and once Owen looked in through a cracked window and saw two children in pajamas in front of a fire, being read a story. He felt a pang of longing as the freezing wind blew sleet against the back of his neck. The district looked like a good place to live, he thought. For all that it was run-down and poor, there was a warmth to it and its people.

The next streets were quieter again. There were few shops open and everyone they met appeared to be

151

hurrying home. Rosie pressed on without looking back, stopping at each junction and checking the roads carefully. They entered a work district where large deserted factories loomed, closed off with ugly barbed-wire fences. There was less cover here and Rosie seemed more nervous. The pavement beneath their feet was black with ice.

"What are these places?" Dr. Diamond asked, as if he was out for a stroll among some ancient monuments.

"Not sure," Rosie muttered.

They turned into a narrow street with tall buildings on both sides. The wind channeled down the street and made Owen's eyes water, and he heard it whistling through the wires overhead. At least that's what he thought until Rosie gave a low groan.

"Specials," she said. She looked around frantically. The whistling noise was rapidly getting louder and Owen could see a blue glow nearing them. "Quick!" Rosie said. "Get in behind these bins."

"What about you?" Owen said.

"I've got ID, so they can't arrest me," Rosie said. "I'll try to lead them away from you."

Owen and Dr. Diamond ducked behind battered steel bins outside a doorway. Rosie walked toward the end of the street, where the whistling was coming from. A group of men appeared around the corner, carrying a magno light. Owen had expected a recognizable police force, but this crew was as villainous-looking as Johnston's men. Their faces were unshaven and rough;

they carried an assortment of cudgels and knives and wore bandoliers of ammunition. The only thing that distinguished them as anything but thugs were the hats they wore—tall, old-fashioned domes with a brass button on top and tarnished silver badges on the front. They had whistles on chains around their necks, which they blew continuously and noisily, interspersed with rough laughter and belching. They came down the street, kicking at doors and swinging cudgels at the few windows left unbroken. They hadn't noticed Rosie yet, and Owen thought she looked very small and brave as she walked toward them. Then, as if at a signal, they stopped and stared at her, like hunting dogs who had just spotted prey.

"Please," Rosie said in a little girl's voice, "have you seen a cat? I've lost my kitty."

As an excuse for being out alone this time of night, it was pretty thin stuff, Owen thought.

"Cat?" one of the Specials said. "What's it look like?"

"Black and white."

"I thought I seen one floating in the river," the man said with a roar of laughter.

"I seen Dogs chasing one," another said. "I think they ate it an' all."

There was more laughter and jeering. Then one Special stepped forward. He was taller and thinner than the others, with a pale, sickly-looking face. He held out his hand. "Papers, please." He didn't raise his voice, but the others fell quiet.

Rosie took a document out of her pocket and handed it to him. He caught her hand and pulled off her glove.

"You won't find much magno down around here," he sneered. "Nor will you find many cats, if you're telling us the truth."

"I am telling the truth, sir," she said, with a half curtsey.

Don't overdo it, Rosie, Owen thought. The little-girl act might fool the other Specials, but this one seemed different.

The man's eyes narrowed as he looked at her. "These magno hunters are a nuisance," he said. "Cocky enough when young, then of course the hands fall off and they end up begging. Just as soon send them to the Terminus jail at this age." He examined her ID and smiled thinly. "It seems we have a financial investment in you, Rosie, so we'd better let you go on looking for this cat of yours. Though you're probably scrounging around in the filth looking for magno shavings. There aren't any left, you should know that."

Owen could feel his face going red with anger at the way the thin-faced man was treating Rosie. He started to get to his feet, but Dr. Diamond put a restraining hand on his arm. "Don't," he whispered. "This is her world. She knows what she's doing."

The man handed her back the papers. Rosie reached out for her glove, but he threw it on the ground at her feet. "You're just outside the curfew zone. Don't let me catch you in it. Who knows what unpleasantness might await you in the Terminus."

The Specials guffawed. Rosie bent down to pick up her glove. "Yes, sir," she said quietly.

He watched her put the glove on. "Don't think I'm fooled," he said. "This city is full of trash like you. I put a dozen in jail every day. If you didn't owe us . . ." He turned to the other men. "All right, let's go." The whistling and roaring resumed as the patrol moved away.

"That looks like a very dangerous man," Dr. Diamond said.

Rosie stood still on the pavement until the patrol was out of earshot, then she beckoned the others out of hiding.

"Are you OK?" Owen asked.

"Course I am." She smiled thinly. "Although I didn't expect to run into Headley."

"Headley?"

"The thin one. The chief corsair himself. Must be something going on if he's running around with that bunch of fools. Let's move before they come back."

They crossed a patch of open ground at the top of the street. The buildings on the other side changed again. This time they looked like merchants' houses, once more boarded up and abandoned. In one window torn brocade curtains flapped in the wind.

"Should be along here somewhere," Rosie said. Owen looked around uneasily. There was something spooky about this part of the City.

"Here it is," Dr. Diamond said. It was a tall building like the others. There were weeds growing out of the stone steps up to the door and there were no lights on, but a brass plaque to one side of the door said MUSEUM and a handwritten notice on the door said OPEN.

"It's about time we got our bums off the street." Rosie walked up the stairs without waiting for them. In her black clothes she looked like a little old lady. Dr. Diamond bounded up the steps and Owen followed reluctantly as Rosie pushed the door. It opened onto a dark hallway, lit only by a minute piece of magno in a glass holder on the ceiling. Rosie looked at it longingly, but it was in a wire cage.

The hallway was full of heavy old furniture—chaise longues, tables, and bookcases crammed with large books with gilt lettering on the spines. There were mirrors on the walls and paintings of men and women in old-fashioned dress. In one, a cruel-looking lady in a blue organza dress held the skull of a small animal in the palm of her hand.

Owen stepped in front of one of the mirrors and felt the hairs on the back of his neck stand up when he realized that he couldn't see his own reflection. Then, as he walked away, his reflection suddenly appeared.

"Fascinating," Dr. Diamond murmured. "The

mirror would seem to distort time. You see your reflection only after you stand in front of the mirror."

"The museum's this way," Rosie said, pointing through an arch surrounded by purple velvet curtains.

"I can't wait," Dr. Diamond said.

Owen wished that Cati was with them. He could imagine her digging him in the back and smiling about the doctor's enthusiasms.

On the other side of the curtain they found themselves in a large octagonal room. Magno ceiling lights cast a dim glow. More velvet curtains covered the walls. There were glass cases everywhere and from the ceiling hung the skeleton of some great, writhing beast.

"Wonderful!" Dr. Diamond breathed.

"More your kind of place than mine, Doc, I must admit," Rosie said. "There's some really strange stuff in here."

Just then they heard footsteps coming down the corridor. Rosie's hand went to the hidden knife inside her jacket. Owen looked around for a weapon. Even the doctor took up a martial arts stance.

The curtain was flicked aside and a man came into the room. He wore a blue suit with black velvet trim on the collar, and black suede shoes. His hair was slicked back in a quiff and his fingers were covered with heavy gold rings. But the strangest thing about him was his face, which was as gaunt as the skull in the portrait.

"Visitors!" he exclaimed, and approached them, his

hand outstretched. "Conrad G. Black, curator. Pleased to make your acquaintance, sir." He shook Dr. Diamond's hand vigorously. "And you, young sir," he said, grabbing Owen's hand. "And if the little magno hunter lets go of whatever weapon she has concealed there, I'll sure as hell shake her hand too."

Rosie looked at him suspiciously and kept her hand inside her coat. Conrad G. Black shrugged. "Entrance is free, gratis, and without charge. Please feel free to look around and ask me questions, if you will."

"I do have a question," Dr. Diamond said.

"Fire away! Shoot! Do your worst!"

"Have you ever gone under the name of Elvis Garnett?" the doctor asked.

Black hesitated. "Elvis Garnett . . . why, I may have. . . . There were charges . . . nothing ever proven . . ."

"University of Leipzig," Dr. Diamond said sternly. "You were blamed for the disappearance of rare temporal matter, the Rocks of North Stynia, precious artifacts capable of straddling two time zones at the same time."

"I don't know, I can't remember . . . ," Black said, moving sideways so that his body obscured a glass case containing two large rocks.

"Then the Dagger of Nemeth disappeared from the dean's study."

"That dagger was a fake and a fraud! 'A blade to rend the fabric of time,' my eye!"

"So you admit to it, then?" Dr. Diamond said. His

voice was severe, but Owen thought he could see a twinkle in his eye.

Black stared at him. "Son of a gun!" he said. "Son of a gun if it isn't Damian Diamond. The glasses threw me. As I live and die, Damian Diamond!" And he flung his arms around the doctor.

The doctor's first name was *Damian?* Owen could only imagine the look on Cati's face when she heard that.

"As soon as I read about the Museum of Time, I thought to myself that Elvis had always said he would beg, steal, or borrow to get a place like that," said the doctor.

"And I did," Black said, "although business is hardly brisk."

"I can see that," Dr. Diamond said. "But surely things were better when you started out."

"Well, you know, I thought this was an up-and-coming area, bought the building cheap. But the up has yet to come. This City is in trouble."

"Why?"

"Simple enough. There used to be a constant supply of time. People bought and sold, and lived happily. Then buyers started coming in from elsewhere. Nobody knew who they were. The price of time multiplied a hundredfold. Suddenly everybody went up the river to prospect. Soon enough they couldn't find any more. And what they had found was sold and gone, nobody knows where."

"I don't understand," Owen burst out. "All this talk about finding and selling time. I mean, time isn't a thing you can find lying about the place."

"It is in Hadima, you know," Black said. "Or was. Let me show you something." He went to a glass display case and removed an object. He put it on top of the case.

"Just an old stone, ain't it?" Rosie asked.

"Look," Black said, turning it over. The stone was hollow. The inside seemed to be made from smooth crystal. "Quantities of time would be trapped in here. Of course, this one has long since been emptied."

"Where does one find these artifacts?" Dr. Diamond said.

"Not artifacts," Black said. "Tempods."

Owen flashed a look at Dr. Diamond. His mouth opened to speak, but the doctor squeezed his arm hard and he shut his mouth again.

"How interesting," Dr. Diamond said. "And where do these tempods come from?"

"They come from space, we think. They fall like meteorites. They're found in the uplands, near the top of the Sound. Well, they used to be. The supply has run out."

"There are none left?" Dr. Diamond said smoothly.

"Alas, no. None has been found for years."

"I don't understand," Owen said. "Time is not a *thing*. How can these stones hold it?"

"Don't be a cynic, boy," Black said, and suddenly his

160

face was dark. He loomed over Owen, a tall spidery figure. "Do you have a soul, boy? An immortal soul? Do you?"

"I suppose . . ."

"Where is it? Can you show it to me?"

"Well, no . . ."

"Is it a thing, an object?"

"I . . . I don't think so."

"Exactly. And is it in a container? Does your body not contain it?"

"I suppose . . ."

"And can it be released from that container?"

"I don't know."

"It can be released. I can release it thus!" Now Black was very close. He pressed a small sharp blade against Owen's throat.

"Leave him alone!" Rosie cried, her own knife drawn.

Owen looked long and hard into Black's eyes. Black slowly released him. His hand flickered, and like lightning the blade flew the length of the room, embedding itself in the timber mount of a surprised-looking stuffed bird.

"So you see," Black said, breathing fast, "time can be enclosed. Do you understand?"

Owen nodded and rubbed his throat.

Dr. Diamond was watching Black closely. He hadn't moved, but his fists were clenched. "The lesson was a little . . . strong, do you not think?" he said mildly.

"The boy was in no danger," Black said, "and he will remember the lesson."

Rosie slipped her knife back into her jacket, but she kept her distance from Black.

"Tell me something," the doctor asked. "What was that beast hanging from the ceiling?"

"A schooner." A look of almost childlike delight crossed Black's face. "Kind of a cross between a shark and an eel, except much larger. The authorities say it swam in time the way fish swim in water."

Owen looked at the skeleton. A creature that could swim in time?

Rosie said nothing, but her eyes shone. Black took her by the arm, suddenly gracious. "I see we have here someone who is really interested in the fauna of time. I would be honored to show you around my humble museum."

"I love beasts and things," Rosie murmured, her mistrust forgotten.

"Please, look at this exhibit. A flightless terfuge. Sadly extinct. Early prospectors found it had the uncanny ability to smell out tempods. This is the only preserved specimen." A brown bird the size of a man with moldy feathers and odd round nostrils stared mournfully at them with glassy black eyes.

"And look at this," Black said. "It was found inside a tempod."

The thing he pointed at appeared to be a fossilized

worm. It was a delicate greenish color and its eyes seemed to be made from coral.

"Amazing," Dr. Diamond said. "What did it eat?"

"Perhaps time itself," Black said. "But many things have been found inside the tempods." He showed them another glass case inside which was an eerie, translucent plant with long delicate fronds, like some kind of strange fern. There was no wind in the case, yet the fronds moved as though stirred by a breeze.

"Why is it moving?" Rosie asked.

"It's time, isn't it?" Owen said. "The currents of time are flowing over it and making it move."

"Exactly right." Black smiled. Dr. Diamond beamed back at him.

They explored the whole museum. There were odd-looking devices that Black said could detect deposits of time. There was a motorized sleigh that could go on water and which had been used by prospectors looking for time. He showed them a photograph of the sleigh fully laden with tempods, being driven by a man with a long, tangled beard and wild eyes.

"The prospectors get like that," Black said. "They spend too long in the wilderness and see strange things."

There were prospector's clothes. There were strange instruments covered with dials and featherlight pendulums, and a five-faced clock that was a smaller version of Dr. Diamond's in the Skyward. And there were books.

Hundreds and hundreds of books on the subject of time.

"What's this?" Rosie pointed at a small glass case. Inside was a paw covered in white fur with sharp little talons. It had four fingers and a thumb, almost like a human hand.

"That? Nothing, really." Black shrugged. "It's the reputed hand of a Yeati."

"What, like the abominable snowman?" Owen asked.

"Well, I've never heard it called that before, but possibly. I think it might be a hoax, a bear claw or something. The old stories say that the mountains were full of them until the prospectors hunted them down."

"Why would they do that?" Rosie cried.

"Yeatis were partial to the odd bit of time. They'd crack a tempod open with their paws, put it to their mouth, and drink the time, like drinking milk from a coconut. Don't really believe it myself, but it makes a nice exhibit."

Rosie continued to stare at the paw. It was delicate, the long fingers and slender curved nails beautiful, yet it also gave the impression of great strength.

"I'm forgetting myself," Black said. "Let's go and have a cup of something!"

Black brought them through to his private quarters, which were decorated with rich hangings and sofas with great rugs flung over them. There was a potbelly stove in the middle of the floor where Black brewed hot chocolate in a little silver saucepan, which they drank with warm biscuits. Then Black made a dark-colored plum liqueur for Dr. Diamond. The two men settled into a long conversation about their university days, full of references to long-dead professors and horseplay in the quadrangles of Leipzig. The two children were bored stiff within minutes. Owen yawned and lay back on the sofa. It was very warm in the room and the sound of voices began to lull him to sleep.

Rosie was wide awake. She was fascinated by the strange animals she had seen, particularly by the Yeati claw. Seeing Owen asleep and the two men deep in conversation, she slipped off the sofa and out the door.

It was much colder in the corridor and she shivered and drew her coat around her. She passed the mirror quickly. She didn't like the idea of having no reflection, but she couldn't help a sideways glance. When she reached the museum door and looked back she jumped at her delayed reflection staring solemnly from the glass.

Inside the museum she moved carefully through the exhibits. The eyes of the sad, extinct terfuge seemed to watch her. She found the case with the Yeati's hand in it. The fur was gleaming white, even though it must be very old. Rosie examined the case. There was a small brass lock at the edge of it. She hesitated, then took a hairpin from under her hat and stuck it into the keyhole. She twiddled it about for a minute, then the lock sprang open. Rosie cocked her head to listen, but all was silent.

Carefully she lifted the hand from the case. It was much lighter than she'd imagined and, even though it was long dead, it had a feeling of life about it. She ran her palm along the furry fingers and felt the nails, which were sharp and hard. She could imagine them cracking open bare rock.

Rosie stroked the fur again and felt something hard near the knuckle. She moved the fur aside with her fingers. Buried in the hair, close to the knuckle, was a delicate gold ring with a single diamond inset. Holding her breath, she eased the ring off the finger and held it up to the light. It looked very old and beautiful, chased around with an almost invisible filigree pattern. Knowing that she should not be doing it, she couldn't resist trying on the ring. Then, hesitating only a fraction of a second, she shoved the paw into her pocket.

Got to get back fast, before they miss me, she thought, moving rapidly and lightly across the floor. She had just reached the door when she heard a noise, like something echoing against an object a long way away. Somehow it managed to sound both unearthly and terribly sad at the same time. She paused and then it came again. It was the sound of something in trouble.

With a quick glance at the door of Black's quarters, Rosie sped down the corridor. There were several doors along the passage. Some opened into darkened rooms full of packing cases. When she heard the noise again she realized that it came from the little door at the end of the corridor, a bare wooden door with a brass lock.

Rosie knew that the locked door meant that entry was forbidden and going in could get her into terrible trouble. But the sound came again, and this time it was sad beyond measure, a moan of infinite pain and loss. She whipped the hairpin out of her hair and went to work on the lock.

This one was trickier than the one on the case and beads of sweat were standing out on her forehead when finally it yielded. She opened the door and saw a staircase leading down into a dark cellar with a cold, rank odor. As Rosie put her foot on the first step, something rustled in the dark and whimpered. The sound was less eerie now—more like a wounded animal. That made up her mind and she walked briskly down the stairs.

There was a window high in the wall on the far side of the room. The glass was broken and a sleety wind blew through it. The window, though barred, let in enough light to see what lay beneath. It was a cage, with bars of tempered steel, barely big enough for a man to stand up in. On the floor inside it was a tin bowl full of foul scraps. And standing at the bars looking at her was a creature the size of a small polar bear, covered in white fur.

It was not as bulky as a bear and its legs and arms were longer. Its head was long and fine-featured, with high cheekbones that gave the blue eyes a slanted appearance. The creature was strange and beautiful, or would have been if its fur had not been matted and dirty and if it had been able to stand up properly in the squalid cage. The creature pushed its arms out through the bars and made a low, musical sound. It was then that Rosie saw that the right hand was missing.

"Yeati!" she whispered, truly astounded. The Yeati made another low sound and without thinking she walked over to the cage. Fast as lightning, the creature's good hand shot out and gripped her by the neck, jerking her off her feet and pulling her roughly against the bars. She hung there, shaking. She could feel the immense power in the slender hand that could crack open bare rock. She could feel its hot breath on her neck. Then slowly the grip relaxed and she was lowered to the ground.

Looking into the Yeati's eyes was the strangest experience. Rosie seemed to lose herself in its gaze, getting the impression of some vast and ancient snowfield. She could almost hear her feet creaking in the snow and hear the wind, and within the wind a voice. . . . There *was* a voice, she realized, trying to tell her something, but she couldn't understand it.

The Yeati seemed to know this. It stepped back in the cage and stooped to pick up a piece of glass fallen from the broken window. It bent over the glass and Rosie saw that it was scratching a message using its diamond-hard claw.

It handed the glass to her. It was too dark to see any more than faint marks on the surface, so she put it in her pocket to examine later. Before she could move away, the Yeati grabbed her right hand, stripping off the ring she'd stolen. Rosie gulped.

The creature peeled off her gloves. Wincing automatically, Rosie suddenly realized that her hands were no longer painful. Looking down, she saw that the terrible sores and open wounds had gone. Astonished, she looked into the Yeati's face and it seemed to smile at her. Then, gently, it slipped the ring back onto her finger, then, her gloves.

"I can't take it," she started to say, but the Yeati shook its head, then paused and listened. It pushed her away from the bars, urging her to go. She didn't need to be told twice and ran for the stairs. But before she climbed them, she turned, her eyes shining. "Thank you!"

The Yeati made another sound, and this time it felt like the coldest and freshest of winter winds carried her toward the door. Swiftly she tiptoed toward Black's quarters and peered through the door, then slipped in beside the sleeping Owen just as Dr. Diamond stood up.

"I think it's about time we were going."

Rosie shook Owen awake. "Rise and shine, sleepy-head!"

"It's good to have a bit of intelligent company. You'll come back, won't you?" Black asked.

"Of course," Dr. Diamond said. "It's been an interesting trip so far. I've always meant to come to the City and learn more about the workings of time, but I've never had the chance before."

"Perhaps you'll come on your own the next time and stay the night."

"Yes, my young friends can be a little . . . demanding," Dr. Diamond said.

Owen sat up and looked indignant, but Rosie choked back a giggle. For an eminent scientist, the doctor was a good liar. He had obviously not been honest about their reason for being in the City.

As they made their way to the exit, Owen noticed a

large, interesting shape in one of the museum rooms that he hadn't looked at before. He went over to it as Dr. Diamond and Black exchanged pleasantries at the door. It was a boat, long and narrow, bigger than it first appeared, with a cabin at the stern end and a forecastle in its upturned bow. Owen reckoned that it could carry quite a few people, but its timbers were chipped and scarred, and the whole thing was covered in dust. What appeared to be a mast was laid down from bow to stern, with a shabby piece of cloth that might have been a sail attached to it.

"What's this?" he asked.

"Just an old boat the traders used on the river," Black said carelessly. "I thought about restoring it, but it's hardly worthwhile." He turned away, dismissing the run-down craft.

Owen rubbed at the bow with his sleeve. Some letters appeared: . . . *arer*.

Then Rosie was tugging at his sleeve. "Come on!"

Owen allowed himself to be pulled to the front door, where Black shook his hand and expressed his delight at meeting him. But Owen could not help glancing back at the boat in the shadows.

Rosie felt the weight of the piece of glass in her pocket. Turning her back to the others, she slipped it out. The scratches formed writing in a strange and fancy script that she didn't understand, but it wasn't the words that made her gasp. In the dead center the Yeati had drawn a face. A boyish face, somber and watchful.

And although it was a simple scratched image and an impossible idea, it was obviously meant to be a picture of Owen.

Cati started awake. It was the middle of the night, but she'd never felt more alert. She had no idea where she was, but she knew that below her there was a cooker, and at the cooker a woman was at that very moment adding bay leaf to stew. She knew that a truck had leaked oil in the street outside. She knew that a man had recently walked past the building and that he had been drinking wine. Then she realized with a start that she knew all these things because she had *smelled* them.

She remembered dreaming. Strange snuffling, running dreams. The sense of a pack around her. Of sleeping in a huddle, curled up side by side for warmth. Of hunting and being hunted. Of nights under the stars.

She jumped out of bed, the blood coursing through her veins. Cocking her head, she could hear a mouse gnawing at a beam in the attic. She could hear a beetle scuttling by under the floorboards. And in the distance she heard howling, voices raised to the moon.

Cati ran to the window and opened it, her feet padding lightly over the floor. The howling was louder now. She could feel her ears prick up. *Like a dog's,* she thought, and at that moment her head filled with dog thoughts.

In one bound she leapt through the window. She

slithered down the sloping roof outside to land in the elm tree, then bounded from branch to branch until she reached the ground. She looked around, raised her face to sniff the air, then loped toward the archway, passed through it, and was gone.

Wesley got up early and went downriver. He had been feeling anxious and guilty about the Raggies, although he knew that if anything had happened to them, he would have felt it in his bones. Something was moving along the seaweed. It was a hedgehog, snuffling frantically through the salty fronds.

That's funny, he thought. *What is a hedgehog doing out in the daytime?* The earth rumbled; Wesley steadied himself against a tree and looked up warily for falling debris. These small quakes had become a part of daily life.

All around was damage caused by the huge tides, dead fish swept upriver and banks of seaweed washed up into the freshwater areas. When Wesley reached the harbor and saw what had happened, he broke into a run. He skidded to a halt at the edge of the fractured ground, staring at the warehouses on their island. How could he have left the Raggies undefended? Without hesitation, Wesley dived from the edge into the choppy ocean.

He swam strongly across the gap and clambered up the other side, his hands and feet grazed and bleeding from the rough surfaces of the broken concrete.

"Halt! Or I shoot!" came a muffled voice.

Wesley hesitated, then kept walking.

"You're supposed to halt when I shout that, Wesley," the voice complained, clearer now.

"Silkie!" he exclaimed in relief. "What's happened here?"

"Johnston," Silkie said. "He attacked us and I had to fight him off with my own bare hands. Well, with a pot of fishy oil. And then when he came back, the ground broke. Now we're stuck over here."

"Is everybody all right?" Wesley asked anxiously.

"I think so, but I'm the only one awake," Silkie told him. "They're not sleeping too soundly, though. What's going on, Wesley?"

Together they went to the Starry and Wesley told her about time running out, and Owen and Cati's journey to the City.

Things in the warehouse Starry were not any better. Many of the children were making sounds of real distress. Silkie took Wesley's hand. She knew how he felt about all of them, and how much it must hurt him to see them in pain and be unable to help them.

"Ain't there nothing we can do?" Silkie asked.

"No," Wesley said grimly. "How come you're awake, Silkie?"

Silkie blushed. She knew somehow that Owen had brushed against her, and that a part of her had reacted to the touch, but she couldn't tell Wesley that, or how handsome she thought Owen looked when he smiled at her.

"I . . . I don't know," she stammered. "I just woke up."

They lingered in the Starry until Silkie could feel her eyes getting heavy. "We should go," she said gently, tugging Wesley's arm.

They went outside and stared moodily out to sea. "It all comes back to the old sea, Silkie," he said. "At least, for the Raggies it does. The Raggies love the sea."

"You go back to the Workhouse," Silkie said. "I can watch here."

"I can't leave you," he said. "I can't quit this place while the Raggies lie sleeping and hurting."

"You have to," Silkie said. "If the Workhouse falls, then this place will fall too. They'll be safe with me, Wesley."

He flashed her a weary grin. "I do believe they will, Silkie."

Silkie cooked them some fish and chips, then they

sat by the driftwood fire eating contentedly, and afterward lay on the warmed stone of the hearth. Neither felt the need to say anything. Raggies had their own rough ways and often were not comfortable in the company of the more urbane Workhouse people, who wore boots and ate with forks instead of with fingers.

Martha had gone back to her own house and was sitting on Owen's bed. She was glad to get home. Besides, she felt Owen's presence in his room. Running a hand over his bedspread, she wondered where he was. Hadima was a distant memory; she knew that it was a place where they'd been pursued, but so much was still a blur.

The old chest, for instance, under the window in Owen's room. It was important, but why? The lock . . . the Mortmain, it was called. The odd tingle she felt when she touched it. She wondered whether she should move the chest to the Workhouse, then decided it was safer where it was. After all, no one knew its location.

Even as Martha was wondering, Johnston was sitting on the roof of his truck, binoculars to his eyes, looking through the bedroom window. The woman was paying too much attention to the trunk, he thought. And the Harsh were pressing him. It would soon be time to act.

It was even colder outside when they left the museum. Dr. Diamond set off at a brisk pace, with Owen following. Rosie slipped the piece of glass back into her pocket and caught up with them.

"I don't think much of your pal," she told the doctor.

"He was never a friend of mine," Dr. Diamond said. "He was always sly, also nosy enough to get to the bottom of things. I learned some interesting facts about the City tonight."

"You seemed pretty friendly," Owen said.

"He is a dangerous man, but such people can be useful. Although I don't doubt that he's on the telephone now, trying to find out what we are doing here."

"I think he's evil," Rosie said. Something about the way she said it made Dr. Diamond turn and look at her.

"What is it, Rosie?" he said sharply.

After a moment's hesitation, she told him what she had seen and done while he had been in conversation with Black.

"Goodness!" Dr. Diamond said. "A real live Yeati? Astonishing. I never suspected such cruelty."

"We should rescue it," Owen said.

"Of course. Later. For the moment we must keep to our quest. The tempod in the museum was empty and seemed to be the only one in Black's possession, but he is a slippery customer. Let me see that glass. . . ."

Rosie showed them the Yeati's message and the drawing. Owen gaped when he saw his own face etched there.

"The Yeati has seen you before, or has seen a likeness of you," Dr. Diamond said. "But I don't understand the writing."

"Could we talk about it somewhere else?" Rosie said. "Apart from the fact that it's freezing here, those Specials could come back at any time."

They returned to the Whin Bush Inn, walking as quickly and quietly as possible. Owen was exhausted now, and looking forward to a bed just like Cati's.

But Mrs. Newell met them at the door with a stricken face. "She's gone!" she said. "She must have got out the window."

They ran upstairs, where they found the bed empty and the window open.

"You were supposed to be watching her!" Owen shouted.

Dr. Diamond went to the window. He could hear dogs baying in the distance. "I don't think that we can put the blame for this on Mrs. Newell."

"You can," Mrs. Newell said heavily. "I never told you."

"Told us what?" Owen said sharply.

"It's about them Dogs. Most of them's just children who've lost their parents, street children. But there are secrets and rumors . . ."

"What secrets?" Owen demanded, his eyes burning.

"The stories say there's this stuff they put on the claws they wear. If they scratch you, it gets into your blood . . . and you become a kind of Dog yourself."

"You mean, Cati's like . . . one of them now?" Rosie asked.

"It's possible," Dr. Diamond said with a frown.

"She's probably gone to join the pack," Mrs. Newell said, sitting down, ashen-faced.

"We must find her!" Owen said. He turned toward the door, staggering with fatigue.

"Wait!" Dr. Diamond said. "Have you forgotten that a whole world's future depends on us? Anyway, you can't walk into the night without any idea where you're going. And you must rest."

"But Cati's my friend," Owen said.

"And mine too," Dr. Diamond said, "as was her father. We won't abandon her. Rosie, tomorrow morning I want you to go and find out what you can about the Dogs and where they live." Rosie nodded smartly. "Mrs. Newell, I'm sure you can pick up some information from your customers. When we know what we're dealing with, we can act. Meanwhile, we need to make a plan based on what I learned from Black tonight."

"I can't leave her out there alone!" Owen cried.

"Think about it, Owen," Dr. Diamond said gently. "What would Cati say? She is the Watcher, a duty she didn't seek, but she doesn't shirk from it. She would tell you that your duty is what matters now."

"The Dogs look after their own," Rosie said. "She'll be all right."

They went downstairs, where Mrs. Newell made them tea and bacon sandwiches. "Eat," she said to Owen, who stared into the fire. "You can't help your friend if you're worn out from hunger."

"Now," Dr. Diamond said when they had finished, "we need to talk about what I learned from Black. It seems that Hadima is under some new government, but no one knows who. The place has been run into the ground, the prisons are full of hostages, and the supplies of time and of magno have dwindled to nothing. An enemy hand is acting in all of this. Tell me, Mrs. Newell. Has the city always had such cold weather?"

"No." Mrs. Newell frowned. "It seems that it is always winter now."

"The Harsh!" Owen said. "They love the cold and dark!"

"I think so," Dr. Diamond said. "No one else is powerful enough. No one else has that hunger to obliterate time."

"We're not strong enough to take on the Harsh," Owen said.

"No. But Black told me some interesting rumors about a man he referred to as 'the Prisoner.' "

"I've heard of him," Mrs. Newell said. "They say he's the smartest man ever lived."

"And the bravest," Rosie added.

"Black seemed to think that the Harsh fear him, yet need his knowledge. He won't help them, so they keep him locked up year after year."

"Where do they keep all these hostages, anyway?" Owen said.

"In the cellar jail, underneath the Terminus," Rosie said.

"This prisoner is kept separate, under special guard, so they say," Mrs. Newell told them.

"That's what Black said. Apparently the man is also an expert in ancient languages. I suspect he may be able to translate the Yeati's writing."

"How do we get in there?" Owen asked.

"You don't, and you don't want to," Rosie said.

They fell silent. The only noise in the little room was the crackling of the fire. Owen thought about Cati, hoping she was all right. He fingered the Yeati's piece of glass which Rosie had given him. Why had he drawn Owen's face, and what did the writing mean? If the man in the Terminus jail was the only person who could translate it, then he had to get to see him.

Rosie's mind was on the Yeati, wounded and alone in its cold cellar. She couldn't stop touching the smooth, healed skin on her hands. One by one they said good-night and went quietly to bed. Despite the cozy blankets, it was a while before Owen fell asleep. There was so much going round and round in his head. And he couldn't stop thinking about Cati, out there in the City on her own.

Cati ran through the night, keeping close to walls, avoiding the few people who were out late. She wasn't following the howling anymore; she could smell where she was going. Memories of Owen and Dr. Diamond stirred in her head. She knew that she was the Watcher and that she belonged at the Workhouse, but a stronger, animal instinct now overrode everything.

She reached the edge of the City and listened to the roar of the Speedway, sniffing oil and exhaust fumes. Then a warm, snug smell wafted through a broken grating in a wall. With one easy movement, she squeezed through it and slithered along a slippery pipe. She emerged on the platform of a deserted underground station, much like the one they had arrived at earlier with Rosie. It was dark and hard to see.

Stepping forward, Cati heard a low growl. She stopped, aware of dozens of presences in the darkness around her, all very still. Something brushed against her, something warm and hairy. She could feel the hairs on the back of her neck stand up and her lips curled in a snarl. From somewhere came a light. She looked around to see that she was surrounded by Dogs. They were all staring at her.

The pack leader was directly in front of her. He looked her in the eyes, then walked around her, sniffing. Cati stood stock-still. She knew without being told that if she moved a muscle she would be torn apart. Strangely, she could sense what the Dogs were thinking, almost as if they had one mind. They were curious but suspicious.

Not Dogs, part of her mind told her. *Children!* The leader was facing her again now. Fast as lightning he leaned in and sank his teeth in the back of her neck, hard enough to hurt, but not enough to draw blood. With a growl, he shook her roughly. She didn't resist. He let go and sat back on his haunches. Then he made a low bark and nodded.

Suddenly a warm wave of friendship and understanding washed toward her from the other Dogs. They crowded around her, jostling, wanting to touch her.

Other noses rubbed against her own and she felt a sense of delight in their companionship.

They surged to the far end of the platform, where there was a fire going and a pot on the fire, from which delicious smells wafted. Two Dogs stood by the pot. One of them lifted a ladle and poured the mixture into several large bowls. The Dogs pushed toward the bowls, some of them grabbing meaty chunks with their hands, others putting their mouths down and lapping noisily.

Cati darted forward and grabbed a bone. Shards of meat and drops of gravy fell from it as she gnawed away. It was delicious. As she ate, she looked around at the pack. They were a curious mixture. Many used their hands and walked upright; others went on all fours. They communicated with words and movements and barks and snuffles. But they all wore the Dog masks, and each mask reflected the nature of the Dog within. Some were broad and friendly with wide-spaced eyes. Others were long and serious. Some were fighters, their muzzles notched and scarred. A lean black Dog with one ear half torn off and a white patch over one eye looked at Cati, growling. She recognized him as the Dog who had attacked her in the truck.

A female Dog came and sat beside Cati. She had an open face with brown on her muzzle and a mouth that seemed to be curled in a smile.

"You're new," she said. "My name is . . . you start to

forget your name around here. Mo, that's it." Mo scratched her side vigorously, exactly like a dog would.

"My name is . . ." It was true. Her name was there, but just out of reach. She concentrated. "Cati," she said firmly.

"You start to forget your name, and after that, if you really let go, the mask gets hard to take off. Nearly like it grows into your skin."

Cati wasn't sure if she liked the thought of this.

"It's not bad here," Mo went on, "if you stay with what the pack wants you to do—and of course Clancy."

"Who's Clancy?"

"Pack leader. Where's he got to? Probably making your mask." Mo gave a sly smile. "You enjoying that bone?"

Cati realized she was still gnawing at the bone from the stew. Hurriedly she put it down. As she did so she was aware of a stir in the pack. Looking up, she saw that Clancy was coming toward her carrying a Dog mask.

"See? It's yours," Mo whispered. Cati stood up. Weirdly, the mask *did* look like her. The black hair woven into the fur between the ears looked familiar and she remembered the hank that had been yanked out as she had struggled with the Dog at the back of the truck.

The pack gathered around as Clancy held the mask aloft with hands that were strong and covered with fine, short fur. Cati stepped forward and he lowered the mask over her head. Instantly she felt more dog than human. The mask smelled of dog and the eye slits seemed to give a dog's-eye view of the world. She felt that, if she really wanted it, the mask would become like part of her, hard to take off, as Mo had said.

She felt approval coming in waves from the pack. *If you had a tail, you'd wag it,* a small human voice said inside. But the voice was silenced when Clancy threw his head back and emitted a long howl. The others joined in, and then they were all streaming out of the station, moving as one, onto the street.

Cati found herself in a wealthy area, near the shrouded Terminus. There were tall silent houses, the inhabitants asleep, and the Dogs rampaged through the gardens, snatching purses from open windows, digging in flower beds, pulling clothes from the lines, grabbing anything that wasn't tied down, stealing it or spoiling it. Everywhere they went, commotion ensued, with lights coming on and angry shouts. And Clancy was always there, encouraging sometimes, nipping at their heels at others.

If there was a high wall to be climbed, then Clancy would shin up a drainpipe. If a guard dog appeared, it was Clancy who charmed it, or threatened it, and few stood in his way. Cati ran with the pack, thinking as they thought, moving as they moved.

As soon as they heard the whistles of the Specials, they moved on to another district, and before Cati knew it, dawn was brightening in the sky. They followed Clancy back down to a market where fish sellers and butchers were setting up stalls. The smells of raw meat made Cati's mouth water.

They gathered by the market wall and Clancy collected up everything they had stolen. Then he stood up and took off his mask.

Cati looked at him, a boy with deep-set hazel eyes and full lips. He smiled at her and his warm, mischievous smile lit up his serious face. Swinging the bag over his shoulder, Clancy winked, then turned and walked into the market.

He was back twenty minutes later, carrying two bulging bags of meat that he could barely lift. There were other things as well. One of the Dogs had a sore on her leg and he had got an ointment to put on it. There was a bottle of medicine for another Dog who had a cough.

As the pack crowded round to see what Clancy had brought, a group of market workers came up the road. With shouts and curses, they began to pelt the Dogs with stones. Clancy slipped his mask back on and picked up a half-rotten turnip from the ground. He lobbed it at a fat red-faced man who took it full in the face. Laughing and barking, the Dogs raced away.

Turning a corner, they ducked into a grating and found themselves in the city sewers. Trying not to look at the murky water, Cati followed the Dogs. Several of them started to chase the large and evil-looking rats that scuttled along side tunnels, but Clancy kept them on course. It was full daylight before they reached the deserted underground station once more.

The Dogs flung themselves down in whatever space they could find, some of them with their tongues hanging out, panting. Clancy curled up on a shelf of the old ticket kiosk, where he could keep a wary eye on the platform.

The black Dog with the torn ear walked up to the spot where Cati had settled. "I'm sleeping there," he growled, and pushed Cati roughly.

Cati leapt up with her fists clenched, but Mo grabbed her arm and pulled her away. "You don't want to mess with Patchie," she whispered. "Thinks he should be leader. He's pretty tough."

"So am I," Cati growled. But she was tired and Patchie did look pretty tough, so she found another spot and curled up. Within minutes she was asleep.

Rosie was woken by Owen shaking her arm. "What is it?" she said sleepily. "It's still dark."

"We're starting early. You have to find Cati!"

"I'm coming, I'm coming," she yawned.

Rosie followed Owen downstairs. The room was full of early-rising workers drinking coffee and eating big breakfasts. A fire blazed in the hearth and when Rosie and Owen squeezed onto a bench, a red-faced Mrs. Newell put plates of bacon and egg and sausage in front of them. The workers talked loudly among themselves and nobody paid any attention to the strangers. By the time Dr. Diamond came down, Rosie was gone.

"I'll find her," she'd promised Owen, "if she's out there to be found. You help the doc."

"Black mentioned a place we must investigate," Dr. Diamond said, between forkfuls of food.

"The Bourse?" Owen asked.

"Indeed. It's the place where time was bought and sold. A visit there may prove useful."

Brushing crumbs from their clothes, they put on their coats and hats and went outside. It was a bright, cold morning and the street outside Cyanite Place was already busy.

Owen was quiet. He knew he must concentrate on what he had to do that day, but he was so worried about Cati. Trying to force his thoughts away from her, he fingered the jagged outline of the glass in his pocket. They walked uphill toward the Terminus, Dr. Diamond reading from the guidebook as they went. The potholed streets gave way to limestone paving and cobblestones. The buildings changed too. The houses here had tall turrets at the corners and the shops had big shining windows displaying only one or two items in each—an expensive-looking dress or a pair of shoes. The people seemed taller and better dressed. There was the smell of good cologne and perfume in the air and the cafes that they passed were full of people with exquisite manners drinking rare coffees. In contrast, on many street corners stood sandbagged gun emplacements, behind which were the distinctive tall hats of the Specials.

Owen was surprised when passersby tipped their hats to Dr. Diamond, addressing him as "Il Professore."

"The scientists around here must all look like you," Owen said, although secretly he doubted it.

As they climbed, the air became misty, a dense, icy fog that reminded Owen of the Harsh. Even with the guidebook Dr. Diamond seemed unsure of the way. After walking for almost an hour they finally emerged into a great, foggy square of gray stone surrounded by monumental buildings.

"Bourse Square," Dr. Diamond read. "A bustling center of the commercial district surrounded by financial houses and dominated by the Bourse itself."

"I think your guidebook is a bit out of date," Owen said.

"I'm afraid so," Dr. Diamond said. The square was far from bustling. In fact, there wasn't a soul to be seen.

"Let's have a look at this Bourse, then," Owen said.

"It's on the north side." As they crossed the square a patrol of Specials appeared, marching in formation. These Specials seemed much more disciplined than the ones they'd seen the night before, with pressed uniforms and steel-gray hair. One flashed a stern look at Owen and Dr. Diamond.

The entrance to the Bourse was a huge stone doorway, reaching perhaps eighty meters into the air, framing ornate brassbound doors. The stone stairs were worn by the passage of many thousands of pairs of feet. As they neared, the doors swung open without being touched and from within a gong sounded a deep note that hung in the air.

"Looks like the day's business has just begun," Dr. Diamond said. Side by side they walked into the Bourse.

A hundred meters away, a pair of shrewd and interested eyes were following their every movement. Headley, the chief corsair, had received a call that morning from a museum owner named Black. Hoping to curry favor with the Terminus, no doubt, the man had described visitors he had received the previous night. Black had described Dr. Diamond as a hopeless rebel he'd known at college, and the children struck him as no better. He added that Diamond seemed interested in the Bourse and might be found there.

As the pair disappeared through the doors, Headley stroked his narrow jaw. There was something familiar about that boy. Should he arrest the pair? But recently he had sent so many prisoners to the jail that it was bursting, so he thought he'd let them go for the moment. The City was troublesome and there was always something to do. Then he realized there was an advantage to be had. The sellers who ran the Bourse had always thought themselves a cut above everyone else and did not welcome Terminus interference. But if they were found to be harboring rebels . . . Headley's eyes brightened and he hurried off to find a troop of Specials.

Owen and Dr. Diamond walked down a long marble corridor. The passageway might have been magnificent once, but now it was gloomy and cobwebs hung from the ceiling. They came to another set of doors and

Owen pushed them open. Then they found themselves in the biggest room that Owen had ever seen.

The great vaulted ceiling stretched on forever, supported by vast carved pillars. The massive stone floor was surrounded by raised stone platforms and on each was a high, old-fashioned desk. At each desk sat a man. These men were immensely tall and thin. They wore pinstriped trousers and old-fashioned shirts and ties with stiff collars. Their faces were narrow and mournful, and they wore celluloid eyeshades above which were extraordinarily long, fine eyebrows that stuck out at each side like wings. There were great ledgers open in front of them and each held a long slender pen.

They were all facing the same direction and when Owen turned to look he saw a vast display of numbers covering one wall. Each number was in its own little window on the display board, but some of the windows were blank, others broken, with springs and bits of mechanical innards protruding. Then he saw a tiny movement in one of the numbers. All the men craned forward, but it seemed to be just some mechanical shift and the number did not change. The men sat back again.

Owen heard footsteps approaching. Turning, he saw a man who looked like the others but was a little more stooped, whose great winglike eyebrows were silvery gray. The hall was so vast that it took him more than a minute to cross it, and when he arrived he was out of breath, but he still managed to stretch out his hand in greeting.

"Welcome to the Bourse! My name is Magnier. I am the chairman and Chief Seller," he wheezed in a high-pitched voice. "What are you here to trade today? A load of magno, perhaps? Don't tell me you've turned up a tempod or two!"

"I'm sorry," Dr. Diamond said, "we aren't prospectors. I'm Dr. Diamond of . . . of Leipzig University, and this is my friend Owen."

"Not prospectors," the old man said, unable to hide his disappointment.

"I'm sorry," Owen said.

"Not to worry," the man said, brightening with an effort. "You didn't really look like prospectors. Or smell like them. They tend to be a bit ripe after a few months out in the wilds. In that case you must be here for the tour. . . ." The man shot a quick puzzled look at Owen. "Once upon a time this was the biggest exchange you could find. Time was traded here, magno, anything. The floor was full of dealers shouting and waving. It was impossible to keep up with the board."

"Things seem a little . . . slack now," the doctor said.

"Yes, the Terminus has . . . well . . . not served as it should. It's hard to know who is in ch—"

Magnier broke off and turned toward the door, frowning. Owen could now hear tramping feet and loud voices, and above it all the sound of whistles.

The doors burst open and a party of Specials marched in. Not the boorish men they had met in the district, but the disciplined, hard-faced men of the

Terminus. And at their head marched the cold-faced Headley.

"This is an outrage, Headley!" Magnier said, his face turning red. "You have no right to be here."

"Do I not?" Headley said with a thin smile.

"This place has always been off-limits to the Specials," Magnier said.

"Times have changed, Magnier," Headley said, "and so have the standards of the Bourse. Since when have you harbored rebels?"

"Rebels . . . ?" Magnier was confused and now he couldn't tear his eyes away from Owen.

"Ask for their papers," Headley ordered his troops.

"Oh, dear," Dr. Diamond said, feeling his pockets, "we seem to have left them at our lodgings. . . ."

"Dr. Diamond is a visiting professor," Magnier said. "And this is his friend Owen."

He was still staring, but Owen didn't notice. The minute Owen had seen Headley and the Specials, a plan had started to form in his head—a plan that he hoped would take him exactly where he wanted to go. Now it was time to act.

"No, I'm not his friend," he said suddenly. "I've never seen this man before. My name isn't Owen and I was just tagging along to see what I could get out of him."

"Indeed," Headley said, smiling unpleasantly. "And if your name is not Owen, then what is it?"

"That's for me to know and you to find out," Owen said.

"Finding out can be arranged," Headley said.

"Stop it, Owen," Dr. Diamond hissed, bemused by the boy's behavior.

"Shut up!" Owen shouted, and Dr. Diamond stared.

Owen darted forward. Before anyone could stop him he had kicked Headley swiftly on the shins. The chief corsair gasped in pain.

"Take him!" he said to his men.

Dr. Diamond stepped forward to protest, but Magnier grabbed him with a surprisingly strong grip. Two of the Specials caught Owen by the arms. Owen struggled and kicked out, then allowed himself to be captured, a sullen look on his face.

"It was wise not to intervene, Doctor," Headley said. "Although I'm sure we could find room for you in the jail as well."

"I'll be speaking to the Terminus about this," Magnier said.

"Do so," Headley sneered. "You think that what the Bourse says carries any weight around here anymore?"

"It carries more than you think," Magnier said, but his boast seemed hollow in the echoing chamber.

"Where are you taking him?" Dr. Diamond said.

"To the jail."

"You just worry about yourself, Il Professore," Owen said as scathingly as he could.

"Come on!" ordered Headley. He spun on his heel and walked toward the door, followed by the rest of the

Specials and the two men dragging Owen. The doctor watched them go with despair.

At the door Headley paused and took Owen by the hair, bending his head back painfully. "Now, young lad, let's go and find out who you are."

"I think I might already know the answer to that," Magnier murmured to himself. Dr. Diamond made as if to follow them, but Magnier restrained him again. "We have to talk."

"I'm going to follow them."

"Later. Right now you should come with me."

Reluctantly Dr. Diamond followed Magnier to a desk, larger than the others, that stood on a dais overlooking the entire floor. Magnier opened the desk and unlocked a drawer at the back. He reached in and took out a large copper coin, which he handed to Dr. Diamond. "Look."

The coin was old. It had a crown on one side, and on the other, worn though it was, a face. The features were unmistakably Owen's.

"That's the second time that I've seen an image like that in twenty-four hours," Dr. Diamond said. "Please explain."

"This is the face of the Navigator," Magnier said.

"Yes," Dr. Diamond said.

"And you know who the Navigator was . . . is?"

The doctor hesitated. "I have an understanding of the term, yes."

"But not perhaps the full understanding." Magnier nodded. "The Navigator was the mapper of time. He traveled and charted all the routes between this world and others—all the pathways in time, in fact. No one really knows how he did it or how he traveled. And now the maps are all lost or destroyed, as indeed was the Navigator himself. Until now."

"But this can't be Owen," Dr. Diamond said.

"No, of course not. But Owen may well be the original Navigator's grandson. But tell me, why did he attack Headley and pretend not to know you?"

"The boy is capable of thinking for himself," Dr. Diamond said. "I think he wants to find the Prisoner that Black talked about. Being arrested is one way of getting into the jail."

The Specials dragged Owen up the hill. If he stumbled, he was grabbed by the hair and hauled along until he found his feet again. He was beginning to wonder if this had been such a good idea after all. Every so often one of the Specials would bash him with a baton. "Soften him up a bit," they laughed.

It took fifteen minutes to reach the Terminus, although he couldn't see it properly.

The next few hours were a nightmare. He was thrown fully clothed into a cold shower that smelled of chemicals, for delousing. He was photographed and had his teeth inspected, then made to run in place for twenty minutes. And every time a jailer walked past, they dealt him a punch or a heavy kick.

In the end it was a relief when they dragged him by the hair and threw him on the floor of an office. On hands and knees, he looked up to see Headley sitting at a polished desk.

"What's your name and where are you from?" Headley barked. Owen shook his head. Headley called the guard back in. "I haven't time to deal with him now. Take him to the holding pen."

Owen was pulled from the office and forced down a corridor where the walls changed from plaster to damp, rough stone. The holding pen didn't sound like the place he wanted to go. He thought quickly. He started to whimper and writhe.

"What's the matter with you?" the guard said. He had a wide mouth with stained yellow teeth and his eyes were too far apart. He didn't look too bright.

"The Prisoner! The one they talk about," he wailed. "The Prisoner is here!"

"Course he is."

"They say he tortures boys like me. That he sucks out their minds and leaves them cold and empty. That he eats their souls! Please don't put me in with him!"

"Well, I wasn't going to," the guard said with an unpleasant grin, "but seeing as you ask . . ."

He forced Owen down a side corridor. Owen wept and pleaded and received several cuffs to his head. It became colder and his teeth started to chatter. Finally they came to an iron door, squat and ugly. Owen was still crying and pleading. The guard put a key in the heavy lock, threw open the door, and put his boot to Owen's backside.

"Enjoy the soul-eater!" the guard said with a laugh, then kicked Owen hard, sending him sprawling onto a wet stone floor. He slammed the door.

Picking himself up, Owen looked around. He wiped away his fake tears with his sleeve. He was in a dungeon with cold, dripping stone walls. But just ahead was a corridor that glowed with a dim light.

The Prisoner! The one who may be able to translate what the Yeati wrote, he thought, his mouth dry, the bruises forgotten.

Owen moved down the corridor slowly. The floor was uneven underfoot and once he tripped over something that felt unpleasantly like a skull. In the end he came to a small doorway. He had to duck his head to get through.

To his amazement he emerged into a small library. Oil lamps gave the place a surprisingly cheerful glow. There were wooden shelves packed with what looked like dense scientific texts. Across the room a man sat at a bench. He was mending the spine of a book. A pot of glue sat beside him and he had a fine brush in his hand.

"Hello," Owen said.

The man stopped what he was doing and turned round slowly. He was wearing what remained of a three-piece pinstriped suit and he peered at Owen through gold-framed glasses, while the lamplight gleamed off his high forehead.

"Yes, is there something I can help?" The man had the faintest of accents. The way he said *somezing* . . .

Owen started to speak, but he felt suddenly dizzy from the beatings. He leaned against the doorframe. The room felt very far away, and his own voice seemed to be coming from a great distance. The ground rushed toward him, and he saw and felt no more.

22

When Owen woke he was lying on a small hard bed. He rubbed his eyes and sat up. The man was sitting on a chair reading a book. When he saw that Owen was awake, he came over and felt his forehead and took his pulse.

"Who . . . who are you?" Owen asked.

"My name is Gobillard."

"The trunk!" Owen exclaimed.

The man looked at him. "What do you know of Gobillard's trunk?" Suddenly he leapt up, seized the lamp from the workbench, and held it close to Owen's face.

"Mon dieu!" he exclaimed, and sat down heavily. "My God!" He turned to Owen. "Your father . . . you look the same as him when he was young."

"My father?" Owen gasped.

"Your father was my friend, but I was told he was dead," Gobillard said sadly. "Together we fought the Harsh before I was captured."

Owen stared at Gobillard. A friend of his father's! A thousand questions ran through his head. "H-how did you know him?" he stammered.

"Through your grandfather—the first Navigator. Your father wanted to follow in his footsteps."

"I don't . . . there's so much I don't understand," Owen said. "My grandfather? And the trunk . . . the Mortmain?"

"The trunk I made for your father. We needed something to contain the evil power of the Harsh. The Mortmain belonged to your grandfather. I harnessed its power to act as a lock on the trunk." The man chuckled. "From what I hear it succeeds, no?" His smile vanished. "The Harsh were very angry. They froze me for a long time. Where is the trunk now?"

"In my room at home," Owen said.

The man's eyes widened. "So it was you that stopped the Harsh. Your father would have been very proud. And your grandfather."

"My grandfather—he was the original Navigator?"

"Yes, he made the maps."

"Like road maps?"

"He made maps of time itself! He navigated *time*," Gobillard cried. "But tell me, how is it that you are here? There has been no travel into Hadima for many years."

"We found the way, me and my friends. We had to. Time is running out, Mr. Gobillard. Everybody is in danger." Owen quickly explained everything.

"The Harsh are so greedy for time!" Gobillard exclaimed when Owen had finished. "I think you need to find a tempod."

"My friends are looking." Owen swung his legs out of the bed. As he did so, the piece of glass he'd been carrying fell on the bed.

Gobillard seized it. "Where did you get this?"

"A Yeati gave it to my friend Rosie."

"A Yeati?" Gobillard snorted. "You say that as if meeting a Yeati was commonplace!"

"Can you read it?"

Gobillard peered closely through his gold-rimmed spectacles. "Let me see. It is a very old language. . . . The first part is a name, I think. . . . Yes . . . *'Mary'* . . . *'Mary White . . .'* "

"Mary White?" Owen almost burst out laughing. There was something very funny about the idea of old Mary having anything to do with Yeati and the like.

"She must be a very great person," Gobillard said, "if the Yeati know her. What else, now? *'It has black . . .'* That's what it says, but I do not know what it means."

Gobillard darted to the shelves and started flinging books from them. Owen wondered if he had gone mad. Glancing around as if there were watchers in the half-light, Gobillard tilted the now empty shelving backward. He scrabbled in the dust underneath until his

206

fingers caught the edge of a flat stone. He lifted it. Underneath the stone was a tin box, which Gobillard seized and placed on the table.

"Look!" Gobillard opened the box and took out a roll of very old, yellowed, and battered-looking maps.

"I don't understand," Owen said.

"These," Gobillard said, seizing Owen's shoulder in a tight grip, "are some of your grandfather's maps. All I have found." Owen stared. The documents were faded and stained and didn't look much like any map he had ever seen. There were no lakes or rivers or mountains, although there were lines connecting different-colored areas. Instead of names there were mystical-looking symbols.

"No one understands them now," Gobillard said. "But maybe a grandson . . ."

Owen traced one of the lines with his finger. As he did so he felt a strange energy coming from the map. He shut his eyes, and although he couldn't see, his finger kept following the line. He could suddenly smell pine trees and snow and mountain air.

"That's the road we traveled to get here," he said.

"Remarkable," Gobillard said.

Owen lifted his finger and put it down at random. He felt a strong sense of salt water and sky. "The Warehouse!" he said. "These are pathways in time, aren't they?"

Before they could discuss things further, Owen heard the sound of keys in the distance and then a crash as the door of the dungeon burst open. Hard voices rang out, and the sound of heavy boots approached. "Take the maps!" Gobillard hissed, thrusting the maps down the front of Owen's jacket. "Keep them safe!"

"But . . . how do I use them?"

"The *Wayfarer*," Gobillard said urgently. "Find the *Wayfarer*!"

"The *Wayfarer*?" Owen said. The name struck a chord with him, but he couldn't quite place why.

But there was no time to say anything more as the light in the little room seemed to fade. Headley was standing in the doorway, his hand on his hips.

"Someone's here to see you, young lad," he said, grinning.

Rosie had spent the whole day in the district, trying to find out about the Dogs and where they lived. Most people weren't inclined to talk about them. They spat on the ground and called the Dogs thieves and vermin. One man even raised a cudgel to Rosie when she asked. It was afternoon before she reached the market. Stallholders were shouting their wares, and delicious smells of food drifted through the crowds. Rosie sat at an outdoor stall and ordered steaming hot soup with big hunks of chicken floating in it. At the corner of the counter she saw two furtive-looking men haggling over a gold ring. A stolen ring, she thought, by the way the two men kept their voices down and looked around them nervously, although they paid no attention to the little girl who sat opposite them.

"Where'd you get it?" she heard one say.

"From the Dogs."

"Pull the other one. Where'd you run into the Dogs? I suppose you went down in the underground for a chat with them."

"Course not. One comes and sells stuff here most mornings. Got this up near the Terminus, so he said."

"You're a good man to tell a tall tale."

"There's nothing tall about it. It's the pure truth."

The two men continued to haggle and Rosie stopped listening. But now she was determined to search for the Dogs in the underground. There were miles of derelict tunnels and all sorts of strange things living down there, but it was worth a try. She might even stumble across some forgotten magno. She bought a loaf and some cheese, then went to another stall and bought an oil lamp and some oil.

A while later she stood at the station they had emerged from the previous day. With a last look at the pale wintertime sky, she ducked under the barrier, lighting the lamp before she left the daylight behind.

For hours she walked the tunnels, going deeper and deeper. Often she heard something scuttling away, just out of range of the light. There were strange moaning noises amplified by the tunnels. Once she heard something and turned to see a terrified, ragged man standing

209

in an alcove beside the track. He flinched from the light, then turned and ran. After that she kept her knife in her hand.

She saw many strange things, but no sign of the Dogs, nor did she find any magno. Eventually she sat down on a station platform to eat her bread and cheese. Her eyelids were heavy and it felt like the middle of the night, but there was no way of telling. The station clock had stopped many years ago.

When she finished eating she found the ticket office. She managed to wedge the door shut with a chair. Placing her knife carefully beside her, she turned out the lamp and went to sleep in the dark.

Wesley was still awake. It was his turn to patrol the riverbank. He didn't mind. He liked seeing the otters and nightjars, the big white moths that flew up from the grass when you disturbed it, and the bats that fluttered along the surface of the water picking up insects. He could smell wet grass and leaves, and the faint salty smell of the sea in the distance. The sky had been cloudy all day and the clouds had continued into the night, but even so the light of the huge moon was visible. Perhaps that was why it took so long for him to notice the single light that moved across the field toward Owen's house.

He hesitated. Martha was alone in the house. He wondered if he should go and wake up Pieta, but she had been so short-tempered recently that he decided against it. Better to look into it himself.

Wesley ran lightly across the tree trunk that bridged the river and into the field beyond. Keeping in the cover of the hawthorn hedges, he crossed the three fields quickly. He scouted the hedge at the back of Owen's house and found a hole in it. He climbed through and lay flat on the grass, alert to whatever was going on.

Yet the house seemed peaceful and sleeping. There were no lights anywhere. Wesley lay very still. The garden was full of shadows and any one of them might hide danger. Then he saw that the window to Owen's room was open and ropes were hanging in the tree outside the window. From the road he heard the sound of an engine starting. Wesley squirmed back through the hedge and ran toward the noise.

As he got closer he heard men's voices. He reached the road just in time to see Johnston closing up the rear of his truck. The man went around the side and jumped into the cab. The truck started to roll forward. Wesley looked back at the house, torn. Should he go back and check on Martha or should he try to find out what Johnston was up to?

He ducked down as the truck's headlights passed him. His impulse was to jump into the back of the truck. But Martha might be injured in the house. What would he say to Owen if something had happened to her?

He turned and ran back toward the house as

Johnston's truck rattled off in the direction of his scrap-yard. The lights were still off. He tried the door and found it open, so he ran upstairs, calling, "Martha!" He found her in Owen's room, sitting on the bed and staring at the spot where the chest had been.

"Are you hurt?" he gasped, out of breath.

"No." The face she raised to him was full of dread.

"What is it?" Wesley asked.

"I remembered what it was, Wesley—the Mortmain, and what the chest was built to contain. I remembered it in a dream and then I came in here and found it gone. I don't know what happened to it."

"I know where it's gone," Wesley said, his voice troubled. "Johnston's got it."

Silkie was also awake. All evening she had watched people flock to the camp on the cliffs, convinced that the world was about to end. Wesley had told her how people did very strange things in times of crisis. As it got dark, the lights of fires had sprung up in the fields around the camp. Then she noticed a crowd gathering on the beach below them. A figure dressed in red stood in the water. One by one the crowd came forward and the red-clad figure took them by the hands, then quickly ducked them under the water. Silkie could hear a raised voice carrying across the water, clear and cold like a bell: "I baptize you."

Silkie looked up. The moon was growing bigger. The people on the beach were evidently not seafarers. The tide was always strong in that part of the beach, but with the moon coming closer, it had turned into a tidal bore that raged up the shoreline at lightning speed, sweeping all before it. There must be a thousand people gathered, Silkie thought, and they would all be lost. She could see white foam at the end of the beach as the powerful tide started to build. She ran inside and grabbed one of the magno bows from the chest. Perhaps they would notice if she fired a warning shot close by.

Her hands trembling, she rested the bow on the windowsill of the big room. She had never fired it before. What if she hit some of the people on the beach? And yet if she didn't find some way of warning them, they would all be swept away. If she fired at the beach, it would be hard not to hit someone. The cliff. It had to be the cliff face. And it had to be now.

Silkie could hear the roar of the water as the tidal surge built. She bent her eye to the bow's sight and aimed at a bush that was growing out of the cliff halfway down. As she aimed her mind became cold and clear, and her hands stopped shaking. She had the bush dead center in the sights and squeezed the trigger gently. With a kick that knocked her backward and bruised her shoulder, the magno bolt shot from the bow. Silkie pulled herself upright and watched the missile arc across the night sky. It looked as if her aim was true. Then, just as it was about to strike, she saw there was a small figure dressed in white standing at the top of the cliff!

Silkie watched in horror as the bolt struck the rock face. There was a blue flash and the sound of the explosion echoed across the water. The white-clad figure threw up its arms. Slowly the cliff face started to collapse and topple into the sea. Silkie saw the white figure stumble and fall forward helplessly. For what seemed like an eternity the figure hung in the air; then it struck the water and was gone.

The people on the beach looked up, startled. One of them turned and pointed. They started to run, in ones and twos at first, then in scores, some toward the harbor and safety, others scaling unbroken parts of the cliffs. The tidal surge had started, slowly at first, then gaining in speed and ferocity as it swept down the beach. Silkie watched it numbly. She put her hand to her face and felt tears streaming down her cheeks. The tide reached the beach, but the magno bolt had done its job. The people were gone and the tide thundered over emptiness.

Silkie sat at the upper window of the warehouse staring at the cliff. Her hands and feet were frozen through. The magno bow lay forgotten at her feet. For the rest of her life, she thought, she would not be able to shut her eyes without seeing that white figure plummet toward the sea. She wondered if it had been a boy or girl, man or woman. She wondered if the person's family and friends were searching, growing more desperate.

She got up. She knew that she had responsibilities and couldn't stay moping at the window forever. The

Raggies were depending on her. She dried her tears with her sleeve and put the bow carefully back in the box. Then she checked on the sleeping children, still tossing and turning uneasily. Silkie was exhausted, though she didn't know if she could ever sleep soundly again. But she had to try.

There was one more thing to do before she lay down. She went outside. A cold wind cut through her thin clothes but she did not feel it. She walked around the warehouse, checking the doors and windows, and looked across the open water for signs of enemies. As she turned back to the warehouse, something in the water caught her eye, a flash of white. A floating seabird perhaps, or the curling foam at the top of a wave. She walked as far as the warehouse door, then frowned and went back to the edge of the dock. Nothing.

She leaned out. At the foot of the dock, where the edge had collapsed, there was an object in the water. As fast as she could, Silkie clambered down the broken concrete, slipping and gashing her knee. A white shape was drifting in the water—a person a little smaller than Silkie, floating faceup.

She reached the water's edge. There was something strange about the water. Her foot slipped in and it made a crackling noise. A film of ice had formed. Reaching out as far as she could, she caught hold of the white shirt and pulled it toward her. The body and shirt were icy cold and she felt the hope that had grown in her die again. No one could have survived the fall from the cliff,

216

and even if the person had, he or she would not have lasted long in the water.

But the least that she could do was get the person out of the sea. Silkie pulled at the clothing until the body, stiff with frost, was out of the water.

It was a boy with blond hair and fine, handsome features, but a deathly pallor. She looked up at the broken dock above her. There was no way she could carry the body to the top. She would have to get rope from the warehouse and rig up some kind of pulley.

Silkie got to her feet and looked down at the boy. His face was perfect, not even bruised by the fall. She wondered who he was and what he had been like, what that pale face had looked like when he smiled. And then the boy's eyes opened.

For all that night and the next day the boy sat in the warehouse room where Silkie had brought him. She put food and water in front of him, but he ignored it. Instead he stared out of the window toward the camp on top of the cliffs, which continued to swell and grow.

"Will someone not miss you?" Silkie asked him, but he merely turned his pale eyes on her and did not answer.

The tides were getting bigger, now flooding low-lying areas of the town. Soon the bottom stories of the warehouse would be underwater. Now when Silkie looked up at the moon, every crater and mountain range was visible. Most of the time she tried not to look; it was too frightening.

That evening at low tide, Silkie heard the sound of

oars. She looked down and her heart leapt to see Wesley rowing out from the harbor. The wind was getting up and he was having great difficulty making headway. Silkie ran to get a rope. She threw it to him, took a turn of the rope around a bollard, and hauled on it. Between them they got the vessel to the little landing place beside the warehouse.

Wesley clambered onto the dock. He was soaked through, but it didn't seem to worry him. "I borrowed me a boat," he said with a grin. "The owner's gone inland, I think. Don't know if you noticed, but we're in the same time as the townspeople now. They can see us and all."

"Have you heard from Owen?" Silkie asked.

He shook his head. "Not yet." He told her quickly about the events of the previous night. "Pieta's not best pleased that the Mortmain's gone missing, along with that old trunk."

"I have some news too." She told him about what had happened at the cliff, about the figure she had seen falling and the boy that had washed up.

"Give us a look then," Wesley said.

She took him to the room where the boy sat. He glanced around as they came in, then returned his gaze to the window.

"Hello," Wesley said gruffly. "What's your name?" The boy didn't answer or move.

"He wouldn't answer me either," Silkie whispered.

"Where are you from?" Wesley asked, but again there

was no reply. He asked a few more questions, but the boy did not even look at him.

Wesley nodded to Silkie, and she followed him out. "He's not one of the townsfolk, that's for sure. I never seen the like of him around here. You all right having him here?"

Silkie nodded. She had never felt any threat from the boy. He just seemed very far away.

"Let's have a look at the Raggies, then," Wesley said.

The sleeping children's condition had not changed and Wesley and Silkie spent the next few hours trying to make them comfortable, plumping up their pillows and arranging blankets. Then they came downstairs and made fish and chips. Silkie put out a plate for the boy.

"Waste of grub, that," Wesley said, but Silkie insisted on leaving it beside the boy anyway.

They ate in front of the driftwood fire, the sweet smell of the burning timber mingling with the smell of the food. For a long time they sat in companionable silence, then Wesley rose to go. "I better get back," he said reluctantly.

They went outside. The wind was blowing violently by now.

"It's rough for crossing," Silkie said, worried.

"The tide is going my way, and the wind. I'll be across in no time."

But Silkie frowned. "What is it?" Wesley said.

"I thought I heard something," she said. "A rumbling noise."

"Could be anything," Wesley said. "Hold the rope till I get into the boat."

"I'm afraid, Wesley," Silkie said.

"We're all afeard, lass," Wesley said. "We must hope Owen and Dr. Diamond and Cati can save us."

In his high window, the boy in white had heard the rumble as well, and seen what happened. Another part of the cliff had started to crumble and a huge section had collapsed into the ocean. The camp folk had moved away from the edge of the cliff and were safe, but the force and weight of the earth had created a massive wave that now swept toward the unsuspecting Wesley and Silkie.

The boy watched Wesley climb into the boat. The great wave picked up speed and height, then struck the edge of the dock. Silkie and Wesley were directly in line. The boy saw their mouths open in horror as the dark wall of water advanced on them out of the darkness, white foam flickering high above their heads.

At the last moment, Wesley pulled Silkie into the boat and held her close as if he could protect her against the malignant power that was upon them. As he did so the boy raised his hand.

Silkie opened her eyes. She thought that she must be dead. The roar of water had been replaced with a dead silence. She started to feel her body to see if she was still there and realized that Wesley still held her protectively.

She looked up at his face. Wesley was staring toward

where the wave had been thundering toward them. In its place was a towering wall of black ice, bent menacingly over them.

"He froze it," Wesley said quietly, and Silkie realized that he was talking about the boy in white. "I seen the power come from his hands. Just as the wave was about to hit us, he froze it."

"He saved us," Silkie said in wonder.

"Yes," Wesley said, "but that's not all there is to it. There's only one sort with the power to do something like that, and that's the Harsh. Looks like you fished yourself a Harsh child out of the sea, Silkie."

They ran back to the warehouse and climbed the staircase to the boy's room, but he was gone.

"Look!" Silkie said.

A long white bridge of ice led from the broken dock to the bottom of the cliffs. Halfway up the cliffs, a small white figure was moving.

The next day Cati went raiding with the Dogs again. Using the abandoned underground system and the sewers, they could disappear and pop up in any part of the City. According to Mo, the daylight raid on the Speedway and the attack on the expensive neighborhood had caused a lot of bad feeling and extra patrols of Specials had been sent out. Patchie was pushing for more daring raids, but Clancy was cautious. He was worried they might antagonize the Terminus to such an extent that the Specials would be sent down to the tunnels to catch them. "Clancy says that the strong would get away, but what about the sick and the young?" Mo said.

Cati was getting used to being part of a pack, of

changing direction suddenly without anything being said, as if each of them shared one thought. In every street where they appeared, they struck fast and ran. Clancy felt that after the two big raids they should steal only enough to eat until things died down. With her pack instinct, Cati could tell that Patchie wasn't happy about that. There was a surly current in the thoughts that passed between them, and often Patchie and a group of thin curs would sit apart from the rest. Sometimes if she was on her own, Cati would remember Owen and Dr. Diamond, but she had only a vague memory of the mission that had brought them to the City.

They raided all day and were on their way home when a thought went through the pack and they veered left and started to climb a narrow tunnel. Up and up they went, until the tunnel narrowed to a ventilation shaft, and still they climbed. After twenty minutes they emerged onto a narrow platform high above the City. In the dusk they could see lights burning, and the smoke of a thousand chimneys. In the distance was the cold foggy outline of the Terminus.

Cati shivered and turned her eyes away from it. Clancy squatted down on his haunches and the rest did likewise. He looked around to make sure that they were ready before lifting his face to the sky and starting to howl. After a few seconds, the others joined in. Cati felt the hairs on the back of her neck stand up; then she too lifted her face to the sky and opened her mouth. She didn't know where the sound, both mournful and triumphant, came from, but she felt a thrill run through her and howled all the louder.

She could not tell how long they stayed there; an hour, perhaps. When the howling had finished they sat quietly. Then one by one the Dogs got up and began to file down the ventilation shaft.

Clancy had howled louder and longer than the others; had he not, he might have been more cautious. There were few places that the Dogs visited regularly, but the top of the ventilation shaft was one. Headley had posted small teams of men around the City to listen for the howling. The minute they started, Headley had been informed. Immediately he sent men into the tunnel where the shaft emerged.

Clancy trotted in front of the weary Dogs. Patchie brought up the rear, snapping at the heels of those who dawdled. Clancy emerged first into the railway tunnel. He waited until all the others had filed out, then turned toward home. Even before he paused and raised his head in the air, the others could sense his uncertainty. The Dogs stopped, confused. Patchie emitted a low growl. Cati could feel the fear sweeping through the pack. Then there was an earsplitting blast of whistles. The Specials were upon them!

The Specials had formed a line across the tunnel on either side, and at the signal they advanced, banging their truncheons and clubs off the walls. The older

Dogs ran to the front and faced their attackers. Clancy was first to leap. He caught hold of a cudgel and almost ripped it from its owner, but another weapon caught him in the ribs and knocked him back, winded.

The Specials struck at any Dog that came within reach. The Dogs tried to fight back, but the Specials towered above them and made sure to cut off any avenue of escape. At the rear, Patchie and his pack were fighting bravely. Cati saw a Special swat several large Dogs aside and raise his club over Mo's head. Cati leapt forward and sank her teeth into the man's ankle. With a cry, the man swung at Cati and caught her behind the ear. She reeled away, half dazed. The man raised his club again, but Mo darted between his legs and he tripped and fell.

Cati looked around. The tunnel was full of yelling Specials and Dogs squealing with pain or rage. Several of the Dogs lay unmoving on the floor. Patchie and his band stood shoulder to shoulder, while Clancy tried to draw the Specials away from the smaller Dogs. She saw Patchie mutter something to his companions. Then, as one, they charged the Specials. Caught off guard, two fell back. It was enough. Patchie and his curs slipped through the gap.

As they ran toward the safety of the empty tunnel, Patchie turned. He stared straight into Clancy's eyes and then he was gone, abandoning the rest of the pack to its fate.

Clancy looked around. The remaining Dogs were

pinned against the wall by flailing clubs. The only reason more of them were not lying injured was that the Specials were getting in each other's way as they tried to hit the Dogs.

Cati was among the Dogs pinned against the wall. Mo had taken a heavy blow on the shoulder and one arm hung limp and useless. Cati tried to shield her as best she could, but it was no good. They were trapped.

Then Clancy was among the Specials, a furious growling, biting, kicking ball of energy. The Specials fell back, some of them bleeding. They hit out wildly with their clubs and cudgels, catching each other as often as not, as they attempted to hit the desperate Dog, fighting like someone possessed.

"Run!" he shouted. Cati realized fleetingly that this was the first word she had heard him utter.

"Quick," she shouted. "This way!" She ran for the gap left where one of the Specials had stumbled. She scampered over the fallen man and felt the others follow. They raced down the tunnel, Cati going to the rear of the limping, bleeding line of Dogs to urge them on.

She looked back. The Specials had turned all their fury on Clancy, who could no longer evade the whirling cudgels. Involuntarily she took a step toward him as he went down under the blows. Her eyes met his and she heard the words as if he had been standing beside her, although he never opened his mouth: *Go! Run! Save the others.*

With her heart feeling as if it would break in pity for their brave leader, she did as he ordered.

Rosie woke in total darkness, almost forgetting where she was. Blind panic swept over her. With a trembling hand she felt around for the lamp. It took a few moments to get it lit. She was calmer then, but more than a little disoriented. Was it morning or the middle of the night? She forced herself to remain calm and eat the last of her bread and cheese. It was hard to swallow. She had forgotten to take water into the tunnel and the air was warm and dry.

When she'd finished, she decided to go back to the surface. She would have to tell Owen and Dr. Diamond that she'd found no sign of Cati and the Dogs. She tried to persuade herself that it was the lack of water that was forcing her to give up her search, but in her heart she knew that she couldn't stand another day alone in the dark tunnels.

She started off marching confidently in what she thought was the right direction before coming to a place where the tunnel roof had collapsed and could go no further. She tried to retrace her steps, but this new tunnel came to a dead end. She attempted to still the growing feeling of panic. It was an underground line, and tracks went *from* somewhere *to* somewhere. So eventually she would come across a station where she could get to the open air.

After two hours she found herself back at the collapsed tunnel and realized she was lost. Worse still, she found that the oil in her lamp was almost gone. She would be trapped underground with no light. And even worse again was the feeling that she was no longer alone in the tunnel.

As fast as she could, Rosie continued moving through the tunnels. And then she *did* hear a sound, and another one. She started to run, not knowing if she was running away from the sounds or toward them. There were shouts of anger and moans of pain. She ran until her heel caught and she fell. The lamp went flying out of her grasp and struck the wall. In despair she watched as it flickered and went out.

But Rosie wasn't in absolute darkness. A faint light was seeping in from somewhere. And in the distance, but coming closer and closer, she could hear the sound of running feet. She shrank back against the wall of the tunnel. The feet were getting closer and she could hear the sound of labored breathing.

Then a pack of Dogs burst into view. She was surrounded in the darkness, and could smell blood and fear in the air.

Pieta looked amused as she turned from the window in the Workhouse. "Johnston has got the chest and Mortmain, and in the meantime you pair of beauties are making friends with a Harsh child."

"He saved our lives," Silkie said.

"Yes, and that is strange."

"What do we do about the Mortmain and the trunk?" Wesley said.

"There is nothing we can do," Martha said.

"Johnston doesn't have the power to do anything with it," Pieta said.

"But the Harsh do," Martha said.

Leaving the adults in the Workhouse, Silkie and Wesley went outside. Apart from the oversized moon looming overhead, it was a fine, cold day on the river-bank. A crisp wind blew and the sun was shining. But when they looked up they saw flocks of birds wheeling through the skies, swallows and pigeons flying aimlessly.

"They can't steer," Wesley said.

"Do you think the Harsh child was trying to freeze us when he hit the wave?" Silkie asked.

"The Harsh don't miss, not from that range any-how," Wesley said. "He wasn't trying to kill us."

"He was in the water too. You know how the Harsh fear the water. . . ."

"Maybe things in the Harsh world aren't as cut and dried as we thought."

"What was he doing at the tent on the cliff?" Silkie asked.

Wesley turned to her with a grin. "Maybe we'd better find out."

Wesley and Silkie walked openly down the road into the town, but no one took any notice. The town was full of strange characters. Preachers had set up on street cor-ners and were competing with each other in predicting the end of the world. Many of the town's inhabitants had moved to higher ground because of the rising tides. Most shops were shuttered, but some of them had been looted during the night and gangs of youths roamed the town after dark.

As they got close to the harbor they saw more and more people wearing white, making their way there.

"Hang on a mo'," Wesley said. He climbed over a garden fence and came back with two sheets from a clothesline. He tore a hole in each and they put their heads through them. "Now we look the part."

Silkie sniffed dubiously. "We look stupid."

"We look the same as everybody else," he said.

They joined the crowds making their way down toward the camp on the cliffs. All normal work at the harbor had stopped. Most boats were abandoned and many had been swamped or sunk by the high tides. The crowd followed a route around the harbor and up the cliff path. Silkie looked down anxiously at the warehouses.

"I know," Wesley said. "I don't like leaving them alone either. We'll only stay five minutes."

The people in the crowd seemed ordinary, Silkie thought, apart from the fact that they were all wearing white. Most of them looked scared, eager to find any comfort they could. For a few minutes they walked alongside a man who was carrying a portable radio. The news was of earthquakes and tsunamis, of people fleeing to the mountains, and of rioting and looting in towns and cities.

When they got to the top of the cliff they saw that another huge tent had been erected, and this was the one people were flocking toward. Hundreds gathered around the entrance and men with whips were beating people back. Silkie found herself turning her head away and wishing she could close her ears to the voices pleading to get in, the moans of those being struck. "Let's get out of here, Wesley."

"No." Wesley was grim-faced. "There's bad being done here, Silkie, and me and you got to find out what it is."

A metal fence prevented people from going around the side of the tent, but the two thin Raggies had no trouble squirming through. They ran, bent double, toward the side of the tent and flung themselves on the ground. Wesley lifted the edge of the canvas and peered underneath. He found himself looking up at wooden trestles.

"Come on," he hissed. "We can get in under the seats." He disappeared and Silkie followed him into the dim space, which smelled of sawdust. The spaces between the benches above them were open, so they could see people's feet. They scuttled toward the front on hands and knees. They could hear a voice, but they couldn't make out what it was saying.

Suddenly the voice rose sharply. Above them the crowd began to applaud and drum on the seats. The noise was unbearable. Silkie put her hands over her ears until it stopped. They moved forward cautiously again. As they reached the front of the seats, they lay flat on their stomachs and squirmed forward so that they could peer between people's feet.

The seats were arranged in a semicircle facing the end of the tent, where a stage had been erected. Above it hung a great silver moon. Below was a raised dais with a podium to one side. And at the podium stood Johnston, wearing a white suit.

"Look!" Wesley said, pointing toward the dais. A small figure in white was sitting on an ornate chair. It was the Harsh boy. He looked straight ahead, seemingly oblivious to the crowd. Johnston had fallen silent, allowing the applause to die down. He started to speak again, his voice low, so Silkie had to crane forward to hear him.

"For centuries an enemy has been sleeping among you," he said. "Rebels and outcasts. They have risen up, not against governments but against time itself, and the leaders of this rebellion have brought this terrible crisis upon us."

Johnston's voice began to rise and Silkie was reminded of a wave in the distance, something that started as a whisper, then grew and grew until it was a thing of raging power.

"These rebels, these Resisters, have interfered with the very fabric of time and are now trying to bring it down so that all that is left is emptiness, nothingness!"

"That's not fair," Silkie said indignantly. "That's what the Harsh want to do. We want to stop them!"

"I know," Wesley said.

"Where are they, I hear you ask?" Johnston went on. The crowd was rapt. "Not a mile from this building, they lie in wait!"

A murmur ran through the crowd. The people above Silkie and Wesley got to their feet and those standing in front of the stage surged forward. Silkie saw that there was another bank of seats beside the stage, filled with villainous-looking men with sideburns like Johnston's, and women with long hair and battered faces. They were all wearing T-shirts with a moon symbol on it. A chant began from somewhere and the whole crowd began to pick it up. "Show us! Show us! Show us!"

A shiver of fear ran through Silkie. She turned to Wesley, but he was looking up at the latticework of seating above their heads with a thoughtful expression. "It's no time for looking at the joinery," she whispered. "He's making them hate us."

"At least he hasn't mentioned the warehouses."

Johnston let the crowd chant for several minutes before holding up his hands for silence. "It gives me no joy to say this, but these rebels are not just misguided. They hate us. They hate the way they live. They hate us so much they have called the very moon out of the heavens to destroy us. But before they destroy us, we will destroy them!"

"Destroy them! Destroy them!" The crowd started to chant again and there was hatred in their voices.

The Harsh boy stared over their heads as though he was alone.

"Come on," Wesley said. He scuttled off under the seats so quickly that Silkie had trouble keeping up. They moved under the seats until they were beneath the bank beside the stage. Above their heads Johnston stilled the crowd once again.

"I would not send you into danger against such an enemy. I would not see you good people put into the way of any more harm. But with your permission my auxiliaries will root out this nest of rats for you."

The crowd was cheering wildly, on their feet and stamping.

"I'm scared, Wesley," Silkie said, but Wesley had disappeared up into the timberwork. His hand appeared suddenly, holding a large metal bolt.

"Grab that," he said. The bolt was followed by another, then a metal hinge, then some pieces of steel with screws in them. While the crowd continued to shout and stamp, Wesley swung himself to the ground. He grinned at Silkie. She'd seen that grin before, when he'd pulled a practical joke. "I think we'd better get ourselves out of here."

As he spoke, there was an alarming creak from the wooden structure overhead.

"Quick!" Wesley grabbed Silkie's hand. She followed unresisting as he pulled her toward the back of the seating. There were more creaks and groans above their heads. Wesley dived for the edge of the tent and Silkie rolled through. Wesley rolled after her. As they did so, there was a loud groaning noise from the stand beside the stage. The clapping and cheering stopped.

"I'd love to see their faces," Wesley just had time to say before there was a thunderous crash followed by shouts of pain and rage. The bank of seats where the brutish-looking auxiliaries were sitting had come crashing to the ground. The thugs themselves had turned to fighting with each other in the confusion. The rest of the crowd was fleeing toward the exits. Johnston tried to call them back, but the cord had been wrenched from his microphone.

"That'll put a stop to their plans for a bit," Wesley said with satisfaction.

Silkie didn't say anything. Her gaze was drawn to the Harsh child, who was sitting all alone in the middle of the chaos, still staring toward the back of the tent.

"Pieta's right," Wesley said. "Don't waste your pity on him." But Silkie could not take her eyes away. She was no stranger to loneliness and the Harsh child seemed completely alone. Then she lifted her eyes and recoiled. Johnston, who had stirred such passions in the audience, was now looking at the panic-stricken crowd as they fought to get out of the tent, and his look was full of contempt and spite.

"Let's go, Silkie," Wesley said. "If they find out that were us, we'll be for the high jump."

Back at the Workhouse, Pieta listened silently while Wesley told her what they had seen at the camp. A frosty smile crossed her face when he told her how he had sabotaged the seating.

"Dr. Diamond always felt that the Harsh were badly damaged when Owen defeated them," Pieta said.

"Perhaps the Harsh child is the only one who was able to reach our time."

"What are they up to? That's the question," Martha asked.

"They are getting ready to attack the Workhouse, that much is clear," Pieta said. "Wesley's quick thinking will hold them for a while, but we had better prepare to defend ourselves."

When all the Resisters were awake, the Workhouse was easily made secure against attack, but with only four it was a lengthy task. For hours they labored, filling in windows with sandbags or with thorny branches dragged up from the river. Pieta uncovered the great holes in the ground that could be covered in foliage so that an attacker would fall in. She even rigged up a few mantraps in among the trees, but the work was hard and not enough. When they took a break, Martha slipped off while Pieta planned lines of retreat.

"In the end we have to make a stand at the Starry," she said. "We must fight to the end to defend them."

"Don't think much of this fighting-to-the-end business," Wesley muttered. "And what about the Raggies? Who will mind them?"

Wesley got to his feet and looked ready to make straight for the harbor.

"It is too late for that," Pieta said. "They will attack here first. The sea will defend the Raggies. We make our stand here. All falls or survives by the Workhouse."

Wesley looked ready to defy her, but then he nodded

weary understanding and sat down again. Martha came back with a tray. When she removed the cloth that covered it there were bacon and mushrooms fried in butter, potato bread, and cured sausage and pickles. They fell on the food, none of them speaking until they were mopping up the last of the juices with the bread. Even Pieta seemed mellow then.

"Wesley can come with me," she said. "We need to put some defenses in at the Starry."

When they were gone, Silkie and Martha sat in silence. Dark water had started to flood up the river. The wind blew in the trees, and the grasses whispered.

"I wonder where he is now," Martha murmured. Silkie did not say that she had been thinking of Owen as well, but, as if she knew, Martha reached out and took Silkie's hand. Silkie gripped it tightly and felt warmth and strength flowing into her.

I could sit here like this forever, she thought.

Headley pushed Owen in front of him along a seemingly endless corridor, its stone walls dripping with cold moisture. "The bosses have taken a special interest in you, though I don't know what they see in a dirty little street rat."

If Owen hesitated for a second, a fist or a heavy boot struck out. They reached a narrow staircase where the steps were winding and uneven. Owen stumbled so often his knees and elbows were bruised and cut. Breakfast that morning at Mrs. Newell's seemed a long time ago. He wondered what had happened to his friends.

As they climbed, Owen noticed that it was growing even colder. The stone walls of the tower glistened with frost and in places he could see icicles forming. The tiny barred windows were covered with frost. He remembered that when he was small, his mother used to tell him about Jack Frost visiting during the night. His mother . . . A feeling of despair washed over him. He was locked in a cold, dark tower, and his mother and home were far away across space and time.

Although he tried to push the thought out of his head, he knew what the increasing cold meant and who was waiting for him at the end of this climb. Only the Harsh could produce this mind-numbing chill and the terrible hopelessness that froze his heart. He would never leave this place. The Harsh would take him and shrivel his mind with cold and despair.

Something rustled underneath his jacket. What was it? *The maps, you fool,* a voice in his head seemed to say. *You have the maps!*

A sudden blow sent him reeling to the floor. Owen looked up. They had arrived at the very top of the tower and in front of them was a wooden doorway bound with black iron bands. Bulbs of ice had formed on the door and there was a sound of wind, although the air was still.

Headley looked down at him with a grim smile. "I can tell you've met the Harsh before. You know what's waiting for you. . . ."

Owen remembered what the frozen Harsh breath had done to Cati. He remembered how the enemy had first presented themselves to him as squabbling teenagers, then revealed their true selves with their longing

242

for emptiness and cold. That was what scared him most, that desire for nothingness. As he looked, the ice frozen into the great lock started to splinter and crack. With a terrible creaking the door began to open. Even Headley backed away a little. But Owen found himself getting to his feet and being drawn toward the opening.

He entered what had once been a room but was now an ice chamber. Everything was frozen: the great embroidered hangings on the wall, the furniture encased in ice. Even the flowers in a vase on a shelf were cold and beautiful and dead. And in the middle, on a chair of black ice, sat one of the Harsh.

At first all Owen could see was white, almost a frozen cloud, but then he made out the face of an ancient king. His expression was lordly and proud, ruined by hatred of the living and greed for emptiness. Owen quailed before the cold eyes, but what really brought despair was what he saw on the floor in front of the Harsh king: Gobillard's chest!

The Harsh king spoke. His lips did not move, but a cold, quavering voice echoed in Owen's head. *You are welcome, Navigator.* There was a kind of amusement in his tone, as though he was mocking Owen.

"You . . . you won't beat the Resisters," Owen said. "You won't win."

Look! the king commanded.

The Mortmain flashed brightly and began to turn, slowly at first, then faster and faster, becoming a blur. The room filled with a strange golden light that made the ice sparkle and dance. When Owen was almost blinded by the intensity, the lid began to open. He could feel his heart thudding in his chest. What would emerge? Would the great black whirlwind, the Puissance that had sucked the time from the world, spring forth in the ice room? The lid swung back and the king leaned forward, reaching into the dark interior. When his hand emerged, on his open palm was a small whirlwind, the size of a child's spinning top.

Look! the king ordered again. In the whirling cone, a face began to form, then another. Cati. Pieta. Dr. Diamond. On each face was written pain and terrible sorrow. They were followed by others. Wesley. Silkie . . .

"Stop!" Owen cried. "Why are you doing this?"

To show you what will happen to them, the king said. *Once the world falls, they will be lost in time. Unless you save them.*

For the first time Owen started to fully understand the Harsh. He could feel the craving from the icy king. They didn't care about the hurt they were causing; they just wanted to amass time for themselves, to hoard it like misers.

But he also sensed that the Harsh king wanted something from him. "How?" Owen said, unable to tear his eyes from the pained faces in the Puissance.

The maps! Where are your grandfather's maps?

"Even if I had them," Owen said in a voice that he barely recognized as his own, "they're no good without me."

He moved and could feel the maps rustling underneath his jacket. If the Harsh king guessed they were there . . .

Then join us, Navigator! We will spare your earth and together we will journey to worlds of time that have never been seen! You would be an explorer and a master of time. Everything you ever wanted would be yours forever!

Visions of far-off universes danced in Owen's head. He was being offered the chance to explore time as it had never been explored before, all its mysteries laid bare for him. He would return home to a spared and healed earth, the acclaim of nations ringing in his ears.

Yes, now you understand!

Owen reached toward his jacket. He would share the maps with the king. They would help him to understand the maps, and then he would break free from the Harsh, overthrow them with his new power and understanding. He could see Cati's eyes shining with gratitude. He imagined his mother's proud smile. . . .

A movement in the Puissance caught his eye. It flickered and the faces of his friends disappeared. In their place was a single face, haggard and drawn, but still familiar . . . the Sub-Commandant, Cati's father, who had been drawn into the Puissance and lost. Owen was held in his stern gaze.

"You fool!" the Sub-Commandant said. "Can you not see what the Harsh king is doing? He will take your maps and suck you dry, then cast you adrift in time forever."

"What . . . what do I do?" Owen said.

Whom are you talking to? the king demanded. Evidently he could not see the Sub-Commandant.

"Destroy the Puissance!" the Sub-Commandant said. "Now!"

"But what about you?"

"The message I left you in the Den took all my strength. I am trapped forever. If you destroy the Puissance, then you release me—"

"Release?"

"I will die."

The maps! The king's voice rose to a shriek. *Where are the maps?*

"*Now,* Owen," the Sub-Commandant said, and this time his voice was warm. "Concentrate on the Mortmain. Let your mind enter it."

Owen knew he must destroy the Puissance. He thought of Cati. She would never forgive him. . . .

"Cati knows what duty is, Owen," the Sub-Commandant said, his voice full of sadness. "This is your duty and your burden. Do it now and tell Cati—"

"No!" Owen felt the Harsh king reaching into his mind. He had seconds to act. He bent his mind to the spinning Mortmain, felt the golden light as if it reflected from within him. He turned it toward the Puissance in the king's hand. The Sub-Commandant's face faded and the blackness of the whirlwind deepened. In the inky dark, Owen could see jagged flashes of lightning.

What are you doing? the king demanded. Owen felt

searing pain, as if a hand of ice had taken his head in a deadly grip. The Puissance began to falter, oscillating in the king's hand. Ignoring the pain, Owen redoubled his efforts. The Puissance was a cone of crackling blue fire. Owen felt as if shards of ice were exploding in his brain. The king was on his feet now, his will entirely bent on the boy in front of him.

From a great distance Owen heard the Sub-Commandant's voice. "Thank you. Hold Cati for me . . . tell her everything . . ."

The Puissance began to disintegrate. Owen could feel the king's fear now, and his vengeance. He sensed rather than saw the Puissance falter and its remnants explode, then heard a shriek of rage and despair from the king.

It's done, Owen thought. *It's all over.* And a feeling of calm came over him. He looked up and saw the frozen tapestry hanging on the wall behind the king. For the first time he could see what was depicted on it, a scene from a time when the Harsh did not rule Hadima. Above the City, a great sail billowed out from a small craft and a figure stood at the helm.

The Wayfarer! Owen thought, before the cold overcame him and he fell to the floor.

Cati crept cautiously toward the place where the Specials had attacked the Dogs. As she approached, she could smell blood and fear and confusion, but she couldn't smell the Specials. There were old odors of sweat and tobacco and unwashed bodies, but no fresh scent. Standing upright, she walked slowly into the tunnel. It was empty, apart from discarded cudgels and pieces of torn clothing, but the smells of the battle were still overwhelming.

She had left the others in a small tunnel under the charge of Mo. She had tried to tend to their injuries as best she could. Some of the younger ones were in a state of shock, but Mo, despite her injured arm, moved among them, calming everyone. When Cati left, Mo was telling a story about chasing rabbits through sunny, wind-tossed fields, and they were licking at their cuts and bruises.

Cati sniffed the ground. Try as she might, she couldn't find the place where Clancy had fallen. She went up and down the tunnel. It could only mean one thing: they had killed him. She sat down, exhausted. Clancy was lost. All packs needed a leader, but few were as brave and resourceful and easy to follow as Clancy. She remembered above all how he had flung himself into combat with the Specials, knowing he had no chance of beating them, but sacrificing himself so that the rest could be saved. She felt a tear run down her face and fall to the ground.

Cati stood there for a long time, unaware now of the scents of battle, lost in grief, her body wounded first by the Harsh, then by Dog gashes that had somehow awakened the instincts of the Dogs in her.

I can't be the Watcher, she thought. *I'm not strong enough*. She remembered how her father had been strong and equal to every situation. And then, as if he was there beside her, she seemed to hear his voice.

Do you think I was always like this? You have to use the gifts you are given. And even the injuries dealt by others can bring gifts.

She was startled. What could it mean? The cold that stayed with her always—that was from the Harsh, and was hardly a gift. But the Dogs . . . she could smell a hundred times better than before. Was that the only gift? Of course not! There was that instinctive understanding that she had developed with the pack. . . .

She shut her eyes. She could feel Mo and the part of the pack that was with her. They were calm now, waiting for Cati to come back. And she could feel Patchie and his followers as well, an angry, gnawing sensation that made her flinch. And then, in the middle of it, a fluttering feeling as if someone was drifting in and out of consciousness. Nearby too! She paced up and down the tunnel but couldn't locate the source of the feeling.

Your ears, she thought, *use your ears as well.* She closed her eyes again. She could hear a rat trotting busily along a pipe. She could hear an insect rubbing its forefeet together in the brickwork above her head. She could hear a mole tunneling in the earth. And then . . . shallow breathing, the way an animal in pain might breathe.

It was very near. She opened her eyes and saw a small opening close to the ground, a drainpipe of some kind, the opening almost too small for someone to crawl into. The breathing was coming from there. She lay down and peered in, but could see nothing. Hesitantly she reached her hand into the darkness . . . and felt a foot. She took her hand out. It was slick with blood. She put her mouth to the entrance.

"Clancy! Clancy!" Something stirred in the dark. With difficulty she got her head and shoulders in, and took hold of the foot.

"Clancy," she said, "I'm going to try to pull you out."

This time there was no response. It was hard to get a proper grip, and the pipe was slippery, but eventually his body started to move. Clancy's skin was cold to the touch. She realized that there was freezing water in the bottom of the drain and he had been lying in it.

"Come on, Clancy," she said. "You're going to be all right." With one last effort she pulled him from the drain.

At first she thought he wasn't breathing. His dog mask was gone. His face was white and his lips were blue with cold. His body was covered in bruises and gashes. Cati put her ear to his chest. There was a heartbeat, but it was faint. She looked around for something to warm him, but there was nothing. So she wrapped her legs and arms around him and held him as tightly as she could, rubbing his hands and feet, talking to him as if she could call him back from the cold depths. She told him about everything that had happened to her, about Owen and the Mortmain, about her father and how she had been caught by the Harsh breath. She told him about being the Watcher and the loneliness, and how they had traveled to the City to see if they could find time that would save their world.

She realized with a start that his eyes were open. And she knew that he had heard every word she had said. She looked into his eyes and could feel what had happened to him. How, in a moment's confusion, he had got away from the Specials and crawled into the drain. They had poked sticks at him for a while, then decided he was dead and left him. He had lain there, too battered and bleeding to move. He never would have made it out if Cati had not come back.

Cati looked around and saw Mo and some of the others. They crept forward.

"We thought he was dead," Mo said, "then we felt you with him."

The Dogs moved forward and surrounded Clancy.

"I thought you was dead and all," came a new voice.

Rosie! Cati thought, but found she could not speak the word out loud.

Rosie stepped forward from among the Dogs, covered in tunnel dirt but looking proud. "I met this lot in the tunnels. They took me along. No choice, really."

"Cati!" The voice was low, but all the Dogs turned, then slowly parted. Clancy was looking at her now, dark eyes in a boy's face, pale and exhausted. He reached to his neck and drew out a small bottle on a chain. He held it out to her.

"Antidote," he said. "Take it. Drink."

"An antidote to the dog poison in you. Take it!" Rosie said.

Cati hesitated.

"Go on," Rosie said, "unless you want to spend the rest of your life sniffing lampposts."

Cati took the bottle and put it to her mouth. The liquid inside was sour and burning, and she grimaced as she drank. But almost immediately there was a change. She looked down at herself.

"That smell . . . ," she said. "That's me! I need a bath!"

Rosie burst out laughing. "Glad to have you back, girl."

Cati went over to Clancy, knelt beside him, and took his pale, sharp-nailed hand in her own. Their eyes met and no one could tell if what flowed between them was Dog or human.

"He'll be all right," Mo said gently. "The Dogs look after their own. But it's time for you to go. You don't belong here now."

Cati felt gentle Dog hands lift her to her feet. And though her voice had come back she did not speak again until they reached the open air. Part of her would always be Dog, she knew.

It was cold and dark in Bourse Square. A tall figure carrying a rucksack moved from shadow to shadow, avoiding the Special patrols. In the entrance of the Bourse itself, the figure stopped. Dr. Diamond took the rucksack from his shoulders and made some adjustments to its steel frame. Then he put it back on. He touched a button on the frame and two jets of pale blue flame shot from the ends. He took a homemade remote control from his pocket, then slowly and silently rose into the air.

Once he was at rooftop level, he turned toward the

citadel, resembling some strange spindly night bird as he flew between the chimneys and rooftops. On he flew, frost gathering in his eyebrows and hair, until he saw what he was looking for: a high window in a tall tower from which a cold white light emanated. Higher and higher he went until he reached the tower. He flew silently over the head of a Special guard standing outside a heavily barred door. There was a barred opening at ground level. Dr. Diamond landed lightly and pressed his face to it.

The first thing he saw was a pair of boots. He followed them upward until he saw two gloved hands. *Headley*, he said to himself. As he watched, Headley turned to an unseen guard.

"Throw the prisoner in the dungeon. He won't last the night."

Owen! I have to hurry! Dr. Diamond thought. He rose into the air again and flew up and up, winding around the tower until he reached the cold window at the top.

He approached with great caution. The cold was different now; his clothes were crackling and freezing as he got nearer. He edged closer until his face was almost against the windowpane. With one hand he scraped an opening in the frost. It was frozen solid and hard to clear, but a small patch was all he needed. He saw a room that seemed to be made from ice, and in the middle, on a cold throne, was the terrifying figure of the Harsh king, whose eyes were cold and black and empty.

Dr. Diamond had suspected this from the moment they had arrived at the City. And then he saw something that disturbed him even more. On the ground in front of the Harsh king was Gobillard's trunk, and in front of it lay the Mortmain!

The doctor stared intently at the Harsh king. The eyes were glassy, but not from the cold. The king was dead! Owen! It had to have been Owen! No one else had the strength to defeat a Harsh king. The boy had defeated him, but what price had he paid?

Dr. Diamond reached into his overalls and took out tools. Within seconds he had the window open. Struggling with the cumbersome rucksack, he slipped into the room. The cold was unbearable, searing his lungs when he breathed, crystals of ice forming at his nostrils and mouth. Under the king's frigid gaze, he grabbed the Mortmain. It was dull and curiously warm in the freezing room, and glittered when he touched it.

He shoved it inside his overalls and climbed over the windowsill again, closing the window behind him. The blue jets were lit again, pale lights against a black sky, as Dr. Diamond flew silently away.

As Rosie and Cati walked back, Rosie told Cati about the Museum of Time and the Yeati. She told her how the Yeati had cured her hands. Cati stared at them in disbelief. Rosie told her how beautiful he was, despite his missing paw and the filth of the cage. The two girls fell silent, then turned to each other and exclaimed at the same moment, "We have to rescue him!" and "I can't bear the idea of him locked up like that."

"How do we get him away?" Rosie wondered.

"The truck."

"Mrs. Newell will have kittens if we arrive back with a Yeati," Rosie said, but there was a grin on her face.

"Let her. Wild things shouldn't be caged."

Ten minutes later they were standing in Cyanite Place. Icicles hung from branches and eaves. They climbed into the cab of the truck. Rosie started it and turned the heater on. They waited for the ice to clear from the windscreen, then, as quietly as Rosie could, they drove out toward the Museum of Time. The streets were very quiet. Even the hardy souls who lived there had abandoned the braziers and gone indoors. Gusts of frozen snow lashed against the windscreen as they drove along in comfortable silence.

The deserted industrial zone seemed even more sinister. Buildings with empty windows looming up out of the darkness, fences swaying in the freezing wind. Cati looked up at the empty windows of the buildings and shivered at the thought of all the people who had once worked there. They drove down to the end of Desole Row.

The museum was locked up for the night. Rosie drove past slowly. All the lights were out. At the end of the block she turned left and left again.

"That's it," Rosie hissed, pointing to a broken window close to the ground. She stopped the truck and they stepped out into the cold alley. There were piles of rubbish everywhere and water spilled from broken gutters had frozen on the ground. They crept over to the window and crouched down to look in. They saw the Yeati's great eyes gleaming at them from the darkness below.

Rosie climbed into the back of the truck and found a rope. Cati attached it to the tow hook so they could climb down.

"How are we going to get the Yeati out of the cage?"

In reply Rosie held up a bunch of strangely shaped implements with hooks at the end of them. "Lock picks."

Looking nervously around, Cati helped Rosie through the broken window. In the darkness below the Yeati watched silently. Cati got down first. Rosie slid down the rope faster than she should have and hit the ground with a thump and a curse.

"Are you all right?" Cati asked.

"Course I am. Just got to sort out these picks. There's a double lock on here. Pretty hard."

The Yeati snuffled in the darkness. Cati went over to it. She held its eye as it reached out and placed its good paw on her hair, stroking it gently. Cati could feel thoughts passing between them, a little like the way thoughts passed between the Dogs. But the Yeati's thoughts were stranger than anything she had ever experienced and she could not understand them. It was like thinking words that were as hard and cold and beautiful as diamonds.

"Man who designed this lock was a genius," Rosie said. The wind outside whistled through the window. As if to echo it, the Yeati emitted a low moan.

"All right, all right, I'm going as fast as I can," Rosie muttered. "Keep your hair on."

The whistling was getting louder. And then Cati realized that it wasn't the wind, but whistles in the distance.

"Rosie," she hissed. "Specials!"

"I'm through the first one," Rosie said. The Yeati moved restlessly. "Pipe down, I'm trying to concentrate."

The whistles were getting louder, closer. The Yeati had started to pace in the cage.

"Got it!" Rosie said. Cati guided the Yeati from the cage, then it allowed her to wrap the rope around its shoulders and knot it. Cati helped Rosie up the rope. She climbed into the cab and began to inch forward. With a sweep of its injured arm, the Yeati lifted Cati off the ground and held her to its side.

From the cab, Rosie could see lights in the distance. She inched forward a little faster and the Yeati's head appeared at the window, followed by Cati. She looked in her mirror. The lights were at the head of the alley, the whistles now joined by shouts. She climbed down from the cab.

The Specials were running toward them, nine or ten of them, shouting and waving cudgels. The Yeati didn't seem to be worried. It stretched and sniffed the air and looked around it.

"Get into the truck," Cati yelled, while Rosie tried to push him. In a leisurely manner he bent down and examined the ground, drew his arm over it, scooping up a sheet of ice. He used his good hand to roll the ice in the crook of his bad arm, forming a hard ball of ice, which he threw, almost casually, toward the Specials. It hit the first one with such force that his feet were lifted from the ground and he was thrown back into the two men behind him, sending them tumbling backward.

The Yeati turned away with an air of satisfaction and climbed into the back of the truck. Rosie put the truck in gear and accelerated out of the end of the alley.

Two hours later Mrs. Newell noticed that there was no hot water. She went upstairs, thinking that one of the children had left the hot water running in the bathroom. When she got to the bathroom, there was steam coming from the cracks around the door, and a smell of shampoo and aftershave and various soaps. Mrs. Newell knocked sharply on the door, meaning to tell off whoever had used all the hot water. That was when the door opened and she found herself facing an immaculately clean, well-groomed, and sweet-smelling Yeati.

It took ten minutes and a large glass of brandy to bring Mrs. Newell back to something of her normal self. "Other youngsters bring home stray cats and things," she said. "You two has to go and bring home a . . . a Yeati?"

Before Cati and Rosie had a chance to explain, the door flew open and Dr. Diamond burst in. His eyes fell on Cati first and he swept her up into his arms.

"Ouch," she said. The doctor's pockets, full of assorted items, were extremely uncomfortable to be pressed against.

He put her on her feet and looked her up and down.

"Ouch is better than woof," he said, his eyes shining. "Welcome back, Cati. Well done, Rosie! But I'm afraid there isn't time to chat. We must be going. Things are worse than I thought."

"Going where?" Cati said.

"To rescue Owen. However, to begin, Rosie, would you kindly give me the Yeati paw you took from Mr. Black's museum."

Rosie jumped as if she had been given an electric shock. She looked as if she was about to deny everything, but Mrs. Newell fixed her with a stern look.

"She's got into some bad habits, for all I did in raising her," Mrs. Newell said, and the tone of disappointment in her voice seemed to sting Rosie more than anything. Eyes lowered, Rosie went to her bag and returned with the Yeati paw.

Dr. Diamond examined the paw carefully, in particular the long hard nails. Then, without looking at any of them, he reached out and struck it against the stone fireplace, drawing it downward. They all looked at the fireplace openmouthed. Dr. Diamond's blow had opened a gash a centimeter deep and almost a meter long in the solid stone surround.

"It cut it!" Rosie exclaimed. "It could've taken my hand off and all."

"No," Dr. Diamond said, running his finger down the hard nail. "It isn't particularly sharp. Obviously the Yeati could not cut through the bars of his cage. There must be some kind of interaction between the claw and the stone. We may be able to cut through to rescue Owen."

"I don't think you'll need the paw," Cati said. And she took a bemused Dr. Diamond by the hand and led him upstairs.

The doctor's eyes gleamed when he saw the Yeati, who was busy combing the hair on its chest. "If we could speak with him," he said longingly, "what wonders he could tell us."

Dr. Diamond tried a variety of languages, but it didn't seem to understand any of them. The Yeati just continued combing its hair.

"Vain big thing," Cati said with a sniff.

"You'd want a wash too if you'd been locked up in that cage," Rosie said. She noticed that the Yeati had found a bandage and had wrapped his stump in it.

"What's the plan, anyway?" Cati asked Dr. Diamond.

"We have to get Owen out," Dr. Diamond said. "I'm afraid after that I have no idea. We have not yet found any tempods." He sighed.

"How many do we need?" Cati asked.

"One would do, I think."

The Yeati was now sitting on Cati's bed and was amusing itself by sketching pictures of them on the windowpanes.

"If only he could help us," Dr. Diamond said.

"Course he can help us, poor thing," Cati said, ruffling the Yeati's fur.

"Cati, a Yeati is a very intelligent being—more intelligent than humans, I suspect—and they are known to be full of ancient wisdom. I'm not sure if petting him like a cat is the best idea."

"We don't even know his name," Rosie said. "Hang on. I've got an idea." She pulled a piece of paper and a pencil stub from her bag. With her tongue in one corner of her mouth, she drew a shaky rose. She gave it to the Yeati, then pointed at herself.

The Yeati looked at it for a moment, then turned and drew rapidly on the windowpane. Rosie peered at the sketch, frowning. "What is it?" she said. The Yeati had drawn a complex series of dots on the window.

Dr. Diamond came over to look. "It's a constellation of stars." The Yeati tapped one of the dots with his claw. "Andromeda—he's pointing to Andromeda!"

"Andromeda it is, then," Rosie said. "Are you going to help us out, Andromeda?"

As if he understood, the Yeati bared a mouthful of extremely sharp and pointed teeth in what looked suspiciously like a grin.

"Let's go, then," Rosie said.

"One minute, young lady," Dr. Diamond said.

"What?"

"Take off your gloves."

One at a time, Rosie peeled off her black gloves. Then she shyly held up her two perfect, pink-skinned hands.

"The Yeati," Rosie said, linking the Yeati's arm and hers affectionately. "The Yeati cured my hands!"

Dr. Diamond looked at the Yeati. The beast met his eyes. Dr. Diamond took off his flying hat and bowed low to the ground. The Yeati bowed graciously back.

Two hours later Dr. Diamond and Rosie waited inside the abandoned subway station. Andromeda had spent a few minutes brushing his hair, then turned to a wall, where he started to inscribe complicated patterns of planets and nebulae.

"You start to think he's some kind of big stupid bear," Rosie said proudly, "then he does something like that."

Cati had disappeared down into the tunnels. She had been gone for an hour, although sometimes they heard a howling from down below.

"Maybe she's run away with them again," Rosie said. Then they heard the patter of feet and Cati appeared, beckoning. Rosie, Dr. Diamond, and the Yeati followed her.

The Dogs were waiting for them at the bottom of the stairs. They ignored Dr. Diamond, but they could not seem to stay away from the Yeati. They followed him around, sniffing. The Yeati didn't look at them, having obviously decided that they were beneath his dignity.

Clancy was moving stiffly and Cati was aware of him wincing with pain every so often. His face was a mass of yellowing bruises and ugly gashes, but when he took off at a trot, the others had difficulty keeping up with him.

"There's a tunnel that comes out right where we want to be," Cati said, "but the Specials patrol it. We need to get there when they go for their lunch. So get a move on." This last comment was aimed at the Yeati who seemed to be looking askance at the filth in the tunnel.

Onward and upward they ran. Clancy did not flag, despite his injuries. The Dogs ran silently on either side of them. Even on her high heels Rosie kept up with Dr. Diamond, who ran in an odd style with his head thrown back and his knees high.

It got colder as they approached the Terminus, a freezing mist billowing through the tunnel. Dr. Diamond and Cati exchanged glances.

"A Harsh cold?" he said.

"Yes. I can feel it in my bones. And it smells of them as well."

The Yeati raised his head to sniff the air and he also looked concerned. On and on they ran, the mist getting thicker and thicker, until Cati found herself depending on her improved sense of smell to guide her. She took Dr. Diamond's hand. Mo dropped back and took Rosie's hand.

They emerged in a station that Rosie had never seen before. Vast chandeliers hung from the ornate ceiling. The walls and platforms were made of marble, and the handrails of the stairs were gilded.

"The Terminus underground station," Dr. Diamond said, "as described in all the books. They talk about the

265

nights here, going to the opera, the way people were dressed—the women in silk organza, the men in top hats. . . ."

"Some of us do our best to keep a bit of glamour going," Rosie said with a sniff.

"So you do, Rosie, so you do," Dr. Diamond said. He looked as if he was about to pat her on the head, but she gave him a warning look and he withdrew his hand.

"Does Andromeda know what we're doing?" Cati said.

"I have a funny feeling he does," Dr. Diamond said, collapsing exhausted onto a red velvet bench, which sent a cloud of dust up to mingle with the freezing vapor in the air.

The Yeati had climbed down onto the track and gone into a tunnel. He started to tap the solid rock wall with a fingernail. Strangely, the rock rang like a bell. He tried several places, walking up and down the tunnel, then he appeared to narrow it down. He tapped several times briskly until the whole wall seemed to ring. With a deft blow from his good arm, he started to cut into the wall. The Dogs watched openmouthed as he cut into the rock so far that he disappeared from view.

"How does he do that?" Mo said.

"It's a molecular process closely allied to structural—" Dr. Diamond began before Rosie cut in.

"Sorry, Doc," she said, "but maybe we should get in that hole after him."

By the time they reached the hole, Andromeda had

disappeared from view. Dr. Diamond produced a powerful magno torch. "Watch out!" he said as pieces of cut rock flew out of the tunnel ahead of them.

"We need to be ready when we get into the jail," Dr. Diamond added.

"Old Andromeda is going like a steam train," Cati said admiringly. And Andromeda had indeed picked up his pace, hammering through the rock as though it was cardboard.

"With two good hands," Rosie said, "he'd be deadly!"

The Yeati slowed. He tapped the rock again and this time they could all hear that there was a hollow space behind it. Andromeda turned to look at them. Dr. Diamond nodded.

Behind Cati the Dogs tensed. "Stay here," she said to them. "Guard the tunnel."

Rosie tapped Dr. Diamond on the arm. "You don't need me here," she said, and turned and slipped away. They looked after her, puzzled.

Andromeda lifted his hand and struck the rock in front of him a massive blow. The rock did not as much crack as dissolve into dust. Coughing, they stepped forward. They had made it. They were in the Terminus.

The Yeati had broken through the wall into the chamber off the Terminus guardroom. Within seconds Dr. Diamond and the others found themselves faced by a group of startled Specials who were armed and ready to go out on patrol.

"Oh no!" Cati said. A frowning Andromeda was picking shards of stone and dust from his fur. "Andromeda, please, can you comb your fur some other time?"

The Yeati looked up from his grooming and the Specials seemed to see him for the first time.

"What's that thing?" one exclaimed.

"A Yeati, by the look of it," a Special with a heavy beard and a glass eye said. "We used to hunt them. There's one thing they're afraid of. . . ."

He took a wooden baton from his side. It had cotton wrapped around the top and Cati could smell paraffin. The Special struck a match and the torch flared up. "Get back, old bear," he shouted, advancing on the Yeati.

Andromeda retreated, fear in his eyes.

"Leave him alone!" Cati shouted. One of the Specials turned toward her. Baring her teeth in an impressively doglike snarl, Cati darted forward and bit him behind the knee. The Special went down. Cati launched herself at the man with the torch, who looked at her uncertainly. He waved the flame, but she snatched it from his grasp. The Yeati moved toward the man, making a low, rumbling sound in the back of his throat. The Special looked from one to the other.

Cati bared her teeth and darted forward. "Woof!" she shouted. The Special jumped back and collided with another group.

"We need to find Owen quickly," Dr. Diamond cried. "We can't fight every Special in the place."

"Wait," Cati said. Her nose twitched. Owen wasn't far away. But his body smelled . . . *cold.* "This way!" she shouted. She charged at the Specials in front of her and the others followed. Caught by surprise, the Specials fell back.

They raced along a narrow corridor. Cati saw a staircase leading upward and recoiled from the cold that came from it. "The Harsh!" But Owen's scent didn't come from there. It came from behind the ironbound door in front of them.

"There!" she shouted. She could hear the Specials cursing and blowing their whistles as they charged along the corridor behind. With one sweep of his paw, the Yeati ripped the hinges of the door from the stone-work around it and it fell inward. They ran through the doorway.

It was very quiet all of a sudden. Cati looked around. They were in a prison. She could smell Owen clearly now, a cold, weak scent from nearby. They followed the narrow corridor and she saw a body lying on the ground with a figure bent over it.

"Owen!" Cati ran forward.

The man leaning over Owen looked up, his face sad and weary. "For him too late almost."

"Monsieur Gobillard?" Dr. Diamond said.

"Yes, I am Gobillard. The Harsh attacked this boy. He is very weak."

Cati knelt beside Owen. His face was white and cold as porcelain. His chest barely rose, and there was frost around his nostrils and his mouth.

"Owen . . . ," she whispered.

There was a commotion at the door. The Yeati had closed it and was now leaning against it. The door bulged and crackled with ice, as though a great cold weight was pressing on it from the other side.

"Quickly," Dr. Diamond said, gathering Owen in his

arms. "The Harsh are here!" As he spoke, the Yeati was forced backward and fell to the ground, the metal door flying out of his grasp. The doorway filled with a white mist and they felt malice like an icy blast.

Cati shrank away, but courage stirred within her. She pressed close to Dr. Diamond and Owen, holding Owen's arm in the hope that she could transfer heat to him.

Gobillard stared with a look of wonder on his face. "A Yeati!" he breathed. "I never dreamed to see a Yeati!"

The mist parted momentarily to allow Headley to step into the room. He stood with his booted feet apart, thumbs hooked into his belt. "A touching scene," he said. "It reminds me of a painting. I think I'll call it *Death of Another Navigator.*"

Cati's fists balled, but Dr. Diamond's hand held her back. "Wait," he said.

"The Harsh aren't best pleased," Headley said. "Their king is dead and they are blaming your Navigator. Seems he made the Puissance blow up in the king's hand."

The Yeati had picked itself up off the ground. Its fur was badly ruffled and there was a tuft of hair torn from its leg. It started to advance on Headley.

"My lords," Headley said nervously, "your servant is being threatened." Cati felt the attention of the Harsh shift from Owen to the Yeati.

"No!" Gobillard cried. "Such a noble beast!"

"My lords, the creature helped the Resisters." Headley backed away.

"Foolish man!" Gobillard said.

"Yes, my lords!" Headley said, sensing their spite was now trained on the Yeati.

"Please, Andromeda . . . ," Cati whispered, but the Yeati reached for Headley. A blast of frozen Harsh breath shot toward the creature as a despairing Gobillard dived forward. He struck Headley between the shoulder blades and, with a cry, Headley pitched forward into the path of the Harsh breath. He fell to the floor, frozen solid, as if he had lain there for a thousand years.

"Now!" Dr. Diamond shouted, holding Owen in his arms. "Follow me!" Blue flame shot from the frame of his rucksack and he rose into the air. With a roar he jetted toward the doorway with Owen. Cati grabbed the dazed Gobillard and the Yeati by the hand and followed. As they ran past the Harsh she felt their terrible dead energy tugging at her, but then she was free and running toward the tunnel.

The Dogs were in among the Specials and this time they were winning the fight. Dr. Diamond roared over their heads and into the tunnel. The Yeati scattered Specials like bowling pins. Cati realized that Gobillard was not holding her hand anymore. He had slipped in the corridor, and behind him the Harsh were advancing. Cati turned to go back, but the Yeati pulled her on. The Dogs were running alongside them.

"Close it!" Gobillard yelled. "Close the tunnel!"

"No!" Cati shouted.

"Close it!" Gobillard shouted again.

Andromeda slashed at the roof. There was a rumble of stone as it started to fall. Cati saw Gobillard, pinned to the rock by an icy blast, a frozen mannequin, his face contorted, his eyes glassy and still.

Numb with shock, Cati ran, tears streaming down her face. *What's wrong with me?* she thought. *I didn't even know Gobillard.* She tried to push the image of his frozen face out of her mind.

It was then they heard a roaring noise in the tunnel. They stopped running. "What now?" Cati said wearily. The Harsh cold had left her bones feeling like jelly. The noise grew louder and with it came a great light that cast their shadows against the wall of the tunnel.

Around the corner came Rosie, at the wheel of the truck. She tooted the horn, stopped right in front of them, and jumped down from the cab. A relieved Cati didn't know whether to hug her or strangle her. But it didn't matter.

They leapt into the truck and Rosie threw caution to the winds. The truck lurched and jolted as it sped down the uneven tunnels, spotlights blazing, the Dogs behind it howling as they ran.

In the back, Dr. Diamond bent over Owen. "He is very low," he said. "Barely breathing."

The Yeati reached into the cab and touched Rosie's shoulder.

"What is it?" she snapped. "Can't you see when a girl's driving?" He pointed to her finger. "What? The ring?" He pointed again, more insistently this time. "OK, OK," she said, letting go of the wheel to take the ring off. The truck veered alarmingly off course before she corrected it.

The Yeati grabbed the ring and ducked into the back of the truck. Dr. Diamond's face was gray with anxiety.

"We're losing him, Cati," he said quietly.

She took Owen's hand. A tear ran down her face and fell onto his. "Owen," she called softly. "Owen?"

Then she felt herself being lifted carefully and set to one side. The Yeati knelt down beside Owen. He took the hand that Cati had been holding and slipped the ring onto the middle finger. For what seemed like ages they looked at Owen's cold white face.

"I think he's gone, my dear," Dr. Diamond said with infinite gentleness. He ran his hand through Owen's hair.

"No . . . ," Cati said. "No, look!" The faintest shade of pink was creeping across Owen's cheeks. She looked up at the Yeati. It was hard to tell in the dim, lurching truck, but it seemed that the beast was smiling.

Owen took a long deep breath. His eyes opened. He seemed to say something, but so faintly that they couldn't hear.

"What is it, Owen?" Cati said.

"Mr. Gobillard got the translation wrong," he said, his voice barely audible.

"Translation?"

"From the Yeati's piece of glass?" Dr. Diamond asked.

"It didn't say, *'It has Black,'*" Owen whispered. "It said *'Black has it.'* Black has a tempod at the museum. I'm sure that's what it means."

As if to confirm what Owen was saying, the Yeati made a low sound deep in his throat.

The attack had come without warning. Before dawn Johnston's crew had crept up along the river. It didn't matter if they made any noise. The earth had started to creak and groan and shudder. If people had been able to watch television or listen to the radio they would have heard news of tsunamis and volcanic eruptions and earthquakes. All around the world each town and each village thought itself on its own. Armed bands roamed everywhere.

Martha had been on watch at the Workhouse and the first wave of hard-faced men and women had nearly caught her off guard. But she saw them in time and grabbed one of the dozens of magno guns that Pieta had loaded and left on the ramparts of the Workhouse. Her first shots were good, and the group scattered for cover. The second wave was met by Pieta's magno whip attacking from the flank.

Wesley joined Martha. He was the better shot and she spent her time loading magno guns and handing them to him. The ground in front of the Workhouse was burning now, and the lurching earth threw him to the side often enough that many of his shots missed. The attackers were using the smoke as cover and swarmed across the river on ladders.

Pieta joined them on the ramparts. Below, a group of men with torches appeared. They set fire to the trees and scrub around the bottom of the Workhouse, then threw a thick, black, oily substance into it. Pieta's whip lashed out from the battlements, but it was too late. Flames and oily smoke licked at the walls of the Workhouse. The defenders were blinded. And then a huge boulder crashed against the ramparts, followed by another.

"We're in trouble here," Martha said.

"I know." Pieta was grim-faced.

Martha looked toward the sea. Where was Owen?

The sea was choppy and dangerous, and out in the rowboat Silkie found the oars hard to handle, but still she worked hard. She could see the tents on the cliff top before her, the warehouse behind her, and, far to her left, black smoke rising from the Workhouse. It took twenty minutes, but finally she beached Wesley's little boat and started to climb the cliff. She needed to help the Resisters at the Workhouse and yet, she had headed here on an instinct. *And if I'm wrong, I'm in trouble.*

She climbed the cliff as fast as she could. The camp at the top was deserted and damaged. Silkie made her way toward the main tent. The kiosk at the front had been knocked over and the canvas entrance sagged sideways. Inside was even more chaotic: banks of toppled seats, ripped bunting, bags and jackets abandoned in haste. And in the middle, on the edge of the dais, sat the Harsh child. Silkie walked slowly toward him. She could feel a faint chill and for the first time noticed the icy mist that hung in the air around him.

He watched her as she approached. She stopped when she was two meters away. She knew that he could lift a hand and freeze her forever in a second.

"Who are you?" she said, her voice faint and scared. He didn't reply. "Who are you? You crossed the water. A true Harsh can't cross water. Who *are* you?"

Silkie held her breath. The Harsh child's eyes narrowed. She shivered as if the cold around him had enveloped her. "Who are you?" she whispered again. "Who are you?" She found herself moving forward. The beads of sweat on her brow turned to ice, but still she walked forward and still his eyes fixed her. When she reached him she took first one hand and then the other. It felt as if she had touched a glacier and her fingers burned with cold. But still she held his eyes.

"Who are you?" she said. "What did they do to you?"

Something seemed to change in his face. The cold stare faltered. A tear formed at the corner of one eye and rolled down his cheek, then stopped, frozen. She held on to his hands. And although she did not see his lips moving she could hear a voice in her head, a distant, faltering voice.

We had an island in time . . . the Harsh came at night . . . they destroyed it with frost . . . I was a baby . . . they took me as their own. They do not have children. I am . . . I am . . . so cold, so cold.

The voice was full of loneliness and Silkie felt as if her heart would break. She leaned forward and put her arms around the boy even though the cold seared her through her thin clothing. His expression did not change, but she could feel his heartbeat now. She started to sing a Raggie lullaby about the sea and the sky and their warm home by the harbor.

Silkie didn't know how long she held him. It was the boy who gently took her arms from around him and she realized that the ground was trembling. This time it was the boy who took her hand. He led her outside. The moon seemed impossibly close. Not white anymore, but a vast expanse of gray, pitted with craters. As they looked, it shuddered and a great fissure ran across the surface.

It's too late, Silkie thought. She sat down on the grass. The Harsh boy sat beside her and together they waited.

At the Workhouse flames and smoke rose around Wesley and Pieta.

"Look!" Wesley said when he saw the crack that had appeared in the moon.

There was a great crackling from the fire below. The smoke was choking, but for a minute the wind cleared it and Wesley saw Pieta standing on the roof, gazing in defiance at the moon, as if she might by force of will drive it away. And then even the wind failed and darkness covered her again.

The street outside Black's museum was deserted. The truck screeched to a halt outside and Cati helped Owen down out of the back. He was pale and weak and his skin felt cold to the touch, but there was a determined light in his eye.

"It is time to say goodbye, Rosie," Dr. Diamond said. "I don't know how to thank you."

"Getting paid would be nice, Doc," Rosie said.

"Of course, of course." Dr. Diamond fished all his magno coins from his pocket and Rosie's eyes widened. "That should be enough to ransom your brother. I would have given them to you before, but I thought I might need them to buy a tempod."

"You're a star, Doc." There were tears in Rosie's eyes. She threw her arms around him and kissed him.

Cati grinned when she saw that Rosie had left a ring of lipstick on his cheek.

Behind the truck Cati saw Clancy. He was standing in the middle of his Dogs. She went up to him and rubbed noses with him. All the other dogs laughed and Cati could have sworn that under his mask Clancy turned red.

Rosie went over to Owen. To his surprise and embarrassment she bowed deeply and formally.

"Stop it," he said.

"No. We are the first people in Hadima to see the Navigator for many years. Travel safely. And come back soon," Rosie said. Owen saw that there were tears in her eyes. Without thinking what he was doing, he put her hand to his lips and kissed it.

"Quickly!" Dr. Diamond said. Owen shook hands with Clancy, who looked long and deep into his eyes before turning to the other Dogs. Then the pack wheeled as one and in the blink of an eye disappeared into the night.

"What about Andromeda?" Cati asked.

"He can come with me," Rosie said. "I'll get him back to the mountain."

The Yeati came over to Owen. It touched the ring on his hand. Owen took it off and, copying Rosie, bowed to the Yeati, who bowed deeply back, then gave the ring to Cati.

"I think he's telling you to keep it," Owen said.

"I can't. . . ." But the Yeati's great eyes were on her, telling her that to refuse the great gift would offend him. So instead Cati said, "Thank you, Andromeda."

The Yeati swept Rosie up in his arms. And if his fur was ruffled, he didn't seem to mind. They walked off down the street.

"Now," Dr. Diamond said. "To business."

The door of the museum wasn't locked and there was no one in the hallway. Dr. Diamond called out Black's name. No answer. They walked through the museum. The tiny magno lights seemed lower than ever. Shadows of the strange dead beasts in cases flickered against the wall. They went deeper into the museum.

"Black?" Dr. Diamond called again, and it seemed as if he was describing the feel of the place rather than someone's name. His voice echoed round the empty room.

They found him at last. He was sitting at a candlelit table under the skeleton of the giant schooner. There was a glass flask on the table and a gun in his hands, pointing at them. Black's face was pale. His hair fell over his forehead and his eyes were like smudges of soot in which a dark fire burned.

"I should have known," Dr. Diamond said.

"Your health, Damian," Black said with sarcasm, "for as long as you have it." He lifted the flask and took a sip.

"I see that horadanum is your drink of choice," Dr. Diamond said. "The curse of the ages. One gulp and you can see time, feel it . . ."

"You are part of it, Damian," Black said, his voice slow with intoxication. "Part of the long deep flow of time. You can sense the mystery, the majesty of it . . ."

"Perhaps," Dr. Diamond said, "but the stuff eats away at who you are. You no longer know right from wrong."

"What is right from wrong when you can see the divine mysteries of time?" Black said.

"Everything," Dr. Diamond said.

"Enough!" Black said. "You have something belonging to me. My Yeati."

"The Yeati doesn't belong to anyone," Cati said indignantly.

"Who is that?" Black demanded. "Is it the little thief, the sewer rat? No? Her friend, then. They have the same ratlike squeak, do they not, Damian? Give me back my Yeati or I will shoot the good doctor."

Black gave a cracked laugh, but Owen saw his finger tighten on the trigger. He felt Cati edging behind him.

"Where did you find the Yeati?" Owen asked, to distract him.

"Find him? He found me. Came here looking for something, I don't know what. Found him in here, looking through astronomy books . . ."

"It was cruel what you did to him."

"He's only an animal, Damian," Black drawled.

"No," Cati said quietly, "he isn't only an animal. Which can't be said for you." She had worked her way around to the pulley that held the schooner aloft. With one swift stroke of her knife, she cut the rope. The skeleton of the great beast plummeted toward Black. He looked up and shrieked, but moved too late.

The schooner crashed down on him and dust flew up from the floor. The surrounding glass cases tottered and some of them fell. When the dust settled they saw that the rib cage of the Schooner had landed right where Black was sitting, the ribs forming the bars of a cage. Black's expression as he peered between the bones was a mixture of fear and rage.

"Where is the tempod?" Dr. Diamond towered over Black.

"Please don't, Damian," Black said. "You were never good at being tough."

"You have one, still full of time," Owen said. "The Yeati told us. It could save our whole world."

"What's a world?" Black said. "There are plenty of worlds. Your grandfather could have told you that." Owen started. "Did you think I didn't notice? There's a photograph in my study. The old Navigator himself. The resemblance is striking."

"We'll set the Yeati on you," Cati threatened.

"No," Owen said. He had seen Black's eyes flicker sideways. Owen picked up the flask of horadanum and tilted it until a few precious drops spilled.

"No!" Black's voice rose. Owen tilted again. Half of

285

the contents ran out onto the floor and were lost in the dust. "Stop!" Black shrieked. "You have no idea . . ." He flailed feebly.

"The tempod," Owen said firmly, tilting the flask one more time.

"The terfuge!" Black said, almost crying. "In the terfuge!"

Dr. Diamond ran to the case containing the gloomy-looking stuffed bird. He opened it and examined the moldy feathers. He felt around before inserting his hand into a gap. Gently he drew out a rock with an intact piece of crystal attached. The crystal was hollow and filled with a cloudy substance, which glittered when he moved it.

"This is it, Owen," Dr. Diamond said. There was awe in his voice as he gazed into the shifting depths. "This is the intact tempod."

From his bone cage Black sobbed. "The most sought-after artifact of my collection," he said. "Perhaps the only one left." Then his expression changed to one of cunning and triumph. "I have one consolation. Look over there, Damian."

Owen followed his pointing finger. In the corner of the room was what appeared to be a television set in an ornately carved cabinet with large wooden knobs on the front.

"A visionater," Dr. Diamond said in wonder. "I thought they all had been destroyed."

"What does it do?" Owen asked, with a feeling of foreboding.

"It sees between the worlds," Dr. Diamond said. "If you had one at the Workhouse, you could see what was going on in the City."

"And vice versa," Black said, his eyes glittering. "Turn it on, Damian. It will tune to the place you desire to see. Let's see what is happening in your world."

Dr. Diamond turned the big knob on the front. At first nothing happened, then the screen flickered and buzzed, and slowly images started to become clear.

"The moon!" Cati exclaimed. It was the moon, but in close-up, each crater and large rock visible. Then the picture opened out and they realized that what they were seeing was the moon from the earth, impossibly close. Great fissures and cracks shuddered across the moonscape as though it was being riven by quakes. The picture changed. They saw the earth, and there were fires everywhere, and earthquakes.

"Look!" Cati said with terror in her voice. "The Workhouse!"

Flames leapt from within and one whole wall had collapsed, and what looked like the ceiling of the Starry too, although the Sleepers were hidden by smoke. As they watched, the Skyward shot into the sky, opening like a telescope until it towered above the flames and smoke. Then it fell with a great crash into the fire below.

"No!" Dr. Diamond cried. Then the visionater

crackled and popped and the screen went blank. Cati stared at it in shock. Dr. Diamond sat down abruptly.

"I let them down," Cati whispered, her hands shaking. "I am the Watcher and I did not watch. They are all gone."

Cati slumped to the floor. Even Dr. Diamond's shoulders seemed to sag. Black's eyes gleamed with malice. Only Owen seemed not to have given in to despair. He took Cati under the arms and lifted her to her feet.

"Come with me," he said. Cati and Dr. Diamond followed him dumbly out of the room and into the hallway. They watched as he knelt beside the battered old prospector's boat that lay in the hall, dust-covered and neglected. Using his sleeve he rubbed at the nameplate on the bow, uncovering the full name.

Wayfarer.

"This is it," he said quietly. "This is the *Wayfarer*."

"I don't understand," Dr. Diamond said.

"The strange thing is that I *do* understand," Owen

said. "I understand in here." He put his hand on his chest. "I just can't explain it."

"I don't know what you're talking about," Cati said dully, "but it doesn't matter anyway."

"It might, though," Owen said, his eyes shining in the dark hallway. "I can't explain, but I can show you. Look." In one easy movement he slid over the side of the craft into the stern and took hold of the slender wooden tiller. A tremor ran through the vessel, the timber itself seeming to come alive. The deck swayed under Owen, then the boat righted itself. Dr. Diamond's eyebrows shot up, and rose even further as the entire craft lifted gently from the floor, hovering above it.

"It feels alive," Owen said quietly.

"I never suspected that such a thing existed," the doctor said.

"What is it?" Cati asked.

"The *Wayfarer*. The Navigator's vessel," Owen said. "My grandfather had maps of time, but he couldn't walk there. It makes sense. There had to be a vessel to carry him. . . ."

"To sail on time the way a boat sails on the ocean!" Dr. Diamond said.

"Yes," Owen said. Cati had never seen him like this. He looked tall and strong, and although there was no wind his hair seemed to stream back from his forehead.

There was a flat board in front of the tiller, and in it was a hole.

"There must have been an instrument," Owen said.

290

"A compass or something . . . we can't go anywhere without it."

"The Mortmain!" Dr. Diamond said. "Look at the shape of the hole. It's a fleur-de-lis!"

"Yes," Owen said, "of course . . . But the Mortmain, the trunk . . . the Harsh have the Mortmain."

"No, they don't," Dr. Diamond said, reaching under his overalls. "I retrieved it. Here!"

Owen, with wonder in his eyes, took the Mortmain and carefully placed it in the hole. It slid in with ease and locked in place. On its dull, battered surfaces, five concentric rings appeared, marked with strange symbols that shone with a bright fierce light. And the little craft was transformed as well. The tiller leapt under Owen's hand and the bow of the boat trembled, seeming eager to be gone.

"I'm not sure if I can hold it! The doors!"

Dr. Diamond ran to the street doors and flung them open.

"Here, Cati!" Owen grabbed her by the hand and hauled her onboard. The *Wayfarer* leapt toward the open door. With one long-legged leap, Dr. Diamond landed on the bow and fell flat on his face. Cati grabbed the side of the cabin, but Owen stood firm and proud at the helm as the *Wayfarer* burst through the open doors and out into the night, its prow aimed high into the sky.

"What's happening, Owen?" Cati gasped, the wind blowing through her hair and her eyes streaming from the cold.

"She's been cooped up for years," Owen said. "She needs to blow the cobwebs off. Can't you feel it?"

And indeed, as the dust and grime of the museum blew away, Cati could see the ship's timber starting to acquire a proud shine. It was no longer a shabby exhibit, but a living thing.

"Marvelous!" Dr. Diamond said, struggling to his feet. "Where are the maps, Owen?"

Owen took them out from his jacket and gave them to Dr. Diamond, who spread them out on the wooden board beside the Mortmain. As he muttered to himself, Cati looked over the side and gasped. They were far above Hadima. She could see the Terminus and the smoky rooftops of Rosie's district. Around the City in a great circle, busy even at this time of night, ran the snarling, choked loop of the Speedway.

"I think I have it," Dr. Diamond cried. "Owen, can you see?" Owen leaned forward. The *Wayfarer* had slowed a little now and was forging evenly through the air.

"You see when you move the tiller, the rings on the Mortmain move as well?" Dr. Diamond said. "And the numbers and symbols on it are matched by the ones on the map?"

Owen looked at the map. He could see the City marked, and what was unmistakably the Workhouse.

"Now," said Dr. Diamond, "it would seem that if you line up the symbols on the Mortmain rings, then we should arrive at the Workhouse."

"But the Workhouse isn't there anymore!" Cati cried.

"Cati," Dr. Diamond said, "we are about to sail through time. And therefore perhaps we can arrive *before* the Workhouse burns down, *before* the moon strikes the earth!"

"This ring looks like a normal clock," Owen said.

"Yes," Dr. Diamond said. "It seems to operate like one . . . the other two are more complex. I can't work out the symbols, but never mind: we can set this one so that we arrive twelve hours ago. That should do it."

"Twelve hours ago?" Cati said.

"Yes," Dr. Diamond said. "It's the most we can do on a twelve-hour clock, but it should be enough. If the moon struck at, say, six in the evening, then we should arrive at six in the morning."

"But we're not flying through time, are we?"

"Not yet," Owen said. "Give me a hand with this winch." Cati took one of the winch handles, and as they turned, the mast, which had been lying flat, was raised into an upright position. It seemed much taller than it had been when lying down. A stained and ragged tarpaulin was wrapped around its crossbeam.

"What's that?" Cati cried. The night sky was suddenly full of lights: great sheets of green that shimmered momentarily and then were gone, reds and pinks that dropped in pillars, fantastic curtains of delicate blue that wavered and expanded to cover the whole sky, then faded away to nothing.

"The aurora borealis," Dr. Diamond said. "The Northern Lights."

"Are you ready?" Owen said to Dr. Diamond.

"Ready?" said the doctor. "I was born for this moment!"

Owen reached out and grabbed a slender rope that fell from the mast. He gave it one hard tug and the tarpaulin opened. Cati gasped. What fell from the tarpaulin was not a sail, or at least nothing like any sail she had ever seen. A sheet of silvery matter that seemed alive draped from the top of the mast to the deck. It was like a cloth so fine that it was barely there. Or perhaps not even a cloth, for it seemed to be made of the same stuff as the Northern Lights that shimmered around them. As she watched, it billowed outward as though it had caught a wind, spreading proudly out in front of the *Wayfarer*.

But it hasn't caught the wind, Cati thought. *Time itself has filled it!*

"And it will carry us home across the worlds," Dr. Diamond said, as if he had read Cati's mind.

"Here goes!" Owen shouted, and the *Wayfarer* leapt forward into time.

Afterward it occurred to Cati that they had actually entered the Northern Lights. She could see them all around, vast distances of shimmering color, and beyond, great wheeling constellations of the stars. And when she looked down they were traveling on a deep dark nothingness, with currents that quickened and slowed, sometimes calm and sometimes choppy.

Dr. Diamond had removed instruments from his rucksack and was busy measuring and scribbling calculations. Owen looked forward, the tiller in his hand, as if he had stood in that spot all his life.

"How did you know?" Cati asked.

"I pieced some of it together," he said. "You know with the maps and stuff, and even the Navigator name—it had to mean something. I knew that there had to be a way of traveling through time, and then when I saw the tapestry in the Harsh's tower, I saw that it showed the Navigator on board the *Wayfarer*. And when I got on board her . . . I don't know. When I put my hand on the tiller, it seemed that she knew me and I knew her. I can't explain it any better than that."

Cati set out to explore the boat. The cabin had four bunks, which converted into a table and chairs. There was a little cooker, and when she opened one of the cupboards, it was full of beautiful silver tableware, forks and knives and tankards, all decorated with the same symbols as on the map. There was a chest full of very old blankets, the beautiful embroidery faded, but still soft and warm. A closet held what looked like chain mail suits that a knight would wear. The forecastle at the front of the boat was full of ropes and spikes and other equipment. There was also an anchor, its spikes tipped with magno.

Cati went to the stern and sat down beside Owen. The sail spread out in front of them like a great silvery mist, and when she let her hand trail idly over the side it left a glittering trail, like phosphorescence, in the black stream on which they sailed.

"I don't understand any of this," she sighed.

"You don't have to understand it," Dr. Diamond said. "Just marvel at it." He produced a bar of chocolate for each of them and they sat eating it.

For five hours they sailed, according to the clock in the Mortmain. Cati went to lie down in the cabin with one of the blankets wrapped around her. Then Owen started to experience an occasional grinding sensation, as if the keel of the *Wayfarer* was grounding on shallows. He told Dr. Diamond.

"I was afraid of something like this," the doctor said. "The stream of time is getting shallow. Keep to your course, Owen. This may slow us."

The grinding got worse and was accompanied by bumping. The shifting patterns of colors surrounding them dimmed. It felt as if they were picking their way through a shallow river, trying to find clear water.

The lights grew dim and the atmosphere began to feel stormy. After a while the keel stopped grating and Owen had a sense of a great expanse on either side of them. "I suppose it's like coming out into a lake," he said.

"Yes," Dr. Diamond said, "and you can be sheltered from the weather on a river, but on a lake . . ."

The *Wayfarer* started to rise and fall as though cresting waves. Sheets of blue flashed up on the horizon, not shimmering like the Northern Lights, but jagged like lightning. The sail billowed and crackled as though the wind had risen. All was still until a sudden gust of minute greenish particles struck them, like a very fine dust.

Dr. Diamond looked at it in wonder. "Some kind of . . . I don't know . . . a new compound," he murmured.

"Whatever it is, it's starting to sting a bit," Owen

said. He lifted his hand to his face and it came away bloody. "More than a bit!"

"Cati said there were suits in the cabin," Dr. Diamond said, and darted inside. The green wind grew stronger, and with it came an eerie sound between a whistle and a roar. The *Wayfarer* rose and fell, and her timbers and mast creaked and groaned.

"Quick!" Dr. Diamond said, reappearing. "Put this on." The suits were like very fine chain mail, almost as soft as cloth. There were tarnished metal helmets with quartz eye guards, which looked like old-fashioned goggles. Owen pulled his on quickly. So did Dr. Diamond and Cati, who had reemerged from the cabin.

"What's going on?" she asked.

"Storm," Owen said. The suit fitted him well. *My grandfather might have worn this,* he thought. Then all thoughts were driven from his mind as a sudden gust caught the *Wayfarer,* pushing her hard over on one side. Cati caught the rail to stop herself being pitched overboard. Owen swung the tiller to try to turn the bow back. He could feel the craft straining under him. The wind, if wind it was, rose to a shriek.

"Get below!" Dr. Diamond shouted to Cati. The *Wayfarer* swung back on course, but seemed to be cresting vast waves that they could not see. Each time the craft plunged into a trough, a black spray rose over the bow. The sky was filled with crackling blue energy, and blue fire ran up and down the mast.

Owen worked the tiller, although the *Wayfarer* seemed to know which way he wanted to go. The deck rose and pitched terrifyingly. On and on they ran, the great sail taut as a drum. In the cabin, Cati could hear every creak and feel every roll.

"The storm's driving us off course," Owen shouted. "We're losing time!"

But the doctor was rapt by what he was seeing. "Marvelous," he said dreamily. "A storm in time!"

Owen's shoulder ached with the strain of holding the tiller. He could feel the little vessel starting to struggle as well. But on they sailed into the storm, until Owen's hand blistered where he held the tiller, and his knees ached from the rolling of the deck. And then, just when the storm reached its pitch, when the *Wayfarer* rose and fell almost vertically and the air was alive with crackling energy, Cati's nose started to twitch.

"I can smell something . . . evil. I can hear something as well," she said. "Music . . . opera!"

"What?"

"It *is* opera. *Don Giovanni,*" the doctor said. Owen stared at him in disbelief. But when he looked over the bow, his heart sank. Another vessel was coming toward them—a vessel made of welded plates of metal, bits and pieces of scrap bolted together. What appeared to be old car tires hung from its sides and rusty stanchions held its mast aloft. Harsh lights glared down from a gantry. The music was blaring from a speaker attached to the battered and corroded wheelhouse. But it was the figure behind the wheel that sent Owen's heart to his boots. A figure with huge sideburns and dark hair and a row of teeth like tombstones that now showed in a huge evil grin. Johnston.

"Of course!" Dr. Diamond breathed. "He has been traveling back and forward to Hadima all along, plotting with the Harsh!"

"But he doesn't have any charts!" Owen exclaimed.

"He doesn't have your grandfather's charts," Dr. Diamond corrected, "but the Harsh must have had a fragment showing this very route, if none of the others."

"Ship ahoy!" Johnston yelled. "Look!" He pointed to their port bow. A huge whirlpool had formed and the substance they were sailing on was being sucked into it.

"How did he do that?" Owen groaned.

"A whirlpool in time, like a small version of the Puissance," Dr. Diamond said grimly. "His Harsh masters have taught him well."

Johnston wrenched the wheel and charged at the *Wayfarer*. Owen couldn't maneuver out of the way. The metal hull caught the boat in the side and she was driven sideways, her planks groaning. Johnston rammed the *Wayfarer* again and Owen felt it like a blow to his own side.

"He's trying to drive us into the whirlpool," Owen shouted. And indeed, they had covered half the distance to it. Johnston rammed again and again. Owen tried to steer the battered *Wayfarer* out of his way, but Johnston's craft was bigger and stronger.

"There's nothing we can do," Owen groaned.

Wesley and Pieta were pinned against the door of the Starry by the attackers. Wesley had long since run out of magno ammunition and was fighting with a sword he'd seized. His torso was covered in cuts and bruises. Pieta's hand was burning from the heat in the whip handle. Her arms and shoulders were weary and the armor she wore was dented and scratched. One eye was almost closed where a rock had struck her.

Pieta and Wesley fought grimly and without hope, but their friends were helpless, sleeping behind the door, and they would not surrender. Their enemies pressed close and they were forced away from the Starry.

We have failed, Wesley thought as the attackers smashed through the door.

Slipping on the pitching deck of the *Wayfarer*, Cati dived into the little forecastle. She came out holding the magno anchor and climbed up onto the bow. The maelstrom loomed terrifyingly in front of her, a whirlpool of darkness. She waited. Johnston drew back, building up speed, then came forward, faster and faster. Owen tried to steer out of the way, but it was no good. He braced himself for the impact.

The opera blared. Johnston's head was thrown back in a great mocking laugh. Then, just before he delivered the blow that would splinter the *Wayfarer* and grind their hopes into dust, Cati threw the anchor.

It caught! The *Wayfarer* jerked to a halt. Instead of ramming them, Johnston's boat overshot at full speed, heading straight for the whirlpool. He wrestled frantically with the wheel, but it was too late. The front of his craft was caught by the edge of the maelstrom and drawn in. Like a toy, the boat was spun around, closer and closer to the center, until at last it was poised on the edge of the abyss.

Johnston shook his fist. As the craft fell into the emptiness they heard a last angry roar and a blast of opera, which then disappeared into silence.

"That's the end of *him*," Cati said, her face fierce and exultant.

Their enemy might have gone, but the storm still raged. Each time they made a little progress, they were beaten back. At last the storm started to abate and Owen set course for the Workhouse again. They made good progress, but the flow of time grew shallow again. Several times the *Wayfarer* seemed to run aground; at one point Owen thought that they might be there forever, stranded on the shoals, until finally the little craft broke loose. They were cold and exhausted, and their mission was poised on the brink of failure. At last they had half an hour left and the Mortmain was almost aligned with the symbol of the Workhouse.

"We have to chance it," Dr. Diamond said, "or there will be nothing left to save."

"How do we get out of here?" Cati said. "I mean, how do we get to the Workhouse?"

"Grab hold of this rope," Owen said. *Where did that come from?* he thought, then realized again that it was the *Wayfarer*. The knowledge of how to sail her was stored in her ancient timbers. Affectionately he ran a hand along her gleaming stern. "Well done, well sailed," he whispered. To the others he said, "On the count of three, pull. One, two, three . . ."

They hauled on the rope and the sail furled back to the crossbeam. The shimmering lights of the aurora borealis changed to the light of normal day, hazy, with the smell of smoke in it. Vapor surrounded them.

"We're in the clouds," Cati exclaimed. Then they were out again, and below was the harbor and the town. And in the middle, surrounded by enemies and fire, was the Workhouse. Overhead loomed the bulk of the moon, a crack starting to appear in its surface.

"Are we too late?" Cati cried.

Dr. Diamond looked at her and did not answer.

"What do we do now?" Cati asked.

"Mary White. That's the other thing the Yeati wrote on the piece of glass," Owen said. "He was right about Black having the tempod, so—"

"So we should go to Mary's." Dr. Diamond nodded. Far below they could see attackers swarming into the Workhouse.

"There's no one to defend the Sleepers!" Cati's face was anguished.

"No, look!" Owen said. From within the Workhouse came a flash of blue.

"Pieta is still holding out," the doctor said. "We must hurry!"

As if the *Wayfarer* responded to their urgency, she dipped her bow and flew toward the ground. Owen could see Mary's shop, half hidden by trees. He steered toward the small back garden, swooping between the branches. As they drew near an earth tremor made the trees shake.

"Not a moment to lose!" Dr. Diamond cried. The *Wayfarer* glided between two very solid beech trees with inches to spare, landing in a potato patch. She skidded along for several meters, then came to a halt, tipping over on one side and looking as though she had been there for years.

They ran around the front. Mary's shop was the same as always, low and whitewashed, the windows gleaming. Owen opened the door and the little bell attached to it rang out. The shop was dark and smelled of fresh tea leaves and tobacco. Owen tapped on the counter.

"The world is about to end and he taps on the counter," Cati murmured. Owen lifted the counter flap and went into the back. There was the fireplace, the sofa, the comfortable chairs, and the grandfather clock in the corner.

He looked around. "I don't know what to do!"

"The answer is here somewhere," Dr. Diamond said, steadying himself as the ground lurched. He reached into his coat and took out the tempod. Then they heard the little bell ring again as someone entered the shop. They heard the counter being lifted.

Martha came into the room, breathing hard. There was blood on one side of her face. Owen gasped when he saw his mother and his face lit up. But this was no time for a happy reunion.

"I saw you coming!" she said. "In the *Wayfarer* . . . Do you have it?" There was a great rumble and the whole cottage lurched sideways. Ornaments tumbled from the mantelpiece and a crack ran up the wall.

Martha reached up into her hair and snatched out the key, which had been acting as a hairpin.

"Quickly!" Dr. Diamond cried, brandishing the tempod. Owen grabbed it from his hand.

"Here!" his mother said, unlocking the clock case. Owen stared in amazement at the endless blue-black space within. He raised the tempod and flung it into the depths.

The tempod split apart and the milky, silvery substance expanded until it seemed for a second to fill all of the space, moving at the speed of galaxies expanding.

"Close it!" Dr. Diamond shouted. "Time might start to flow the other way!"

Martha slammed the case shut and locked it. The house gave one more sickening lurch to the side and then was still.

No one spoke.

Finally Dr. Diamond broke the silence. "Three minutes," he said, a slight shake in his voice. "That's all we had left. Three minutes."

"Is the Workhouse all right?" Cati said, fear in her voice. "Is it? We saw it destroyed on the visionater."

"No, it is safe," Dr. Diamond said. "We arrived back

just before the moon struck the earth. It is safe, Cati. At least it is if Pieta has won her fight. And she rarely loses."

"Mum," Owen said hesitantly, "these are my friends. They are Resisters . . . they . . ." He stopped in confusion. She must know about the Resisters! And where was Mary, if they were in Mary's house?

"Yes, I know who the Resisters are," she said, coming over to him and touching his face, almost in wonder. "I know who the Navigator is, and I know that you have done the thing that your father dreamed of. To find the *Wayfarer* and sail her in time. He would be very proud of you now."

Owen blushed. Cati had tears in her eyes and Dr. Diamond turned politely away, a smile on his face.

"Your father was brought here by your grandfather from Hadima as a child for safety when the Harsh started to rise to power, as was I. When we met we didn't know our histories, but we knew there was something different about us."

"We knew the Navigator as guardian of the Mortmain, and as a leader," Dr. Diamond murmured. "We didn't know anything about the *Wayfarer*. . . ."

"Neither did we at first," Martha said. "Owen's dad pieced it together gradually. Then he came across the road to Hadima. We went there in a truck."

"The truck!" Cati said.

"Your father found out the true meaning of the Mortmain. It has many features and was part of the chest for a long time after Gobillard put it there. But it's really a time compass."

"And my dad . . . ?" Owen felt his voice falter.

"He took the Mortmain from the Resisters," his mother said, "but not to give it to Johnston. He hoped that it might lead him to the *Wayfarer*."

"That wasn't what I wanted to know," Owen said. "I wanted to know if . . . if he is still alive."

His mother turned her head away as if she had not heard him. But Owen knew that she had. He opened his mouth to ask again, but Cati interrupted.

"What am I doing? What am I thinking?" she cried. "I am the Watcher, and the Sleepers are under threat!"

Without waiting for the others, she dashed out the door.

Owen had no choice but to follow.

In the Starry all was quiet and dark. The Resisters slept, even as the attackers broke in. The first, a swarthy man, looked up at the ceiling and grunted in contempt. He moved toward the nearest bed where a girl slept. If he had known to smell the air he would have realized that the staleness had gone and that there was a wakefulness in the Starry.

He lifted his cudgel to bring it down on her head. The blow never fell. A battle-grizzled Resister shook sleep from his eyes and sat up. With one hand he plucked the cudgel from the man's hand and with the other sent him flying across the floor. Others were waking now. A lean, sour-faced man in brightly colored robes sat up, just as more attackers burst in, whooping and shouting. The man's eyes narrowed. He reached under his bed and drew out a magno gun.

The grizzled man charged at the attackers. "To me, Samual!" he shouted to the man with the gun.

"What do you think I'm doing, Rutgar, you fool?" Samual muttered, jumping to his feet. The two of them drove the attackers back toward the door. Soon the whole Workhouse was a mass of fighting men and women.

But the attackers were many and the Workhouse defenders were weak after their long sleep, and not everyone was awake yet. Rutgar and Samual fought desperately back to back, but the battle had started to turn against them.

"There's too many!" Rutgar shouted.

"Wait!" Samual said. "Look!" From the direction of the sea came a great crowd of Raggies, with Silkie at their head! Alongside her was a small figure in white. The Raggies charged from behind and a cry of dismay went up from the attackers.

"Now!" Silkie shouted. A bolt of ice from the Harsh child flew toward them.

"The Harsh!" they cried. "The Harsh are among us!"

Within minutes the attackers were in disarray. First they were beaten back from the walls, then they threw down their weapons, turned tail, and ran.

Wesley slumped to the grass, weary beyond measure. He looked up at the moon. Was it his imagination or was it smaller, further away?

A small figure skidded to a halt in front of him. "Wesley! What are you doing sitting here? Look at the place! Fires everywhere! Get up!"

Wesley grinned wearily. "Good to see you too, Cati." He held out a hand. "At least you can help me up."

"I've better things to do," she said furiously. She darted off into the smoke and Wesley clambered to his feet.

Suddenly Cati reappeared from the smoke and threw her arms around him. "I thought you were all dead!" she said, a catch in her voice. Wesley saw tears in her eyes. She let go of him and stepped back, dashing the tears away angrily.

"Come on," Wesley said with a broad smile. "Them fires got to be put out."

When Owen and the others arrived there was no time for talk. The earth still rumbled, although the moon was retreating to its proper orbit, and fires still raged. The Resisters and the Raggies formed a chain and relayed water from the river to the Workhouse. They worked until the flames had been quenched and they stood in a charred and smoking landscape. Owen recognized many of the smoke-blackened faces.

Rutgar, the leader of the defense, came over to him,

his smiling teeth shining out from the soot on his face. He wrapped Owen in a bear hug. "Good to see you again, Navigator," he boomed.

The gentle Contessa took his hand and smiled. He had forgotten how much he had missed the Resister leader's wise counsel. "I have to talk to you," he said, and she saw pain in his eyes.

"Come to me later," she replied.

Some of the Resisters were still waking and leaving the Starry, looking around them in amazement at the scene of battle and at the retreating moon. Owen saw Wesley among the Raggies and went over to him.

A smile creased the skinny boy's tired and blood-stained face. "If it ain't the Navigator himself!" he exclaimed. "I hear tell you come out of the sky to save the lot of us."

Owen grinned. "If it hadn't been for you, there wouldn't have been much to save."

"I'll have to get a look at this sky boat," Wesley said.

"Not just a sky boat—a time boat!" Owen said, and Wesley looked at him in astonishment.

But Owen turned away. They had saved the world, and he had found the *Wayfarer*. So why was his heart so heavy?

The Resisters set about preparing an urgent Convoke for that evening. Ordinary life was resuming in the town and the Resisters had no place in it.

Owen saw Pieta, limping through the crowd, supported on either side by her two silent children. Cati called to her and ran over, but as she reached out to embrace the woman, Pieta flung her aside. Grabbing her magno whip, she tried to lash out with it, but her injuries prevented her and she fell to the ground with a groan of pain. "The Harsh!" she whispered.

Cati spun around. Silkie was standing there with the Harsh child. Samual and several of his men took a step backward and produced weapons.

"Kill it!" Samual shouted.

"No!" Silkie leapt in front of the child, her arms outspread. "He helped us."

"It's a trick!" Samual cried.

"Wait, Samual," Contessa said. "It's true this child fired ice bolts at the attackers."

"And he saved me and Wesley's life," Silkie said.

"This must be discussed at the Convoke," Contessa said. "Can you guarantee his behavior until then, Silkie?"

"You don't have to ask," Silkie said.

"Then take him out of here."

"He's only a boy," Silkie protested. "A lost boy."

"Get it out of here!" Samual yelled. Silkie and the child turned and left without another word.

Owen went to sit in his Den until it was almost dusk. One part of him wanted to be with the Resisters, but another part wanted to be on his own. He was startled by a polite cough at the entrance.

"I thought I would find you here," Dr. Diamond said. "May I come in?" The scientist sat on the sofa while Owen made tea.

"Dr. Diamond," Owen burst out finally, "can I come and join the Resisters?"

"Why do you ask?" the doctor enquired, his head to one side.

"I could be a Watcher with Cati."

"There can only be one Watcher."

"I don't see why I can't join," Owen said stubbornly. Dr. Diamond put down his mug of tea and stood up with a sigh. "Come with me," he said. He led Owen out onto the riverbank, but instead of turning toward the Workhouse he went the other way.

"Where are we going?" Owen said, but Dr. Diamond didn't answer. They walked for ten minutes under the trees, then emerged onto a pathway which they followed until they reached an ancient stone wall with a gateway in it.

"A graveyard!" Owen said in surprise. "I've never been here before."

"It can be hard to find," Dr. Diamond said. "Go in. There is someone there you need to talk to."

Dr. Diamond stood back as Owen entered the little graveyard and walked between rows of old headstones in the dusk, the names on the stones worn away by time and weather. He reached a freshly dug grave. His mother knelt by it, putting flowers on it.

"Who is it?" he asked, kneeling down beside her.

"Mary White," his mother said. "I brought her here the night she died."

"You carried her?" Owen asked in wonder.

"And buried her. You find strength when you need it, as you know, Owen.

"She was a good friend to us, and to the Resisters. Her heart gave out in the end. It's because of Mary that I was so sad and distant."

"Why?" Owen asked. "Why did she do that to you?"

"I fled with your father from Hadima. He had the Mortmain and the Harsh were in pursuit."

Owen shivered. He remembered the Harsh cold in his bones.

"We abandoned the truck at Gobillard's shop—"

"Gobillard is dead," Owen said quietly. "The Harsh froze him."

His mother bowed her head and her eyes gleamed with tears. "Another one gone," she said at last. "You must tell me more later. . . . We were attacked by the Harsh. They put ice in my mind. I was in terror, screaming with pain. Mary turned off that part of my mind."

"Why?"

"So the ice could thaw. It took years. But that's why I was sad and forgetful. I'm sorry, Owen, but I couldn't have lived with the pain."

"You wouldn't talk about my father when I asked you today in Mary's shop," he said in a quiet voice. "I need to know if he is really dead."

There was a pause before Martha spoke.

"I wish for a place like this I could come to, a grave where I could lay flowers for your father. I didn't answer your question, because I didn't want to say it out loud. But in my heart I know. I know your father is dead. When his car crashed into the harbor with you in it, I knew. . . . You were saved, Owen, but he was lost."

Owen reached out and took his mother's hand and they knelt there as the shadows grew long around them. Then they rose and walked slowly back toward the Workhouse.

As they approached they met Rutgar.

"You're just in time," he said. "The Convoke is about to start."

Owen looked around and saw Contessa. "I have to talk to her first. . . ."

He broke away from Martha and approached the woman. Contessa could see the anxiety in his face. "What is it, Owen?"

"The Sub-Commandant . . . ," he began.

She looked at him, puzzled. "Cati's father? He is gone, Owen, drawn into the Puissance. You were there."

"No." He told Contessa about the brooch and the message, then about how the Sub-Commandant had appeared when the Harsh king held the Puissance in his hand. How he'd told Owen to destroy the Puissance, even though it would mean the end of his own life.

"I did it, Contessa. I destroyed the Puissance. Cati . . . I killed her father."

Contessa could see that the full horror of what he had done was just dawning on him. "You did not kill him, Owen. You had no choice, as he had none. He commanded you to act, and because you did, this world is safe for a while longer."

"But Cati . . ."

"Cati is a Resister, and she is the Watcher. Her father's daughter."

"Do I tell her, Contessa?"

"I cannot make that decision for you."

• • •

The Convoke met in the great hall of the Workhouse, roofless now, as they had not had time to repair it. The Raggies perched themselves where they could find space along the wall. Samual's soldiers were there in brightly colored uniforms, as were Rutgar's men and women of the guard. Owen sat on the dais with Contessa and Cati and Dr. Diamond. Martha sat with the Resisters. Wesley joined the Raggies, but there was no sign of Silkie or the Harsh child. Pieta sat in her customary place at the fireside, her son and daughter standing solemn-faced beside her.

To Owen's surprise it was Cati who stood up and called the Convoke to order. Her voice was firm and precise, and he was reminded of her father. She called on Dr. Diamond, who stood and bowed to her gravely.

"We thank you, Watcher, from the bottom of our hearts. You have done great service." Cati blushed and bowed back.

He told the assembled Resisters everything that had happened since he, Cati, and Owen had left for the City, and there were many interruptions for questions and gasps of astonishment. When they learned about Owen and the *Wayfarer* and how he had brought the tempod back, they rose to their feet and cheered him. He bowed, red-faced, and thought about the first time he had met the Resisters, when he had stood alone and almost friendless in front of the same Convoke.

When Dr. Diamond had finished, Wesley stood and

told his part and was cheered again, the Raggies shouting themselves hoarse.

"This is all very well," Samual said, getting to his feet, "but what do we do now?"

"We must return to sleep," Contessa said. "Time is safe again. We are not needed, for now."

"But we've just been woken," someone protested.

"Contessa is right," Dr. Diamond said. "The townspeople are coming back."

"It is a hard thing to do, but our lives were meant to be hard. We are Resisters," Cati said firmly.

"And no life is harder or more lonely than that of the Watcher," Owen found himself saying. Cati shot him a grateful glance and was puzzled when he looked away.

There were a few grumbles from the Convoke, but mainly they accepted Cati's words.

"I have prepared a feast from stores," Contessa said. "Later we must return to the Starry, but tonight we shall celebrate."

The Convoke was about to rise when Samual spoke. "Wait. Have you forgotten? The Harsh walk among us. Where is the Harsh child?"

"He has gone," a small voice from the back said, and Silkie walked forward, looking miserable and very alone.

"You were supposed to guard him!" Samual shouted. "What harm is he doing now?"

"I went outside and when I came back he was gone," Silkie said, sounding close to tears.

Dr. Diamond watched and said nothing. It was he who had secretly beckoned to the Harsh child and led him to the edge of the sea. "You must go," he had said, "for they are afraid and may kill you."

The child turned to him without a word, and Dr. Diamond felt the loneliness, but also saw the beginnings of a small, cold smile. *His little heart may thaw yet,* Dr. Diamond thought. He watched in silence as the Harsh boy raised his hand and began to build a bridge of ice, casting it in front of him as it melted behind. In minutes the child was a speck on the ocean, and then was gone.

"Wretched girl!" Samual snapped. "I told you we should have killed it when we had the chance."

"Leave the girl alone." The voice was low but carried a menace they all recognized. Pieta rose slowly to her feet. "If it was not for Silkie rousing the Raggies and befriending the Harsh child, we would all be dead."

"We saw it," Owen said, remembering the visionater. "We saw the future and the Workhouse burning."

The Raggies started booing Samual, and others in the Convoke began arguing loudly. Dr. Diamond held up his hand.

"Pieta is right. Furthermore, this is something that has never happened with the Harsh before. Silkie forged a connection that may help us in the future." He turned slowly, looking around the silent room. "And apart from all of that, I'm hungry!"

A great roar drowned out Samual's protests. The

Resisters started to stream toward the doors. Then Owen stood up.

"Wait!" he said. His voice sounded very small and feeble to his own ears, but they all stopped and turned toward him.

"In the City . . . in Hadima . . . I stood before the Harsh king. He held the Puissance in his hand and I saw many faces in it. But one spoke to me: that of the Sub-Commandant."

He could see Cati's face in the crowd. She had turned very pale. He knew what she was thinking. He had seen her father and had not told her. Why? The hall was very still.

"I had to destroy the Puissance." His voice sounded firm now, echoing from the great stone walls. "It was a thing with the power to undo worlds. I had to destroy it, and by doing that, I ended the life of a great man, the Sub-Commandant. We knew he was lost; now we know he is gone."

There were gasps of shock, then all eyes turned to Cati.

"He told you to do it, didn't he?" Cati said. Owen nodded dumbly. "My father told you to destroy the Puissance, knowing it would end his life. But you didn't say that because you wanted to take the responsibility on your own shoulders."

"I—" Owen began.

"I know what you did. I pay tribute to your bravery, Navigator, and I thank you for obeying my father's wishes. He can sleep in peace knowing that he died the way he lived his life."

"I'm sorry, Cati."

"There is nothing to be sorry for. He was the Watcher. He did his duty."

A murmur of approval went around the crowd, then a shout went up as the Resisters saluted their fallen hero. "Watcher! Watcher!"

Cati walked to the dais where Owen stood. She took him by the hands and embraced him. The hug was warm, but as her cheek touched his, he could feel tears.

They feasted long into the night. There were smoked hams and cured meats and bacon and sausages, and fish that the Raggies had brought from the harbor. Rutgar had gone out with his men and dug potatoes and vegetables from abandoned fields.

Wesley and the others listened openmouthed to Owen as he told them about the *Wayfarer*. Wesley asked shrewd questions about how she sailed. Silkie listened enthralled to Cati's tales about the Dogs, and was fascinated to hear about Rosie and how she dressed. Martha sat with Contessa, and they talked long into the night about Owen's father.

It was late when Martha went over to Owen. The Raggies were singing sea shanties, and Dr. Diamond was dancing an old-fashioned waltz with Pieta.

"We should slip off," she whispered to him, "before

the party is over. There will be sadness later, when it is time for them to sleep."

Owen nodded. He couldn't bear to say goodbye to his friends. Hearts heavy, Martha and Owen slipped out of the Convoke. But they didn't get far. At the tree trunk that bridged the river, Cati and Wesley awaited them, and they heard footsteps behind them as Dr. Diamond ran up.

"Off slip you'd thought," he gasped breathlessly, agitation causing him to speak backward. They all laughed, but still the parting was hard. Wesley gave Owen a firm handshake and then turned away, blowing his nose on his ragged sleeve. Dr. Diamond also shook hands.

"There is one more thing." The doctor's face was serious. "You went against the will of the Convoke. The path to Hadima was sealed and you opened it."

"If he hadn't, the world would have fallen!" Martha protested.

"Nevertheless, there must be punishment. I have met with Contessa, Pieta, Rutgar, Samual, and Wesley. We have decided."

Owen waited. What would the punishment be? Would he be sundered from his friends forever?

"We have decided that you should replace Mary White as our Watcher in the visible world, with all the duties that entails."

His voice was solemn, but Cati laughed in delight.

"That means I can contact you from the shadows of time!"

"It is no longer against our law to call on Owen," Dr. Diamond said, "but only in times of concern or danger. Your father only contacted Mary in time of great need. Remember that, Cati."

"I do," Cati said, "for I never contacted her once. I had no need until it was too late."

"I suppose, with Johnston gone, things will be quieter," Owen said, sighing in relief.

"I don't know," the doctor said. "We saw him fall, but has he gone forever? We'll see. In any case, we know the Harsh are not gone. We won a battle, Owen, not the war. Stay vigilant!"

Cati started to speak, then threw her arms around Owen. He could feel tears on his shoulder.

"See you soon, Watcher," he said, feeling a dampness in his own eyes.

"From the shadows, Navigator," she said, smiling.

There was another surprise when they got to the top of the hill. Instead of turning toward their house, his mother went up the road toward Mary's shop. "Where are we going?"

"Mary left the house to us, and we're going to live there now. We have to guard the clock, and the *Wayfarer*, of course."

The little shop was quiet and dark. Owen hesitated at the door. "I'll come in a minute," he said. His mother nodded.

He slipped around the back into the garden. The *Wayfarer* lay on her side, looking as if she had been shipwrecked. But when he ran his hand along her rail, he felt a shiver run through her timbers. Owen climbed on board. He put his grandfather's charts under his jacket. They would be safe in the Den. Then he went to the tiller.

He reached down for the Mortmain, expecting that it would be stuck fast, but it came away easily, the brightness of the map rings now faded. He put it under his jacket to keep it safe. Then, with an affectionate pat for the ship, he jumped back into the garden.

He walked down the road until he stood at the field gate looking at the river and the Workhouse. He could feel the weight of the Mortmain against his skin. The moon was still large, but almost in its proper place. A faint light in the east signaled that dawn was close. At the Workhouse all was quiet and very still. He wondered if they were all asleep, if Cati watched.

"See you soon, Watcher," he whispered.

END OF BOOK TWO

ABOUT THE AUTHOR

Eoin McNamee was born in County Down, Northern Ireland. He is the author of *The Navigator,* the first book in the Navigator trilogy. He is critically acclaimed as a writer of novels for adults, the best known being *Resurrection Man,* which was made into a film. He was awarded the Macaulay Fellowship for Irish Literature, and has also written three adult thrillers under the name John Creed.

Eoin McNamee lives in County Sligo, Ireland.